DEATH AT THE DOLPHIN

An absolutely gripping WW2 historical
murder mystery full of twists

GRETTA MULROONEY

Joffe Books, London
www.joffebooks.com

First published in Great Britain in 2022

Cover art by Nick Castle

ISBN: 978-1-80405-455-0

For Daisy Randall, Darragh's little sweetheart

NOTE

Oxfordshire and Oxford are of course real. The author has invented Fernfield and surrounding villages.

CHAPTER ONE

If only.

If only I hadn't been distracted by the cat.

If only I hadn't been obsessed by work and a crucial message from Antwerp.

If only I'd remembered to turn and check the hearth.

If only.

I'm convinced that I was responsible for my mother's death. Her regular refrain, wailed through a dense fog of fag smoke, used to be: 'Daisy Moore, you'll be the death of me.' It demonstrated a certain prescience on her part. I was a headstrong, curious, accident-prone child, breaking limbs, tearing my skin, falling — usually onto my head. The first time I did that, I was two and came tumbling down the narrow, lino-covered stairs. Maybe all the bashes on my skull accounted for the way I turned out.

I view myself as an accidental killer. That might be why I take to solving crimes. A kind of restitution.

* * *

I hang my damp socks to air over the fire just before midnight, securing them under the clock on the mantelpiece. They'll be toasty in the morning. They dangle beside the photo of my dad in his infantry uniform, our two well-thumbed ration books and a signed photo of Pius XII, which Father Hickey brought back from Rome for my mum. There are greasy smudges on the glass where she fervently kisses it. I'm not sure about the aptness of this gesture to the pontiff, who is supposed to be unworldly and celibate. There are no such smears on my dad's photo.

Puddle is scratching at the back door, wanting to be let in after her usual evening ramble. I go to open it and tell her she's a sensible cat to be home, out of the way of buzz bombs and things going bump in the night. She pauses inside the door, ears pricked, scanning around warily for my mother. She's my cat and Mum is scathing with her, grumbles about having to feed her, claims Puddle gets under her feet. We'd had a big row about her at the start of the war. Mum argued that Puddle should be culled with all the other pets who were being put down in a national panic, because animals like her would be a burden when there were going to be food shortages. I'd said that if she insisted, I'd move out. That had put a stop to Mum, because she hated the idea of living alone, but I did worry for a while that I'd come home and find Puddle gone, with my mother insisting it was nothing to do with her.

'It's OK,' I whisper to Puddle now, 'you-know-who is in bed. You've ages before she gets up and nags you.'

I give her a drop of milk and sneak a wedge of cheese from the larder for her. She's in seventh heaven. I watch her for a while, puzzling over the message I was working on all afternoon. It's locked in my desk drawer in the office. I have an idea about a different approach and I can't wait to get back to it in the morning. My brain's buzzing as I lock the back door and head for bed.

I forget the fireguard.

Later, I remember what my dad once said. *The disaster that happens is rarely the one you were expecting.* That was his wry observation in a letter home from the front, after we'd had to tell him that one of his best mates had been killed by a lorry while he was home on leave. Ronald had survived a fierce naval battle and returned to London for a well-earned break, only to be flattened by a vehicle with faulty brakes.

My forgetfulness with the fireguard wouldn't have surprised Dad. He often said I was a wayward angel.

He was being kind regarding the angel part.

* * *

I wake, coughing, in the dark. I can hear screams, shouts, glass breaking. My bedroom is full of hot smoke and my chest is heaving. The smoke has me by the throat, penetrates my lungs, fills my eyes. I stagger out of bed towards the window and manage to yank it open. There are blurry shapes below, shouting at me to jump.

The next thing, I come to in a hospital ward.

A nurse tells me that I've been very lucky because I landed in the blanket people were holding out for me. A miracle really. My mother, on the other hand, is very poorly, and my cat is dead. Puddle fills my thoughts more than Mum does. That renders me horribly guilty the next morning, when the nurse returns to explain that my mother has died, 'due to complications'.

I lie, staring at the ceiling, not feeling much, just stunned, my chest aching, a horrible taste in my throat. When I cough, I produce greyish mucus.

'Better out than in, you get those lungs cleared,' the woman in the next bed says. Mavis is a motorcycle messenger who had an argument with a bomb crater at speed and now has two broken legs.

I'm happy to listen to her chatter and grumble about her cumbersome plasters because when she's quiet I succumb to dreadful memories. Then I suddenly remember the socks, and an awful suspicion sneaks into my mind. I try to recall if I put the fireguard in place, take myself back through my actions after I heard Puddle clawing at the door. I'm sure that I forgot. I picture a sock falling, the embers catching it, flames licking. I'm convinced that I caused the fire.

When I'm not fretting about that, I worry over the message I was so near to cracking at the office. They'll have gone into my drawer for my tray of work, but will my colleagues follow my reasoning? I can't ask anyone at the hospital to ring in, given the nature of my work. When I ask the nurse if there's a phone I can use, she replies reprovingly that I'm to rest and not bother my head about such things.

The parish priest, Father Hickey, visits me, despite the fact that I'm not one of his flock. My dad was C of E and refused to allow my mum to raise me as a Catholic. It was one of the few things he got his way in during their marriage. I've always liked Father Hickey, who's a free thinker for a man of the cloth and wears his beliefs lightly. He once stunned my mother, who invested heavily in the catechism concept of the one true church, by commenting that he was only a Catholic because he was born in the bogs. He told her cheerily that if he'd grown up in Kashmir, he'd have been a happy Hindu.

A handsome man from County Offaly, Father Hickey turns heads with his thick dark hair and film star glow. Several nurses get into a flutter when he appears and sits on the end of my bed, facing me, his legs pulled under him lotus-fashion. He's brought a bag of slightly squashed strawberries, which we share. Their fresh, clean aroma, a reminder of gardens and sunshine, is an antidote to the antiseptic confines of the ward.

When I claim wildly that the fire was all my fault, the priest assumes that I'm mad with grief.

'Don't be talkin' that oul' nonsense, Daisy. Yer not yerself at all right now. Yer mammy wouldn't want ye to be sufferin' like this.'

He blesses me, reassuring me that my mother is safe in God's bosom. I consider my mum's temper and I'm sorry for God at that moment, because He'll be getting a tongue-lashing.

'He's a bit gorgeous for a vicar. Is he married?' Mavis asks when he's gone.

'He's a priest, he can't marry.'

'What a waste. He's a dreamboat, like William Holden.'

A do-gooding lady at the hospital, called an almoner, comes to sit by my bed with a doleful manner that fails to console me. She's brought me some clothes, large serge knickers and a sensible, middle-aged skirt and sweater several sizes too big. I wonder if they're from a dead woman and imagine a hospital cupboard full of garments no longer needed by their owners. The almoner is saddened by my plight — she wouldn't be so charitable if she could guess what's bothering me. She sighs that at least this awful war should be over soon, and informs me that she's found me a temporary berth at a place called Hailsham House. I understand from her face that I'm not conveying enough gratitude, so I thank her profusely.

A nurse appears soon after the almoner leaves and hands me a brown envelope. When I open it, I read a brief note, unsigned, typed on plain paper.

All fine here at the office, tasks proceeding apace, including success regarding your work in progress. We wish you well.

At least they haven't forgotten me and that last message is being dealt with. I take a small crumb of comfort from the dry communication.

The hospital discharges me six days later, the day before my mother's funeral. I'm reluctant to leave the warmth, the three meals a day and Mavis's tales of riding her Triumph through the night across Dartmoor to Plymouth, using a torch instead of the broken headlight. She's been blown off her bike in Woolwich and is an expert in evasive riding techniques. I could happily lie there for weeks in a hazy lethargy, safely tucked up, listening to Mavis. I stay meek and quiet, the first time I've been so docile in my life, hoping that I'll go unnoticed. But the doctor wields his chilly stethoscope and says cheerily that my lungs are fit for parade now and he's giving me my marching orders. Everyone talks in military metaphors these days.

The first thing I do when I leave the hospital is to visit our house, which I now regard as the scene of my crime. My serge knickers are so big, they're like an extra layer of rough skin and I have to keep hitching my skirt up, folding it over at the bagging waistband. I walk around the gutted house, which still has three walls standing, but no roof and layers of scorched plaster. I can find no trace of Puddle. I expect the fire crew disposed of her.

I peer carefully at what's left of the fireplace. And sure enough, there's no sign of the fireguard in the hearth. I spot a charred sock toe lying in the grate. Matricide by arson, I tell myself, and sit on the blackened front wall, riddled with guilt.

Mrs Braden from across the road emerges from her front door with her shopping bag and trots over. 'Oh, Daisy, I'm so sorry! Your poor mum! I don't know what to say.'

'Yes, thanks.'

'You got a place to stay?'

'A hostel, in Tottenham.'

'Not far, then. That's good.'

'D'you know what happened to Puddle?'

'Sorry, dear, I've no idea. Your mum, she used to go on about that cat eating her out of house and home. Want to come in for a cuppa?'

'I'd best get on, thanks anyway. Stuff to do.'

'I'll pop along to the shops, then, see what I can scrounge today. Come and see us sometime. News is, it'll all be over soon. At least there's that.'

She bustles away. I sit for a while longer in a daze. Eventually, I rouse myself, return to the back yard where my chest of drawers is lying, almost intact, where it's fallen. I take out a few items of clothing which will have to do me until I can find some new things. At least the knickers will fit.

No one ever asks me any questions about the fire. For weeks, I expect the police to turn up with a *we know you did it* attitude. I discover that a Doodlebug landed in the next road in Walthamstow the same night I caused the conflagration, so there's no investigation into why a terraced house went up in flames. So many homes were destroyed, one more was of little significance.

By the time I'm well enough to fully absorb what's happened, London is hysterical with relief at VE day and I don't see much point in telling anyone.

* * *

I never hit it off with my mother, who was a moody, sharp-tongued woman and always ready with a barbed comment, but I am ashamed that I've incinerated her.

My father died at Dunkirk and I was an only child. Although I was raised in the East End, ours wasn't one of those families surrounded by networks of aunts, uncles and cousins. There'd been just the three of us in our rented house, so I'm on my own at twenty-four, stranded at Hailsham House with just the clothes I stand up in plus the few that I rescued from home.

The day of my mother's funeral is blustery and change-able, with a snapping breeze, which is appropriate, given her personality. My dad would often come home from work, catch me in the hallway and murmur, 'Is there a storm front or are the skies favourable?' I would reply along the lines of, 'Cloudy with a chance of sun,' or, 'Light rain, building to a persistent downfall.'

There are around twenty mourners in the church, more than I expected as my mother didn't cultivate friendships. Father Hickey relishes the dramatic potential of the funeral mass and declares that my mother had a big impact on every-one she met and won't be easily forgotten. I suspect that his words are double-edged. A wizened old lady who I've never seen before, and who I suspect is one of those professional mourners who turns up for any funeral going, is almost blown into the open grave by a sudden gust of wind. She teeters like a silent film character, arms windmilling, before

Father Hickey grabs her and pulls her back. Afterwards, we have tea and sandwiches in the presbytery. Father Hickey furtively produces a hip flask and tips a good splash of brandy into my cup, saying, 'That'll cure whatever ails ye.'

I return to Hailsham House warmed with the brandy. My temporary accommodation bears a grand name, but it's a scarred, shabby building that used to belong to the Quakers. In 1945 it's become a hostel for waifs and strays. I'm another bit of the flotsam and jetsam bobbing on the grim tide that ebbs around the world.

I left school at fifteen and joined the biscuit factory where my mother worked. I hated it there, but with no qualifications, I couldn't see a way out. So, I packed ginger nuts and digestives, occasionally knocking some to the floor for light relief. The one advantage to the job was that it satisfied my love of sweet things.

The war freed me from my biscuit prison and brought me unexpected opportunities. For many, it meant persecution, injury and a brutal death. I got a chance to shine and flourish. In fact, I enjoyed myself, although I couldn't admit that to anyone. In 1940, I drove empty buses around London, ferrying them to replace broken-down vehicles or between garages for maintenance. I loved that job, even if I wasn't allowed to carry passengers because I was female. Being on the move suited me, as did the casual swearing and matiness. I felt liberated, and with the odd exception I was treated as one of the lads. When any of the men got frisky, I'd lie solemnly, 'My fiancé was killed in France. We were going to marry when he came home on leave.' That was a potent anaphrodisiac.

Then in late 1941, I landed a job that suited me even more. I can't say what it was. Official Secrets Act. I replied to an ad that Father Hickey alerted me to in the evening paper and was summoned to Whitehall. I had to spend an hour in a room on my own, decoding and encoding complex ciphers and puzzles. I was then interviewed by two tweedy men with pipes, plummy voices and a list of razor-sharp questions. I didn't rate my chances. I was bright but chippy, and I had a cockney accent. Not their sort, and a girl to boot. To my amazement, I impressed them enough to find myself working for the government in Central London. Apparently, I had exactly the kind of brain they needed. My mother assumed that I was a secretary and reckoned that I'd got notions about myself — the biscuit factory had always been good enough for her and so on.

* * *

Soon after I've moved from the hospital to Hailsham House, I receive another note from Whitehall, telling me to take it easy for a couple of weeks. When I eventually return on a Monday morning following VE day, my section manager, Peregrine Bowles, a man who actually twirls his moustache, informs me that my group is being disbanded and I won't be needed anymore after the end of the week. I mind terribly. I understood the day would have to come, but I hadn't expected it to be quite so soon. What needles me more than anything is the satisfaction that Bowles takes in telling me. He's never really accepted women doing important work, and I'm the only female in our group. I'm not pretty enough to offer him any compensation with my figure or my face. I sense that he's always been deeply disappointed by my short stature, flat chest, dark, wiry hair, abrupt manner and general lack of social graces.

On my last day, he pats my shoulder. 'Time for you to find a husband, my dear, and settle down with a family.' His smirk indicates that he doesn't hold out much hope.

My camp bed in the dormitory at Hailsham House is hard and unforgiving. The building echoes day and night with people coughing and spitting, babies bawling and women crying. Now and again, men try to grope me.

I take stock. Mother gone, home gone, cat gone, job gone. Despite several washes, the clothes I retrieved from our house are still tainted with smoke. I smell like a smouldering bonfire. What am I going to do?

Father Hickey brings me the answer. He arrives at Hailsham House one day, sweeping in with his cassock billowing. For a priest in a working-class parish, he has friends in surprisingly top-notch places, and I'm aware that he frequents the Chelsea Arts Club. He gleans information from many sources and I've always suspected that he has an idea of what I've been doing for most of the war. At times, I've speculated that he might have had a hand in my securing the Whitehall work.

We stand in the corridor outside my dormitory. It's littered with prams, bags of clothes and dirty laundry and cigarette stubs. There's a terrible stench of blocked toilets and dodgy drains. Father Hickey pronounces Hailsham House a holy shame and no place for a tender young woman. I'm not sure that he can be referring to me.

'Any port in a storm,' I tell him.

'Well now, darlin' Daisy,' he says, 'I've a different port to offer ye, a safe harbour. A job and a home, if ye want it, and Mr Berrow likes the cut of your jib.'

'Who's Mr Berrow?'

'He's a friend of mine. We were on stage together one time, first met in a production of *Elizabeth of England* at the Cambridge Theatre. I played the Earl of Essex and he was Thomas Seymour. I can't recall now who was Queen Bess — she wasn't much good, didn't have the pipes. Mr Berrow did quite a few documentaries for the Ministry of Information in recent years — rousing propaganda about the power of the RAF and the marvels of our navy. Ye've probably seen some of them at the pictures. He lives in Fernfield.'

My interest is piqued. Father Hickey has always exuded a certain air of glamour in the parish because he enjoyed a brief acting career in Dublin and London before entering a seminary. He enjoys projecting a stage Irishman, littering his speech with *begorrahs* and *top o' the mornin's*. I suspect that he has far less of a brogue at the Chelsea Arts Club.

I ask, 'Where's Fernfield?'

'It's beyont in Oxfordshire, a darlin' little town by the Thames. About eight miles from Oxford, the city of scholars. A doty place, so it is. Jeffrey — Mr Berrow — needs a general factotum. He has a little hotel and when I told him about ye, he said ye sounded ideal.'

I have no idea what Father Hickey means, but I'm not going to let on. I've learned it's often best to pretend understanding in life. A little hutzpah goes a long way. I assume a deeply contemplative pose, which is my forte and has always stood me in good stead.

'And,' Father Hickey adds, 'this is where there's buttermilk in the tay and salt on the spuds — there's accommodation with the job. Your own room, Daisy darlin'.'

Oxfordshire might as well be another country, and I have only a vague notion where it is. The furthest I've been from London was a day trip to Southend. 'Sounds interesting, but I like London. It's my home town.'

'Ah now, Daisy dear, don't be standin' on yer dignity. Jobs are going to be like hen's teeth with all the troops comin' home, and beggars can't be choosers.'

'I'm not a beggar,' I shoot back, aware of my shoddy clothing and the singed soles of my shoes.

'Don't be misunderstandin' me. Ye grasp full well what I mean. I owe it to yer poor departed mother, may God and all his saints protect her, to try and take care of ye. She always said, "Father, now her dad's gone, if anything happens to me, make sure Daisy's all right."'

This has the ring of Hollywood, the kind of line that someone might have delivered to Bing Crosby in *Going My Way*. It certainly doesn't sound like my mother. On the other hand, she was a fan of Bing's, so maybe she mimicked one of his films in a rare moment of affection.

Father Hickey seizes on my hesitation. 'Ye'll go and take a gander? Jeffrey's a gas character. I'd say ye'd get on with him. Ye're both . . . unusual, shall we say. Free spirits. And I can guarantee ye'll like his sense of humour.'

I suppose I won't lose anything by checking this Jeffrey Berrow out. At that moment, someone is sick on the floor by the dormitory door, projectile vomit that catches the hem of my skirt. My decision is made.

That afternoon I walk to the nearest library and look up 'general factotum': *a person employed to do all kinds of jobs.*

CHAPTER TWO

Jeffrey Berrow has a jolly manner and a rich, fruity voice. Very actorish. He's average height, in his late forties with auburn hair and twinkly, bright blue eyes. His purple cravat strikes me as unusual afternoon wear. He lives in Brize Lodge, a single-storey house which resembles a mansion to me after years in a two-bedroomed terrace with an outdoor lav. It's set in a good-sized garden, half a mile from Fernfield and the Dolphin, the small hotel he owns.

My first impression of Brize Lodge is the smell of polish and soap. This delights me after years of bombing, of sniffing burning wood, cinders, petrol fumes and unwashed clothes and bodies. Tall vases of flowers adorn antique cabinets, and the place has a placid, contented atmosphere. The war might not have happened. There might not be streets of rubble, dirt and ash throughout London.

The sitting room has an arched door and windows, with glossy oak floorboards covered by a couple of dark green rugs. A well-stacked fire burns brightly. There's a piano against one wall, lots of bookshelves and sketches of famous writers on the walls. I examine them while Mr Berrow makes tea: Eliot, Shaw, Woolf, Dickens, Fitzgerald and all the Brontës. I only know who they are because their names are beneath their faces. I hope that Mr Berrow won't ask if I've read any of them. When I pick up a book, it's an encyclopaedia or something factual. My head is full of random snippets of information on all kinds of subjects. I've never been attracted to fiction or poetry.

We sit in deep-red velvet armchairs with a little table for our cups. The tea is weak but manages to taste simultaneously stewed. I assume that Mr Berrow is using the leaves several times, like most people. The cup is fine, posh china, patterned with butterflies, but mucky around the rim, and when his back's turned I wipe it with my hanky. I might have crawled from the ashes and charity accommodation, but I have standards and I once stood in the same room as Churchill.

'I'm terribly sorry about your mother and what's happened,' Mr Berrow says hesitantly. 'Horrible for you.'

'Thank you. I'd rather not discuss it.'

'Enough said. I expected you'd have a real cockney accent, but it's modified. Is that deliberate?'

'It was to start with. Now it's just how I speak.' I'd worked on it for my job in Whitehall, not wanting to sound too alien among the Oxbridge graduates.

'You're quite small and thin. Declan told me you're stronger than you appear.'

'Declan?'

'Declan Hickey.'

'Oh. Stronger in what way? Physically or mentally?'

Mr Berrow laughs. 'Haven't a clue. Maybe he meant you're a survivor.'

'Thanks. My dad used to say that I was light on my feet and I could turn on a sixpence. Is that any good to you?'

He throws his head back and chortles, flashing his teeth. 'I'll take that as a character reference. Is that how your dad meant it?'

'Search me,' I say. 'Maybe he reckoned I'd make a good cat burglar. And why is my accent, build or height of any significance? Do you need someone to do heavy lifting or ploughing?' I resent the idea that the priest and Mr Berrow have been discussing me.

He smiles. 'No need to be prickly. Usually, when one is applying for a job, one aims to present one's best side.'

That riles me. 'According to Father Hickey — Declan — I'm here to take a gander. He reckoned we'd get on. You asked me to come here, so I came.' I'm wishing I hadn't bothered and I'm not keen on Mr Berrow's upper-class accent — it reminds me of Peregrine of the twirling moustache — and the chortling might be wearing. But the next thing he says endears him to me.

'Priceless. You're sharp, aren't you? Declan said you were quick, but he didn't mention delightfully waspish. Repartee goes a long way in life and I'll be frank, I don't get much with the *kommandantin*.'

'Who's that?'

'My wife, my other half, my wifey or, as you say in the East End, my old trouble and strife. It's alright, no need for alarm, she doesn't live here.'

'Where is she?'

'She's ensconced in her own version of the Eagle's Nest at Brize Manor, up the way. We have an arrangement.'

'I see.' I haven't a clue what he means.

Mr Berrow recites with a sly tone, '*I see, said the blind man, a hole in the wall. Oh no, said the dumb man, you can't see at all.*'

He flutters his fingers. His hands are shapely and smooth. 'Now, I'll tell you what this job is, shall I?'

'Please.'

'I need a general help. I have an eight-bedroomed hotel, the Dolphin. The army took it over between forty-one and forty-four for training accommodation, but we've been back in business since then. The staff are trustworthy and reliable, so I let them get on with the day-to-day functions. I take acting jobs when they're available, which is thankfully pretty often.'

'What kinds of things are you in?' The acting sounds much more interesting than the hotel. I'm a great film fan — it's the one interest I shared with my mother, although I've never liked Bing Crosby, who's too oily for me — and I hope Mr Berrow is going to name-drop some stars.

'I have been in a few British films and did quite a bit of theatre pre-war, then during the war I had parts in information films about emergency campaigns and national security. At present, it's mainly wireless work. Although with the theatres opening up again, I'm hoping for auditions. I'm no Cary Grant, but I do have a good range of accents. I have to go to London for rehearsals and recordings, so I really need someone to keep this place ticking, make me breakfast — I'm terrible in the mornings, more of an owl than a lark — and help out at the hotel. Also—' he gives a modest cough — 'I receive a small amount of fan mail and I do like to respond, so you'd send the replies for me. There's a backlog, I'm afraid, I haven't had the time in recent months and I'm a one-finger typist. How are you on a typewriter?'

'Self-taught but proficient.'

'Jolly good. All in all, you'd be giving me a hand with lots of bits and bobs. A sort of here-and-there deputy.'

'Father Hickey said "general factotum".'

'Couldn't have put it better myself.'

'Did someone do this job before me?'

Mr Berrow shifts in his chair. 'Yes, a chap called Joe Casey. He was called up in forty-two, died in Italy.'

'I'm sorry.'

'Thank you. I miss Joe.' He takes a breath. 'So, you see, I've had to captain my own ship for a while and I'm hopeless at it. I really do need someone to keep me organised.'

I admit, 'I haven't a clue about running hotels.'

'Neither have I, frankly, but what's the difficulty? It's not so mysterious — people book, they stay and then they go. But listen, you strike me as the kind of woman who's a fast learner and who'd take a stab at anything.' He taps his nose. 'I'm pretty sure you weren't a *secretary* in recent years.'

I answer starchily, 'I've no idea what you mean.'

'Agreed.' He gives an exaggerated wink. 'Now, you'll have your own free accommodation in an annexe at the back of the lodge, buckshee meals here or at the hotel and six bob a week in your pocket.'

That's a more than decent wage. It all sounds too good to be true. I'm getting worried that Mr Berrow might include sexual services among general factotum duties. He doesn't appear at all lecherous, but his geniality could be a smoke-screen. 'Won't your wife mind?'

'Mind what?'

'Well . . . a young woman living here.'

Mr Berrow bats his eyelashes and says gravely, 'No, that really won't be a problem at all. Unless you're strait-laced and it would bother you. I can assure you that I'm not seeking a mistress. I wouldn't want to cause you any embarrassment, so if that's a difficulty, just say and we'll call it quits.'

Now I've got past the plummy accent, I'm warming to him. 'I wouldn't be embarrassed.'

At that moment, two identical black cats appear around the sitting-room door and freeze, glaring at me.

'Meet Tybalt and Oberon, brothers-in-arms and my trying and trusty companions,' Mr Berrow says. 'How could I not mention them? Feeding them would be among your most important duties.'

'How do I tell which is which?'

'Oberon has a tiny white mark on the tip of his tail, but they have different personalities. Tybalt is the saucier one, Oberon likes to please, although he can be deceitful and I don't entirely trust him. Now, what do you say to giving this job a try?' He stands, clasps his hands together, sways and sings in a convincing East End accent, 'Daisy, Daisy, give me your answer, do.'

The cats, unimpressed, leap onto the cushioned window seat, oblivious to the fact they've clinched the deal.

I laugh. 'OK.'

'Marvellous. Let's sort out dates and such.'

* * *

Before I leave London, I call round to see Father Hickey at the presbytery. He's in the back garden in mufti, shirtsleeves rolled up, cotton trousers tucked into wellies, hefting a spade. A tall, blonde man wearing shorts and a vest is with him, shaking potatoes in a large metal sieve.

'Daisy! It's good to see ye out and about and just like yerself!' Father Hickey jabs a finger at his companion. 'This is Abe. He's helping me dig up the last of the main crop spuds. Give us five minutes and we'll have a brew.'

Abe flashes a fulsome smile at me and rattles the potatoes. A fine spray of soil drifts downwards.

'I just wanted to say thanks and cheerio, Father. I've taken the job with Mr *Berrow*.'

'So he told me. He was impressed with ye. I take it ye liked what ye saw.'

'I enjoyed his sense of humour.'

'Good, good. And Jeffrey hates being on his own. He's a divil for needin' company, so he's delighted. When do ye head off to the far shires?'

'Beginning of next week.'

The priest leans on his spade and wipes sweat from his brow with the back of one hand. He's even more handsome out of his clerical garb, his skin flushed from the sun. Abe puts the sieve down, takes a hanky from his pocket and leans forward, patting it to Father Hickey's temple.

'There, you missed some.'

They smile at each other and for a moment, I feel excluded.

Father Hickey turns and winks at me. 'It'll be strange at Brize Lodge to start with, but I'm sure ye'll settle soon enough. Ye're adaptable and that's a great talent in life. 'Tis a fine house, isn't it?'

'Lovely. I'm in seventh heaven at the notion of having my own bathroom.'

'Oh,' he laughs, 'that's reason enough to up sticks to the landed gentry. Yer mammy would be delighted if she only knew. I'm saying a mass for the repose of her soul tomorrow.'

'Thanks, that would mean a lot to her.'

I perch on the handles of a wheelbarrow as the priest and Abe finish their task. It's hard to imagine my mother in repose, she was always a blur of movement and fuss. Abe picks up a worm, dangles it in the air and murmurs something to the priest. He chuckles, glances at me and upends the last clod of potato-filled earth.

* * *

I move in to Brize Lodge at the end of August, and have a hot bath for the first time in weeks — or, as JB insists on calling it, 'a luvverly hot larf'. (We agree that I'll call him JB, as he's not that fond of Jeffrey and Mr Berrow is too formal.) He delights in my cockney accent and enjoys mimicking it for his entertainment: 'Make us a cuppa rosie lee, Daisy.'

The lodge isn't big, but all the rooms are a good size. Apart from the sitting room, there's JB's bedroom, a tiny spare room, a bathroom, a square kitchen with a pantry and a dining table, a utility room and what JB calls the gubbins room, a repository for boots, old coats, the cats' bowls and beds and anything that hasn't found a place elsewhere.

The annex is a converted stable at the back of the house. There's an L-shaped sitting room with a tiny kitchen off it, a bathroom and one bedroom with a watercolour on the wall of laughing fairies sitting on toadstools in a greenish glen. I note the initials RB in the bottom right-hand corner. JB says to take the fairies down if they bother me, but I tell him I don't mind them, I like to wonder what they're laughing at.

'Probably at me,' he says. 'I've always assumed it's malicious humour. The *kommandantin* painted it. She dabbles. When you encounter her, you can ask her the source of their amusement.'

'Who used to live in this lodge?'

'The groundskeeper. He died, conveniently, leaving it available for yours truly.'

'Is there a groundskeeper now?' I listen to myself, sounding so grand all of a sudden.

'Oh yes. Winters lives in another cottage, north of the estate.'

JB adds that he hopes I won't find my accommodation too poky, but it's bliss as far as I'm concerned. I have my own door to close and a view of roses climbing a trellis from my kitchen. It's as if I've moved into the cover of a chocolate box.

I binned my cindery clothes before I left London and gave the almoner's offerings to a woman in my dormitory, glad to get rid of the unfamiliar skirts that made my legs feel naked. I'd got used to wearing trousers since the start of the war and I bought several pairs and some shirts and tops from a charity shop near Victoria.

After my bath, I dress in clean things and lie for a moment on my comfy bed. It's covered by a thick, feather-filled eiderdown, encased in yellow cotton with tiny sprays of daffodils. It's the first time I've been on my own, with any privacy, for months. A wisteria frames the window, the leaves tapping gently against the glass. I study the laughing fairies, trying to work out if their mirth is spiteful or benign and can't reach a decision.

I stretch, wiggling my bare toes.

For once, I've fallen on my feet, not on my head.

CHAPTER THREE

By late September, JB and I have a routine going, and it's as if I've lived at Brize Lodge for years.

I feed Tybalt and Oberon when I get up. Tybalt's pushy, making a fuss while his brother watches and waits. The outer door of the gubbins room is left open for them at all times so that they come and go as they please. This is where they hang out and snooze when they're not hunting or swapping chairs in the sitting room. They eat what they catch as well as a mush made of stale bread mixed with rabbit stew. (The *kommandantin*, JB explains, shoots the rabbits and cooks them herself. She also shoots pheasant, partridge and woodcock on her estate.) The cats have inspected and accepted me. I understand that I've been fully approved when they take to sleeping on my bed, usually separately, as if they've worked out a rota, but sometimes together.

I make breakfast around half eight every day — soft-boiled eggs for JB, toast and marmalade. The eggs come from the *kommandantin*'s hens and appear mysteriously and regularly by the back door. I'm adjusting to the amount of food available in the countryside. It's a marvel and makes London rations seem very meagre. JB cuts his toast into long fingers and dips it in the yolks. I like my eggs hard-boiled, so let them simmer for longer. Then I peel them whole and sprinkle them with salt.

'Is that an East End tradition?' JB asked the first time he saw me do it.

'Not sure. It was the way my dad ate them.'

Otherwise, we don't converse at breakfast. JB doesn't like talking until he's finished eating and reading *The Times*, which is fine with me. I sit and devour one of the many magazines I find in the house, of a type I've never come across before. In *Variety*, I see that the music business is bullish despite paper shortages and there's to be a new theatre production of *Arsenic and Old Lace*. The *Naturist* has articles on the importance of sunbathing for a natural, healthy life. (Is JB a naturist? I hope I'm not destined to stumble upon him nude in the garden. I should be safe for now, as it's autumn and too chilly for stripping off.) I read Hollywood gossip in *Stage and Screen*, lingering over photos of wholesome Americans who are so vigorous compared to us war-ravaged, food-deprived Brits.

Once JB has woken up properly, he's charming, good fun and often plays the piano for a while, ranging through classical pieces and popular songs. 'This is one for you, Daisy, me old china,' he'll say in mockney, launching into a London tune: 'Underneath the Arches', 'The Lambeth Walk' or 'Any Old Iron'.

After that, I might help him learn some lines for plays he's rehearsing. I've never been a theatregoer but I become familiar with *Private Lives*, *Peril at End House* and *Flare Path*. JB has smallish parts, and he walks up and down the sitting room, smoking a cigar and waving it in exasperation when he forgets a line. (He does an excellent Churchill impression with the cigar too.) It's on the tip of my tongue one day to tell him I've been in the great man's presence, but then I catch myself. I like the smoking; it reminds me of my mother and at times I get quite nostalgic and remorseful, forgetting her bad temper.

On days when JB is due in London, he drives to Oxford station and gets the train. I tidy up after breakfast, although the *kommandantin*'s surly cleaner, Mrs Milligan, comes once a week bearing a vat of rabbit stew and does what she calls a turn-out, which includes laundry. On quite a few mornings, I have to dispose of the mangled corpses of mice and birds in the gubbins room. I gradually clear most of the backlog of fan mail, about sixty letters. JB doesn't bother with lunch and eats out most evenings, in London or Oxford. Once a week, he dines with his wife — according to him, 'by royal command'.

If he sees my light on when he gets back at night, he'll call, 'Last snifter, Daisy?' We have a whisky, sitting on either side of the fireplace like a married couple and talk about the grim aftermath of the war. The wireless plays dance music softly in the background: Geraldo and His Orchestra, Glenn Miller, Joe Loss, Carroll Gibbons and His Band. Sometimes, when one of his favourites comes on, JB stands, beckons to me and sweeps me around the floor. If the cats are in, they watch us, unblinking, ears back. He comments that it's strange to dance with a woman wearing trousers, but he likes it. The first time it happens, I worry that he's getting fresh and I'm ready to stamp on his feet, but I quickly realise that he just wants to show off. He's a terrific dancer, light and fast. We sway to 'Somewhere in France with You', 'Russian Rose' and 'You Started Something'. I've never danced, but I like it and I get quite adept. *If Mum could see me now!* I have a guilty pang as we twirl. She'd probably say, *You're no better than you ought to be. Mark my words, he's only after one thing!*

One morning, after JB has gone to London, curiosity gets the better of me and I walk up the wide lane that leads to Brize Manor. It's about a quarter of a mile, the lane shaded by beech trees. My feet crunch on the gravel as I walk. The only other sound is a tractor in a field. I round a bend, halt and catch my breath as I see the house in the distance. It's majestic and stunning, built of sand-coloured stone, with a central tower, tall chimneys and ornamental caps and balconies. More like a small palace than a house. I'm mesmerised by it.

Why was JB banished from here to the lodge? How must he have felt, being relegated from this glorious home to the lowly groundskeeper's place, yet still married? Adam being ejected from the Garden of Eden comes to mind. Why did JB agree to the demotion? He's no walk-over. It strikes me as a very strange arrangement, but then my dad always said that the ways of the upper classes were a mystery hidden in a conundrum. And if she can't bear to live with him, why does the *kommandantin* want him so near and expect him to dinner every week?

As I ponder these matters, a rangy woman strides around the side of the house, wearing a pleated wool skirt, a thick sweater and gumboots. She's carrying a shotgun in one hand and a brace of dead birds in the other. I can't see her features, but her brunette hair is in a topknot. I step back as she stops and glances around, her nose lifting, before she goes through the front door.

I've seen the *kommandantin*, and although I'm sure she can't have spotted me, I sense that I've been scanned.

* * *

Each day, I cycle to the Dolphin on a Raleigh ladies' bike with a basket. JB unearthed it from his garage and got the *kommandantin*'s groundskeeper to spruce it up. It's army green and has a habit of pulling to the left, but it does me fine and I like having my own wheels. It also has an intermittent squeak and I work out that this fits the scansion of a song I learned at school, 'A North Country Maid'. As I cycle, I sing and pause for the squeak.

'A North Country maid up to London had . . .' *Squeak.*

'Although with her nature it did not . . .' *Squeak.*

'Which made her repent, and so bitterly . . .' *Squeak.*

'Oh I wish once again for the North . . .' *Squeak.*

I bowl along lanes, winding past harvested fields and stretches of newly ploughed earth that birds are thronging. There's a lot of sky and few people. Being here is a novelty, but not always a comfortable one. It takes me a while to stop feeling unnerved. Despite the empty landscape, I keep glancing around in a way that I never did in London. The space is strange, the dark fields and swooping, calling crows alien.

I find little to do at the hotel. There aren't many guests, people having neither the funds nor the inclination to travel just yet, and the place runs on a small staff, nearly all part-time. A no-nonsense, thirtyish woman called Vera Crampton is the manager. She's somewhat moody, but switches a smile on for guests. Vera covers reception during the day and oversees the bookings. It's hard to tell if she likes or dislikes me. I decide that she's indifferent. Some days she barely speaks, others she chats away. I'm not bothered by this, having spent years navigating my mother's temperament. Vera can't really decide what to do with me, but doesn't appear to resent my presence, despite the occasional sharp comment. She lives next door to the hotel in a flat above a bakery, which is run by her husband, Ray. If any guest has an emergency, Vera is available after ten at night until seven in the morning, via a push-button bell.

'Isn't that intrusive, being disturbed at night?' I ask her.

She stares at me as if I'm half-witted. 'It's been used once in eight years, when someone had appendicitis. This is Fernfield. Our guests don't have emergencies.'

There's a breezy cleaner, Dora Sullivan, about the same age as Vera, who also covers reception between five and ten in the evening. She has a slot-shaped mouth which barely opens when she speaks, giving the impression that the words are trying to escape. Dora informs me that she likes her late shift — it gives her something to do in the evenings, which are a terrible drag, especially in the winter. This strikes me as a poignant remark for a young woman to make, but Fernfield gives the impression of being sleepy and dull, so perhaps there's little to provide inspiration after dark.

The cook, Leslie Mathis, makes breakfasts and evening meals — lunch is a case of fending for yourself. Leslie also works for Ray in the bakery, which means there's warm, fresh bread and rolls every day. One waitress serves in the dining room, a pallid, jumpy sixteen-year-old girl called Susan Bates. She has a permanent sniffle and was evacuated from Stepney during the blitz.

Ray Crampton does any maintenance required. Leslie tells me that Ray's a Stalinist, which must be an unusual calling in Fernfield, so I'm keen to meet him and when I do, he doesn't disappoint. One of the bus drivers in London had been a communist and he'd chatted about the highlights of party membership, mistakenly hoping that he might recruit me. I'd got the impression that the comrades spent a lot of time falling out with each other, working out positions and then arguing against them, purging their leaders and reversing policies. It all sounded dizzying yet tiresome. Ray is dogmatic and dull, but he bakes well, so he has his compensations.

Leslie has a bullet-shaped head, black hair slathered in brilliantine and gaps between his teeth that give him a cartoonish appearance. He wasn't called up for active service because he had too many allergies, and working in a bakery was a reserved occupation. He's a fair, but uninspired cook — not that there's been much to inspire a chef in recent years — and a gossip. He tells me that Vera makes no secret of the fact that she's trying to 'fall for a baby', so he reckons Mr Berrow wants me to learn the ropes for when she has 'a bun in the oven'.

'Take no notice when Vera's having one of her off days,' Leslie says confidentially. 'She has trouble with her baby machinery some months.'

I take a few seconds to realise that he's referring to her periods. 'Did she tell you that?'

'No, Dora told me. Something about awful cramps. Dora's always urging Vera to take vitamins and herbal remedies, makes her drink milk stout. What I know about female plumbing could be written on a postage stamp, but it certainly makes our Vera down in the dumps.'

I'm finishing a bacon sandwich Leslie's made me — more bread than bacon, given rationing. 'Does Mr Berrow come in here much?'

'He's what you might call a hands-off owner. Pops in for my fish pie sometimes. He's partial to that.' Leslie eyes a paper parcel and opens it to reveal some scrawny sausages. 'Toad-in-the-hole tonight, then. A lashing of batter with powdered eggs conceals how little meat there is, Daisy. But don't tell anyone I said that or I'll have to mince you up for rissoles.' He pokes me in the ribs, a habit he has that annoys me. 'Mind, there's not much meat on you, so you'd be gristly.'

'You're no Mr Atlas yourself,' I reply, moving out of range of his finger.

I take over reception when Vera needs a break, chase the meat and grocery deliveries when they fail to turn up and help guests with queries and problems along the lines of: 'What time does the post office open? Can I make a long-distance call? The bedside lamp in my room needs a new bulb.' Hardly mind-stretching.

I miss the stimulation and importance of my war work and I'm mildly bored, but reckon I'll give it a year and save some money. Maybe I'll emigrate, or apply for further education or training. It's hard, not being at the centre of things, part of a crucial cause. Sourcing scarce toilet paper doesn't really match up. Sometimes, I close my eyes and recall the hushed intensity around my desk, the quiet cheer when there was a success, the sheer exhaustion after a long shift. Still, I remind myself, this is a lot better than Hailsham House, blocked drains and projectile vomiting, and there are plenty of people in the world with no roof over their head. And I should rightly be in jail for causing my mother's demise.

The hotel itself is a handsome, three-storey Georgian building on the High Street, with silvery-grey dolphins in the stained glass that edges the windows. Like many places after the long years of war, it's shabby, with faded curtains, carpets and fabrics. Much of the paintwork is scratched, probably damaged by the soldiers who stayed during the army occupation. It was originally a merchant's home and was converted to a hotel in the late nineteenth century. There are oil portraits throughout the ground floor of generations of the merchant's family: bewigged, simpering ladies and gentlemen with dogs lying at their feet. Downstairs, there's a spacious dining room with a bar off it, a parlour and a small walled patio at the rear.

The eight bedrooms are situated above, four on each floor. They all have marine names, presumably to fit with the dolphin theme — Porpoise, Marlin, Shark, Seahorse, Whale, Seal, Walrus and Sea Lion. When I ask JB why an inland hotel carries sea-faring references, he says that the original hotel owner must have been contrary or a retired mariner.

'I presume JB bought this hotel because acting's an unreliable income,' I say to Vera one morning when she's light-hearted and forthcoming.

'Oh, he doesn't own it,' she tells me, 'Mrs Berrow does. She bought it for him to run years back when he moved out of Brize Manor into the lodge. A sort of pay-off, I suppose.'

'Pay-off for what?'

'I don't have any details. I'd be surprised if this place turns much profit, the way things have been, and Mr Berrow doesn't take that much interest, just lets it tick along. The acting's his thing. I listen to him on the wireless. He's ever so good, can do all kinds of voices. He's a kind man, very decent. He lets Susan have the small single room on the top floor for next to nothing. He's a sucker for a hard-luck story.'

'What's her story?'

'Her mum died in the blitz and her dad's missing in action, presumed dead. She hasn't got anyone else. She stayed in the village as an evacuee and didn't want to go back to London when the war ended. Mr Berrow offered her a job this spring. She's cack-handed and can't waitress for toffee. You're as likely to get your soup in your lap as on the table with Susan.'

I detect a lack of charity in Vera's well-upholstered bosom. Perhaps JB sees me as a hard-luck story. 'Does Mrs Berrow visit the hotel?'

'She arrives once a year on Christmas Eve to do her lady of the manor bit and give the staff presents. My Ray says that come the revolution, her sort will be put against the wall and shot.'

'What's her sort?'

'Oh, big house and grounds, old money — her people have always been rich bankers. She inherited it all, never had to work for anything. Doesn't bother me, that's just the way of things, but Ray says there's a reckoning coming.'

This is startling talk in quiet, rural Fernfield. I've read that the Communist Party got two MPs to parliament in the general election, but a revolution is still a distant prospect.

'Is Ray a member of the Communist Party?'

'Oxford branch, joined two years ago,' she says in a long-suffering way. 'Fills his head with all their nonsense. I don't have any truck with politics myself.'

'You don't want Mrs Berrow shot, then?'

Vera snorts. 'Hardly! She pays my wages, indirectly. She and Mr Berrow might not live together, but she still holds the purse strings.'

I digest this. 'I haven't met her yet.'

'You will, when it suits her. She'll have approved your employment, especially as Father Hickey was involved. Mrs Berrow worships the ground he treads on, loves his blarney and the attention he pays her. Mr Berrow might call her the *kommandantin*, but he realises which side his bread's buttered.' She laughs. 'Careful what you say to Maureen Milligan, by the way. She takes everything back to Mrs Berrow.'

Mrs Milligan is frosty and tight-lipped with me at first, so there's little chance of saying anything incautious to her. She's a taciturn woman, one of those people who can express disdain with a lift of the shoulder. She sounds like one of the upper-class actresses in a Noël Coward film who try to assume chirpy working-class accents, but in fact she's a local whose husband is a farm labourer. I assume that she's worrying that I'm a fallen woman, shipped here by JB as a live-in mistress. I'm struck by the irony of this — from what I've learned about the *kommandantin*'s control of the land, properties and money, JB is a kept man. I coast Mrs Milligan's chilliness and sideways glances for a couple of weeks, and then decide to address the problem. I've never been one for silent antipathy.

She's putting shirts through a wringer — strangling them, apparently — when I approach her.

'Mrs Milligan, I just want to say that I'm not here to replace you. I'm what Mr Berrow calls his general factotum.'

'Indeed,' she says. 'Well, sounds very grand, I'm sure.'

'Hardly. Do I come across as grand? I boil eggs and do errands, basically. I've taken Joe Casey's role.'

'Oh yes, Joe. Gone but not forgotten. Quite the lad, he was.'

'And I'm not in any kind of liaison with Mr Berrow,' I add.

She stops strangling the clothes, her lips twitching. 'Now, dear, I was never going to make that mistake! Out of my way, must get on.'

I back off. Mrs Milligan does thaw towards me after a while, but it's a slow defrost, and bearing in mind Vera's comments, I keep our meetings to pleasantries.

CHAPTER FOUR

The week when my crime-solving career kicks off is a slow one. There are just five guests in the Dolphin. Joan Dean has taken a district nurse post in the area and is waiting for a rented flat. Dr Jessop and Iris, his wife, are staying while their house is being rewired. Amelia Ward is a widow who booked in after her husband's death and took up permanent residence. She has all her meals in her room, rarely ventures out and Vera refers to her as 'fixtures and fittings'. Simeon Lancaster is a solicitor from London, here for several weeks while he attends to business at Granville Grange, a large estate a couple of miles from town.

When there isn't much to do at the hotel, I walk around Fernfield, taking in its limited attractions. I set out for a stroll just after ten on a Monday morning in late October, when life suddenly becomes much more interesting.

It's a small town, self-sufficient, handsome, with a prosperous air despite the attritions of war, which luckily didn't involve any bombing. An idyllic, tree-lined stretch of the Thames passes through the town. I idle by the river, glad that it gives me a connection to London. Nobody in Fernfield spits on the pavement, jostles me or yells at me to get out of their way. There are no shoeshine stands, newspaper kiosks or three-card trick chancers on street corners. The town's sedate gentility makes me a tad uneasy after London. If it was a person, I decide, it would have a smug expression.

When I've had enough of its charms and rain starts spitting, I head to the Napolina café on the High Street. The café is a long, narrow room with a low ceiling that traps cigarette smoke and recirculates it, as if it might benefit us. The Napolina is good value, although it sticks out like a sore thumb alongside Fernfield's traditional array of butcher, greengrocer, chemist, baker, pub, dairy, newsagent and hairdresser. It's an unusual place, with its Italian name, Scottish owner — inevitably called Jock — samba music and a little grey monkey called Rindi who sits on Jock's shoulder and throws nuts at the customers. This causes great merriment and applause, except from yours truly. Rindi wears an embroidered orange jacket, a green fez and a little cloth bag stuffed with his ammunition. The monkey has taken a dislike to me and I'm sure he throws more nuts my way than at anyone else. Perhaps he doesn't care for cats, and can detect Tybalt's and Oberon's feline scent on me.

Rain is hammering down when I reach the café and order coffee. While I wait I glance around. There are just a handful of regular customers, women with wicker shopping baskets, some with freshly styled hair which they're checking in make-up mirrors. Pincurl, the hairdresser, is next door, and customers tend to migrate to the Napolina when they've had a perm or a set. This week, Pincurl's window is advertising a Greer Garson full, soft pompadour. A woman seated near the counter has just had one, her hair styled in a huge roll high above her forehead.

There's a young man I haven't seen before, sitting by the window in a long grey raincoat. He doesn't strike me as a local, with his halo of curling black hair and slim, elongated face. He wears round, dark-brown glasses and his chin is cupped in his hand as he reads a book. A student, I decide. The woman at the next table to him drops her bag, some of the contents spill and he jumps, a hand braced on his chair, as if he might run. Then he takes stock, gathers a powder compact and purse from the floor, replaces them in the bag and hands it back to her. When she thanks him profusely he bites his lip and retires behind his book. He has a sweet expression and a strong jaw that gives his pale face character.

My coffee arrives in a glass cup and it's watery, but hot and frothy. I add sugar from the tiny bowl on the counter. Sugar is still rationed, so Jock only fills it once a week and it's first come, first served. I pick a nut from my hair and carry on reading a discarded copy of the newspaper. I'm scanning an article about the founding of the United Nations and how it will be the hope for lasting peace in the future, when a commotion catches my attention from further up the café.

'Please, please get this thing off me!' The young man by the window has leaped from his chair and he's spinning around, swatting at the back of his head. His open raincoat flaps. The monkey is on his back, bouncing up and down and grabbing a handful of his curly locks. Customers are in stitches at the performance. The man yells again and Jock arrives from behind the counter, clicking his fingers at Rindi. The monkey obediently hops to his shoulder.

'So sorry, sir,' Jock soothes. 'Rindi forgets himself sometimes. Can I get you a free coffee?'

The man sounds tearful and terribly distressed. 'No, you can't. I'm not staying.'

He dashes out of the door, into the downpour and vanishes as if it had swallowed him. Rindi takes a bow and nibbles Jock's earlobe. The customers are still laughing when I notice that the man has left his book on the ledge beside his chair. I wait for a few moments, then wander over to his table, pick up the book and take it back to my seat. It's a thick blue hardback with yellowing pages, well-thumbed: *A History of Italian Architecture*. I flick open the cover and see several crossed-out inscriptions. The last legible one is:

This book belongs to Lucinda Laidlaw, 12 Market Avenue, Fernfield.
Loaned to Felix Koller, September 1945

I like the fluid, attractive handwriting. I might take a trip to Market Avenue that afternoon to return it. After all, I don't have much else to do.

I am able to return the book, but sadly, not to its owner, who I never get to meet.

Lucinda Laidlaw is a fresh corpse.

* * *

I find mayhem when I return to the Dolphin, running through the blinding, lashing rain with my head down. I almost bounce off a large policeman standing four square at the closed door.

'Careful, miss!'

That's when I see a gleaming black police car parked at the kerb. 'What's going on?'

He counters, 'Who's asking?'

I've had plenty of chats and cups of tea with the police when I was driving my buses around London. Some of the regulars patrolling my routes became friends, so I'm not in awe of this substantial bobby with a dripping helmet.

'I work here. I'm Daisy Moore.'

He opens the door for me with a meaty hand. 'You'd better go in, then, and report to Inspector Thaxted.'

I hang up my coat and see Vera, perched on her stool at reception. She has two red spots on her cheeks and she's talking to another constable, who is making a list.

'Nurse Dean is out on her rounds, Dr Jessop is at his surgery and his wife went into Oxford after breakfast. Mrs Ward is in her room and Mr Lancaster is also out at work. Oh, here's Miss Moore now.'

The constable flicks a glance at me and says he'll escort us to the parlour in a minute and not to go anywhere.

'There you are, at last!' Vera says to me accusingly. 'It's been madness here.'

'I was only in the Napolina. It was quiet when I left.'

'Yes, well . . . I've been trying to get hold of Mr Berrow. He's not answering the phone. I rang Mrs Berrow and she just said let the police deal with it. She's a cool customer and no mistake.'

'JB is in London today, rehearsing *The School for Scandal*. He's playing Sir Benjamin Backbite.' We'd spent half an hour the previous night running through lines, before dancing to Glenn Miller. 'What's happened?' The door to the dining room is shut and a policeman is loitering in the passage to the kitchen. The place is silent but the air is turbulent.

Vera cradles the back of her neck in cupped hands, elbows pointing forwards. There's a smudge of lipstick on one of her bottom teeth, where she must have been biting her lip. 'Someone's been murdered in room one. It's all blood up there. The police are here from Oxford.'

'Who's been murdered?' I glance upwards. Last time I checked, room one (Marlin) which is at the head of the stairs, was empty.

'Dora said it's Miss Laidlaw. She found her.'

That rings a bell. I take the book from my bag and open the cover. 'Lucinda Laidlaw?'

'Yes. How do you know her?'

'I don't, I found this book . . .'

I break off because a man is being led down the stairs in handcuffs. It's the young man from the Napolina, his rain-coat stained with damp patches. I see him glance at the book and then raise his large, haunted eyes to me. The lenses of his glasses magnify the appeal in them. I recall his distress in the café and I almost offer him the book, but he can hardly take it with his hands cuffed behind his back. Then he's gone.

'Who's he?' I ask Vera.

'The murderer,' she replies grimly.

* * *

The constable who'd been talking to Vera escorts us to the parlour, saying that Inspector Thaxted will question us in a while. Dora is being interviewed. Mrs Ward is the only guest in the hotel at present and has been asked to stay in her room, a request she'll have no problem with. Leslie and Susan are already in the parlour, sitting in the floral armchairs. Leslie is in his blue-striped chef's apron and reeks of pungent onions. I recall that onion soup is on tonight's menu. Susan is tearful and picking at a ladder in her stocking.

'Leave it alone, Sue, you'll only make it worse,' Leslie says to her.

He has a soft spot for Susan, calls her 'our war baby'. She laughs at his jokes and hangs around the kitchen whenever she can. I suspect she has a crush on him, despite the fact that he's spoken for, with a fiancée who works in the local bank. Leslie has a smart tongue, but isn't too quick on the uptake where women are concerned and appears oblivious to Susan's yearnings.

'I hope the police don't make me cry or nothing,' she says, pushing her lank brown hair back. She has a little rash of spots across her forehead, which she tries to conceal with a pinkish foundation.

I bet that JB loves her unmodified Stepney accent. 'Why should they do that?'

'I ain't done nothing wrong,' she replies with her irritating habit of answering questions elliptically.

'You don't need to worry, then,' I tell her.

'I'm not so sure,' Leslie grins. 'I've heard that Thaxted is a demon of a detective, just stops short of thumbscrews.'

Susan lets out a little scream and wriggles.

'Just joking — honest, Sue,' Leslie says. 'Don't get aerated, there's a pet.'

'What happened here?' I ask him.

'No idea. One minute I was slicing onions, and the next Dora was yelling the place down. She'd found Miss Laidlaw with her head bashed in. Vera'd popped out for change so I ran up there. The old dear was lying at the foot of the bed. Whoever did it used the stone dolphin from the window ledge to smash her head in. There was a lot of blood. I wouldn't be surprised if the carpet will need replacing.'

Susan shudders. 'Oh, Les, don't! It's too horrible!'

He reaches across and pats her hand. I imagine that's what she was hoping for. There's a hefty stone dolphin on a window ledge in every bedroom. They've been a feature since the hotel opened and would make a nasty weapon.

'What time was that, when Dora found Miss Laidlaw?' I ask.

'About half eleven.'

'Why would Miss Laidlaw have been in room one?'

'Anyone's guess,' Leslie replies. 'I called the police straight away.'

Vera's been sitting with her eyes closed but she straightens her skirt and takes charge. 'Miss Laidlaw had no right to be up there,' she comments. 'I've no idea when she arrived, but I didn't see her go past me. I was in the store cupboard at one point, sorting extra pillows for Mrs Ward. She's been complaining that hers are too lumpy. Nothing's ever right for that woman, she's always criticising. I suppose the police will ask me what time that was, but I'm just not sure. Dora told me she went in Marlin around ten fifteen to open the window and give it an airing. Then she started cleaning up on the top floor. She heard a thump from Marlin when she was in the first-floor bathroom, so she came out to check and she saw that chap in a raincoat running out of the room and up the stairs to the top floor. The police found him up there and arrested him.'

'He might've murdered all of us!' Susan sits bolt upright and puts her hands to her face. The ladder in her stocking soars above her knee.

'The police will be asking where we all were this morning,' Leslie says. 'I was in the kitchen and Sue was in and out. What time did you go out, Daisy?'

'Just after ten.'

'I was on reception, except for going to the store cupboard and for change,' Vera tells us, 'and Dora was cleaning, so we're all accounted for.'

'Not necessarily.' Leslie smirks. 'It wouldn't take long to nip to Marlin and do the old lady in. Any of us could have done it.'

'But they've got him, ain't they?' Susan stammers. 'That man, they've arrested him. It's all sorted.'

We fall silent. I'm wondering why he ran upwards instead of downstairs and away.

I ask, 'Do you all know Miss Laidlaw?'

Leslie cracks his fingers. 'She used to be head at the school, been retired a while now, must be in her sixties. She was there when I was a pupil — a strict old biddy, she was. I remember—'

We're interrupted by a constable who asks Leslie to accompany him to see the inspector. Vera rises and stands at the window, watching the rain whip the courtyard. She rubs her abdomen gently. Maybe her 'baby-making machinery' is aching. Susan blows her nose loudly and asks if I have any nail varnish with me.

It's a strange time to worry about cosmetics. 'I don't wear it. Do you need it now?'

'Yeah, for my stocking — stop the ladder spreading.'

I examine the wide rent. 'I'd say it's a lost cause.'

She grows teary again, wails, 'I ain't got no more and they're hard to get.'

She's so young, with no family to care for her. I have a couple of pairs which are still in good nick as I've been in trousers for so long. 'I've some spare, I'll bring them tomorrow.'

'Thanks ever so. I hope they don't give Les a terrible grilling in there.'

Vera snorts. I'm startled, thinking Susan's made a witty, kitchen-related pun, but her face is blank and she's twisting her stocking, trying to hide the worst of the ladder.

* * *

Inspector Thaxted appears mildly bored when I sit opposite him at a dining table. Susan has already set it for the evening, with a white cloth, cutlery and cruets on a little tray. The inspector has shoved the cutlery to one side. He turns the salt and pepper around and then pushes them away. I see a walking stick hooked over his chair.

I place him in his thirties, but his hair is paper white, wavy and brushed straight back from his bloodless face. His arched black eyebrows provide a startling contrast beneath. It's arresting, the old man's hair framing the lined yet young face, and I make an effort not to stare.

The table has a wobble because of the uneven flooring by the fireplace, so I lean down and adjust the piece of card under the leg nearest me. 'This is a quirky table,' I explain. I test it. 'There, that's firm now.'

He has a well-educated, dry, scratchy voice, as if a crumb's stuck in his throat. 'Thank you, it was annoying me.'

'Yes, if I was interviewing, I'd find it distracting.'

He gives me a measuring look and pinches the bridge of his narrow, straight nose. He's sitting sideways on and has gangly, spidery legs. His hollow, blueish appearance puts me in mind of the skull beneath the skin. He doesn't seem strong enough to question anyone, let alone make an arrest. I imagine a gust of wind blowing him away.

He perks up suddenly when I tell him how I came to Fernfield.

'You work for Mr Berrow and you live with him?'

'I live in accommodation attached to his home,' I correct. 'I'm a general factotum.'

He's amused, his thin lips lifting. 'Explain.'

I describe my roles, judging it best to leave out the dancing. It all sounds lame and uninteresting as I recite my litany of cat feeding, tidying, helping JB learn his lines, answering fan mail and pottering at the hotel. Thaxted flicks a pen between bony fingers as he listens, staring out of the window, but I'm not taken in. He's paying close attention. *You'd be impressed if I could tell you what I was doing this time last year.*

When I trail to a halt he says nothing, but scratches an eyebrow. He's wearing a brown worsted wool suit that dangles on his emaciated frame and, beneath the jacket, a home-knitted V-neck sweater in mustard and green stripes.

Maybe whoever made the snot-coloured garment doesn't like him. I picture a vengeful wife getting her own back with the knitting needles, although nothing about Thaxted indicates that he'd have the zing to annoy anyone that badly. And there's no wedding ring on his slender left hand.

'And you said that Mr Berrow is in London today?'

'That's right. He's an actor; he's rehearsing a play.'

'Which one?'

'*School for Scandal.* He's been in lots of stuff, some films and theatre. At the moment it's mainly wireless work.'

'Interesting combination, a thespian and a hotel owner.'

'Well, actually, that's not quite true. I've been told that his wife owns the hotel.'

'Where is Mrs Berrow today?'

'No idea. She lives in Brize Manor.'

He lifts eyes that hold a speculative glint. I can't imagine that anyone would see me as a kept woman, but I can hardly blame him for wondering about my domestic arrangements.

'She lives in the manor and he lives in the lodge.' Thaxted spins his pen on the table. 'Sounds like a play — possibly a farce, wouldn't you say?'

'I suppose it does. I haven't met Mrs Berrow yet. She likes shooting things and she paints fairies.'

He suppresses a laugh. 'Where's Mr Berrow rehearsing?'

'I'm not sure. It's a BBC production, so I suppose they could tell you.'

'It can wait. What time do you expect him back?'

'Hard to say. It depends on how well the rehearsals go. It could be very late.' For the first time, I wonder how JB will react to the murder. 'Can the hotel stay open?'

'The guests who are already resident can remain. No new guests allowed for now. No one can enter room one. We'll lock it and take the keys when we go.'

'I doubt new guests will be a problem,' I say. 'Business is slow.'

The rain has paused and the sun has escaped the clouds, pouring honey through the window. A glow catches

Thaxted's eyes and he shifts his chair back. 'Talk me through your morning, from when you arrived at work.'

I tell him that it was uneventful until I went to the Napolina café. I picture the inscription in the book I found, and take a guess as I continue. 'I saw Felix Koller, the man you've arrested, in there. A monkey was annoying him and he ran out.' I'm about to mention the book, but decide in that instant not to.

Thaxted sounds bemused. 'You know Koller?'

I reply evasively, 'Only from the café.'

His bored mask is back but I've grasped that it's deceptive, concealing a watchfulness. 'And the monkey?'

'It's called Rindi and it throws nuts at customers. A lot of them find it amusing. I don't and neither did Mr Koller.'

'What time was that?' He's making notes now in tiny handwriting. I imagine he'd be good at codes.

'He left about eleven fifteen. I stayed there for another twenty minutes or so, then I came back here. Did Mr Koller come to the Dolphin when he left the café?'

'I'm here to ask the questions,' Thaxted replies.

'Neither he nor Miss Laidlaw were guests in the hotel.'

'So I understand.'

'Do you think he killed Miss Laidlaw?' I've never seen anyone who looked less like a murderer than Felix Koller. He has exhausted, victim's eyes.

Thaxted makes an impatient noise. 'He's assisting with enquiries. How about Miss Laidlaw, had you met her?'

'No. Leslie said she was the head teacher at the school here before she retired.'

'You're well informed for someone who hasn't been here long.'

'You say that as if it's a problem. I like to ask questions, find out about people.'

Thaxted gazes at me — eyes are supposed to be windows to the soul, but his have the shutters down. His eyelashes are so fair, they're like gossamer. 'So, to recap, you left the hotel just gone ten this morning, walked around town and then called at the Napolina. You left there soon after eleven thirty and returned here.'

'Yes.'

'You didn't see Miss Laidlaw or Mr Koller enter the hotel this morning.'

'That's right. I understand that the weapon used was a stone dolphin.'

He ignores that. 'Why are empty rooms not kept locked?'

'No idea. They just aren't. It's that kind of easy-going place.'

He's unimpressed and waves a hand dismissively. 'That's all for now. Ask the constable to bring Susan Bates in.'

'What time did Miss Laidlaw die?'

'We've finished this interview, Miss Moore.'

I head to the door and turn. 'Why would Mr Koller run upstairs rather than down to the front door for a quick exit? If he's the murderer, it doesn't make sense.'

Thaxted has turned back to the window. 'That question had occurred to me. I'll be sure to ask him.'

CHAPTER FIVE

The rest of the day passes in a blur of policemen and Susan's tears while the rain drums down again from a dour sky. At one point, we're all asked to stay in the parlour again while the body is removed. It's claustrophobic as we huddle in the fading light. Cue more sobs from Susan when we hear heavy steps on the stairs. I study her, wondering if she's always been tense or if what she witnessed during the Blitz has rendered her a bag of nerves. She found a sanctuary at the Dolphin and now death has invaded it.

Leslie hands her a hanky. 'Here, pet, it's wet enough outside. You've got more water than Niagara.'

Vera says sharply, 'Do pull yourself together, Susan. We still need to deal with the guests we have and I don't want your blotchy face upsetting them. Go and have a lie down when the police have gone so that you're presentable for dinner. Take a leaf out of Dora's book. She saw a terrible sight and she's not blubbing.'

Dora has recovered well from her gruesome discovery. She's a square-set woman with little imagination, whereas I guess that Susan is cursed with too much.

'No good crying over spilt milk,' Dora observes. Her permed curls, dyed a daffodil yellow, hug her scalp tightly, sitting high on her wide brow. She has a pleasant, unremarkable face and a smooth, creamy complexion. 'That man, the one they've arrested — he was staying with Miss Laidlaw. I told that reed-thin inspector. He could do with one of your steak-and-kidney puds inside him, Les.'

'That and a good dose of Vimaltol. I swear by that stuff,' Leslie agrees.

I shudder. My mum used to buy Vimaltol for us, a disgusting mixture of malt extract and halibut liver oil. The advertising slogan lied, *They all love it because it's Delicious*.

'Is Mr Koller a relative of Miss Laidlaw's?' I ask Dora.

'That his name, Koller?' Leslie interrupts. 'Foreign, isn't it? Sounds kraut to me.'

I've been wondering who'll be the first to mention it. 'Could be German, or from any European country.'

Dora lifts her curls with a cupped hand. 'I've no idea where he's from, except that he's a Johnny foreigner. But he looked guilty as sin when he was running to the top floor. He appeared at Miss Laidlaw's place a little while ago. She was a close one, never told anyone her personal business.' She makes a zipping movement across her lips. 'When she chatted, it was all about the awfulness of war and her collections for refugees and the poor and homeless. I did say to her once that war was dreadful but this one had to be fought. I mean, what was the alternative? Lie down under the jackboot?'

I prompt, 'What did she reply?'

'Oh, offered me one of her pacifist leaflets. She was always hawking those around, had a stack of them in her bag wherever she went. I can tell you one thing — she wouldn't have lasted two minutes if the Jerries had won.'

Leslie gives her his cartoon grin. 'They'd have snapped you up, Dora. Everyone needs a good cleaner, especially those mucky Nazis!'

She's sitting next to him and gives him a friendly elbow shove. 'Get away with you!'

I persist. 'How did you know Mr Koller was staying with her, Dora?'

'I live half a dozen doors up. Saw him in and out a couple of times. He went for a walk every morning, always in that grey raincoat.'

'You never can tell who's around these days,' Vera observes. 'Maybe he has a family connection to her.'

'Hardly, with a name like Koller,' Leslie says. 'Her dad's people have been around here for years and her mum was from Banbury way. Could be he's some sort of refugee. We're going to be awash with that sort now. Loads of *wals* coming in.'

I ask, 'What's a *wal*?'

'It's a word we sometimes use around here for outsiders who come to town,' Leslie replies.

'I'm a *wal*, then,' I say. 'So is Susan. We lost our homes and families, didn't we, Sue?'

She sighs and murmurs, 'Yeah, I suppose.'

Dora leans over to Vera and taps her knee. 'You OK, Vee? You're knocked out, I reckon. If you need to have a rest, just shout.'

'I'm fine, no need to worry about me. It's just a lot to take in.'

A policeman opens the door. 'All sorted now, you can get on with your work. I just need the keys to room one.'

Susan stands up and wobbles. I go over to her. 'Vera's right. Go and lie down for a while.'

'But I have to sort out the dining room after that inspector's been . . .'

'Leave it to me.'

'Thanks ever so.'

Vera accompanies the policeman to fetch the keys, saying that she'd better check that Mrs Ward is OK. Dora announces that she'll make everyone a strong cuppa. Susan drifts away to her room and Leslie says he's all behind, and he'd better get back to his onion soup or there'll be no dinner tonight. I offer to help him and he sets me to whisking batter with powdered eggs that don't want to dissolve.

* * *

I don't set out for Brize Lodge until nine thirty that evening. It takes a while to inform all the guests about what has happened as they gradually return to the Dolphin. Luckily, none of them decide to leave, at least not straight away. Then Susan is clearly a nervous wreck when she appears early evening. It doesn't help when Leslie comments that he's sure he can smell the blood from upstairs, which inevitably sends Susan into a tear-storm. I send her back to bed and serve dinner in the dining room. The atmosphere is very quiet, just the clink of cutlery and, judging by the amount of toad-in-the-hole left on plates, the murder has affected appetites. Or perhaps it's the clumps of undissolved powdered egg in the batter.

I cycle back through the dark, my front light dancing through shadows and catching the silvery sprays of surface water on the tarmac. I'm tense as I listen to my own breathing and sniff strange scents that I can't identify. At least the rain has stopped. The air is autumnal, woody and smoky and there's a light mist hovering near the ground. I suspect that I will never grow fond of the countryside. To bolster my courage, I sing my squeak version of 'North Country Maid' very loudly. I reach the lodge just after ten and find that JB is back, sipping whisky and warming his hands at the fire.

'The weary wanderer returns! Come in, come in and take a dram. I hear we've had a murder. Inspector Thaxted phoned me with the sanitised, official version. Sit down, I want all the gory details.' He straightens his yellow cravat, pours me a tot of whisky and wrinkles his nose. 'You smell . . . savoury.'

'I served dinner — onion soup and toad-in-the-hole. Susan was in a state, what she referred to as "off her legs", so I stepped in.'

'You see, I knew you'd earn your keep. You've just missed the *kommandantin*. She was here waiting by the fire when I got back. Deemed it very bad form that there'd been a murder at the hotel, acted as if I was personally responsible.'

I am tired, although my brain is fizzing. It hasn't occurred to me that the *kommandantin* will have a key, which is dim of me because, after all, she does own the lodge.

As if he's read my mind, JB says, 'Don't worry, my trouble and strife doesn't make a habit of popping by. Her biggest concern was that all the guests might abandon ship.'

'Hasn't happened so far.'

'Excellent. Now, tell me all about it.'

I recount my visit to the Napolina, events at the hotel and the details of my interview with Inspector Thaxted. 'I don't believe that Felix Koller is the murderer.'

JB raises his bushy eyebrows. 'And what do you base that on, a fleeting glimpse?'

'His eyes are kind and anxious. A monkey made him nervous. He jolted when a woman dropped her bag in the café. He's twitchy like Susan, but worse. And he reads books about architecture. I can't see him killing an old lady.'

'*Koller the Killer* has a good ring to it though, especially as he must be foreign. I'm just articulating what others will say, not my own views,' he adds hastily when he sees my face.

'Good, because I might fall out with you. I've already heard about *wals* from Leslie.'

'Fascinating local term that, from the Old English *wealh*, meaning foreigner. Not many people use it nowadays.'

'Maybe not to your face, but probably quite a few say it silently.'

JB taps his chin. 'But why did he run, our Mr Koller?'

'And more to the point, in the wrong direction.'

The fire flickers and a drift of soot falls down the chimney. We drink companionably. The whisky — Tullamore Dew, provided by Father Hickey from his home town — is smooth and smoky. Oberon is stretched on the hearth, one paw over his eyes.

'Dora opened the windows in Marlin at ten fifteen and she found the body about half eleven,' I muse aloud. 'Felix Koller left the café at eleven fifteen, so technically, he could have committed the murder. He'd been staying with Miss Laidlaw. Perhaps they fell out, although if that was the case, why not murder her at home? Why go to a public place where there would be far more chance of being caught, and the

47

murder would be discovered pretty quickly? It would make more sense to kill her in her house and then stage a break-in to cover himself, or more likely, leave town and be far away by the time someone found her body.'

'Remind me never to cross you and put myself at your mercy,' JB comments. 'What did you make of our Inspector Thaxted?'

I've been reflecting on the infirm detective during my journey home. 'Painfully thin and not well — has to use a walking stick. But he has a good brain, he's perceptive.'

'I have a family connection of sorts to him. His deceased father was a relative of the *kommandantin*. Peter — our inspector — was in the police before the war, then sustained a nasty injury at El Alamein and was invalided out, so returned to police duties once he was well enough.'

'That explains why he's old before his time. Witnessed too much, suffered too much.' I've seen soldiers around London with similarly crumpled, weary faces, consumed by their bitter experiences.

'He lives with his mother in Oxford,' JB adds. 'The *kommandantin* sees her from time to time. His mum's a member of the Peace Pledge Union and, like Miss Laidlaw, a lady who does good works.'

It explains the awful V-neck — a misguided demonstration of maternal love. Now that I've learned about the inspector's link to the *kommandantin*, I'm trying to recall if I said anything about her that she could take exception to. It was sneaky of him not to mention his relationship and pretend ignorance of the Eagle's Nest/Brize Lodge set-up. I have to admire his guile, as it's just how I would operate.

'Is your wife involved in peace pledge activities?'

JB gives a deep belly laugh. 'Not likely! She's fond of all manner of violence — war, hunting, shooting, hanging. A thirst for blood, you might say.'

'Did you know the victim, Lucinda Laidlaw?'

'I was dimly aware of her as a churchy lady with a name attached to causes. It'd be interesting to find out why Felix

Koller was living with her.' JB pokes the fire. 'If he didn't do it, who did?'

'It could have been any number of people, including hotel staff and residents.'

'Exactly. I sincerely hope that nobody in my pay did it.'

'I wouldn't assume that. We all had easy access to Marlin during the morning and we're aware of the handy stone dolphin. It's an open field.'

JB puts a hand to his chest. 'You're not confessing, are you?'

'No, it wasn't me.'

'That's a relief. I have to admit, I'm taking this personally. I'm fond of the old Dolphin and I don't approve of someone selecting it as a venue for murder, let alone using one of the stone ornaments as the weapon. We need more details, Daisy. Fingerprints and such.'

'I'll see what I can do, but Inspector Thaxted is good at stonewalling.'

The fire flames dark gold, the same colour as my drink. I sip it, glancing at the photo standing on the little table by JB. It's of a young man with a tentative smile and a curved mouth.

He sees me noticing, runs a finger along the top of the frame. 'That's Joe, taken a couple of months before he died.'

'He was gentle-looking.'

'Wasn't he just! And Joe was a rare soul.'

There's a silence that I'm moved to break. 'How did your rehearsal go?'

'Bit naff. Lady Sneerwell had flu. We ploughed on. I have to be there again tomorrow, but I expect full reports on my return. Suppose you're too tired for a twirl?'

'As Susan would say, I'm off me legs. I'm heading for bed.'

In bed, I lie for a while, turning over the day's events. I keep seeing Felix Koller's terrified expression. Sitting up, I examine *A History of Italian Architecture* again, flicking through chapters on the Etruscan civilisation, ancient Rome, the Middle Ages and Byzantine style, the Gothic period and Renaissance and Baroque. Near the back, I find a folded note on blue paper in Lucinda Laidlaw's handwriting.

Dear Felix,
Please meet me this morning in the Dolphin hotel at 11.15. Come to room 1 on the first floor.
With thanks, Lucinda.

No date, but unfortunately for Felix Koller, this places him at the crime scene. What was Lucinda doing in that room and why had she wanted Felix there? I decide to hold on to the note and see what comes into play tomorrow. I fold it and slip it into the side pocket of my bag.

I lie back down and focus on the painting on the wall. The fairies have a sly air tonight. My door nudges open and Oberon, the fairy king himself, glides in and hops on my feet, a living, breathing hot-water bottle.

I switch off the bedside lamp and pull up the blankets.

CHAPTER SIX

I'm enthused as I cycle to Fernfield the following morning, recapturing that positivity I used to have travelling to
Whitehall each day. At last, I have something more than
deliveries and domestic trivia to interest me. The police are
back at the Dolphin when I arrive, busying themselves in
Marlin. I ask a constable if Inspector Thaxted is around.

'He's based at Fernfield station for a couple of days.
Shouldn't be more than that. We'll get this wrapped up sharpish as we've already made an arrest.'

'Has Felix Koller confessed?'

The constable straightens his helmet. 'Quite the opposite, but given his guilty behaviour, it's hard to believe his
insistence that he didn't do it.'

'Is he being held in Fernfield police station?'

'For now.'

Vera's busy on the phone, so I wander into the dining
room, hoping to gently quiz some of the guests. Simeon
Lancaster and Joan Dean have already gone. I do spy Dr and
Mrs Jessop finishing their breakfasts.

I stop by their table. 'I hope you slept well after yesterday's drama.'

Tim Jessop forks sausage into his mouth, which is heavily camouflaged by a thatch of moustache. He has a genial enough manner, but doesn't bother much with conversation. 'Oh, nothing ever keeps us awake, does it, Iris?'

'Just your snoring,' his wife responds fondly. 'But that never wakes *you*. It's a dreadful business. Got a minute for a cup of tea, Daisy?'

This suits me fine. I'd stopped at the surgery door on the way in and noted that there wasn't a clinic on Monday mornings, but in the afternoon, two until six. So, I'd love to know what they'd been doing yesterday. I pull out a chair. 'Thanks.'

Iris is playing with the toast. She's four months pregnant with their first child, content and moon-faced, but she's also glamorous, with foundation and a red bow of lipstick, her hair artfully curled. She pours tea with her capable hands. At present, she's working as her husband's receptionist and claims that she's going to continue after the birth. (The surgery is in a ground-floor extension to their house.) This is the cause of some gossip and comments along the lines of: 'Mothers shouldn't be working, and you don't want to hear a baby bawling while you're seeing the doctor.' Ray Crampton, of course, is all for it, referencing strong Soviet female comrades who take their infants to work. He'll be picturing posters with broad, head-scarfed women wielding scythes in cornfields, their babies strapped to their backs. Iris doesn't fit the type. She favours high heels and floral scents.

'Did you enjoy your trip to Oxford yesterday morning?' I ask her.

'It was very wet. I window-shopped and had an early lunch so I could be back for afternoon surgery. I did manage to get a lovely little padded jacket.'

'Was the bus on time?'

'Amazingly yes, both ways. I travelled back with Mrs Dacre on the one fifteen, we had a good old chat.'

I top up my tea from the pot and prompt the doctor, 'I suppose that gave you a peaceful morning.'

'Yes, if sorting out drawers of patients' notes counts as peace. I was just about to get myself a bite of lunch when the police came calling, asking me to pronounce on Miss Laidlaw's body. First murder I've ever attended, hope it's the last. I can't imagine that an old lady like her could have done any harm.'

Tim Jessop doesn't have an alibi for the morning, then, but his wife's in the clear. 'Did either of you know Miss Laidlaw?'

'She was my patient, but I can't comment on that,' he says.

'I worked with her in the church guild,' Iris sighs. 'She was lovely, full of verve. Fiery and quick-witted, a real ball of energy. She did loads for refugee causes. That might be how she met Mr Koller, the man who's been arrested.'

'He's a refugee?'

'I'm not sure, but I remember her saying something about him being Austrian. I heard that the police have him in custody. That was quick.'

'Bit of a giveaway, being found at the scene,' her husband mutters, spearing another chunk of sausage.

Iris rubs her forehead. 'If it was him, that's so awful. Lucinda showed him hospitality and that was her reward . . .' She trails off and sips tea, her eyes glistening.

As I'd expected, the rumour mill is working well. I'm about to ask if they've heard anything else of interest when Vera puts her head around the door.

'If you're here to do any work today, there's a veg delivery missing,' she calls tetchily.

I gulp my tea. 'Just coming.'

When I've chased down a box of turnips, cabbage and parsnips, I run into Ray Crampton, who's popped in to sort out a toilet flush. He's a beefy man, older than Vera by a good few years and dressed in navy overalls with deep pockets. He has receding hair, a trim beard just like Lenin's and always appears mildly depressed.

'I've fixed that flush,' he tells me.

'Thanks so much.'

He clutches his tool box and gestures around. 'It's a crime, a place like this standing half empty when there are people needing homes. Mr Berrow should offer it to refugees and the like. People in desperate straits who've been bombed out. I expect he would, but his wife wouldn't allow it.'

I'm reluctant to be drawn into a discussion about my employer's ethics. 'Mr Berrow has helped me and Susan. We both needed homes.'

Ray shakes his head gloomily. 'All these unused rooms. Dreadful. It's the same all over the country. Stately homes and big houses with hardly anyone in them, landed gentry not giving a toss. That Mrs Berrow lives in a six-bedroomed place all on her own. You could fit a couple of families in there, dead easy. Come the revolution we'll . . .'

I'm grateful that two constables clump through the door at that moment, as I imagine I'm about to hear tales of walls and shootings. I escape upstairs to the first floor. I'm itching to peek in Marlin, but the door is closed and I can hear movement inside and deep voices.

I head to the other end of the landing and knock at number 4, Mrs Ward's room — Porpoise. She might have heard something yesterday. Her bedroom is the largest, with double windows giving a view to the back of the hotel. She's parked in her usual chair beside her bed with her feet up on a padded stool. Her massive left leg is bandaged because of an ulcer. Dr Jessop has told her that she needs to keep mobile and lose some weight, advice which she ignores. Sometimes, there's a whiff of decay in the room and it's infecting the air this morning. I recall a history teacher once telling us about Henry VIII's ulcerated leg and contemporary reports that it stank. That information had caused me to ponder that it would be bad enough being married to a man who chopped your head off, but having to put up with his suppurating leg before being led to the block added insult to injury. (When I went home and related this tale to my mother, she commented darkly that it was God's retribution for Fat Harry's disobedience to the Pope.)

Mrs Ward is huge, with a vast appetite, and each time I see her she flows a little more over her chair. As usual, she's staring at the view of the park across the road and listening to the wireless. She has a flat, unengaging way of speaking. I've never seen her reading, sewing, knitting or absorbed in any other pastime. Either she's shallow and easily amused, or a woman of deep resources and contemplation. Conversation with her indicates the former.

'Hello, dear. I do like your trousers. So practical.'

'Thanks.' Mrs Ward always says that when she sees me.

'I was just listening to that new *Light Programme*. I'm not sure I can take to quizzes. Will it rain again today? I do hope it doesn't.'

'Probably not.' For someone who rarely goes out, Mrs Ward takes a baffling interest in the weather. 'I just wanted to check on you, in case you were upset after yesterday.'

She has a mannish face, dotted with several large moles. 'I'm tucked away up here, out of sight, out of mind. I doubt anyone wants to murder me. I wouldn't care much if they did. I could be with my Harold again,' she says, matter-of-factly.

This is Mrs Ward's constant lament. She just wants to join her dead husband, Harold. It's a shame therefore that Miss Laidlaw, who sounds as if she loved life, has been deprived of it in Marlin while the woman at the other end of the corridor lives reluctantly on.

'Were you friendly with Miss Laidlaw?'

'Oh yes. We were at school together, although I wouldn't exactly say she was a friend. Such a busybody, into everything. She was head girl.'

Lucinda sounds like a woman I'd have got on with. I perch on the end of the bed. It's covered with a flounced, red sateen spread that slides under me. 'She never married?'

A snort. 'I doubt any man asked her. She was very opinionated. A man doesn't want that in a woman. He needs peace and quiet when he gets home. No wonder she was left on the shelf.'

At that moment, I wish fervently for Mrs Ward that she could be with her Harold.

'A pacifist too,' she adds. 'I've no truck with them.'

'Did you hear or see anything yesterday?'

She yawns, her chins wobbling. 'The police asked me that. No, nothing. I was in here all morning, listening to my wireless and minding my own business.'

Why is minding your own business regarded as a virtue? To me, it's an excuse for indolence, or perhaps more disturbingly, given recent world events, the justification for doing nothing when you hear your neighbour being carried away screaming by uniformed thugs. 'I wonder what Miss Laidlaw was doing in the Dolphin?'

'It was just like her to be where she shouldn't, that's all I can say.' Mrs Ward shifts her bandaged leg with a little grunt. 'Can you ask that doctor chap and his wife to be quieter at night? Sounds like they march up and down above me, comes right through the ceiling.'

'I'll mention it to them. Have you met Mr Koller? He was staying with Miss Laidlaw.'

'That the chap Dora mentioned, the one who did it? No, but if he's a foreigner, she was asking for trouble. Play with fire, your fingers get burned. Is Nurse Dean coming to dress my leg later?'

'If she's due to, I'm sure she will.'

'It's not as if she has far to come, just along the corridor. Mind, I'm not that gone on her, she's too clumsy for my liking and she doesn't listen. The nurse before her was really gentle. I might have a word with Dr Jessop about her, see if he can get her to buck her ideas up. Can you ask Dora to fetch me a pot of tea?'

I leave her and return downstairs. Vera says that the place is as dead as the grave and she doesn't mind if I pop out.

She grumbles, 'I've just had to turn down a booking. Hope this ban on new guests doesn't last long. At least the person who enquired hadn't heard about the murder, but then he was ringing from Hampshire.'

'Some people with ghoulish leanings might find it makes for an interesting visit.'

Vera shudders and clasps at her necklace. 'Ray says Miss Laidlaw was probably murdered because she was a pacifist. He reckons there'll be lots of people with grudges coming out of the woodwork now. Like these stories about collaborators being rounded up in France.'

I reflect on this. It's an interesting theory and well worth considering, although I can see a flaw. 'Wouldn't her pacifism have made more sense as a reason for murder *before* the war ended?'

Vera stares at me. 'It must be funny, having a brain like yours.'

'What kind of brain is that?'

'Always examining things. Must be wearing.'

'I find having things to work out gives me energy.' *Instead of solving major problems like missing veg and blown lights.*

'If you say so.'

I fetch my coat and bag, deciding to forget about Mrs Ward's tea. It'll do her good to haul herself from her chair, walk downstairs and ask for it.

* * *

The day is fresh and breezy, with fast-moving clouds. I reach the police station, a small, detached stone building next to the post office. When I open the door, I step straight into a space that resembles someone's sitting room. It has a couple of armchairs, a square of floral carpet on parquet flooring and a standard lamp in a corner. I almost go back out to check that I have the right place, but then I spot a very young constable sitting to one side behind the scarred table that serves as reception. He's reading the *Daily Mirror*. The headline is about Attlee and the miners.

'Good morning,' I say politely. 'Is Inspector Thaxted in?'

He flickers sleep-crusted eyelashes. He has plump, red cheeks, a scarlet birthmark on his neck and an air of mild puzzlement. 'Not at the moment, miss.'

Good. 'That's a shame. I've come to visit Mr Koller.'

He blinks. 'Who are you?'

'Daisy Moore. I work in town and I'm a friend of Felix Koller's. Inspector Thaxted — Peter — said it would be OK to call in and see Felix. I won't be long.'

The constable is suitably impressed that I casually dropped the inspector's first name, but he scratches his cheek, trying to work out the situation. 'I'm on my own here at the moment, there's been a robbery out Kingham way.'

'I'm sure you're all busy, so I won't take up much of your time.' I prise the book from my bag. 'I brought a book for Felix to read. I expect he's in a cell with nothing to do.'

The constable reacts as if I'm speaking in tongues. 'Well . . .'

'Just ten minutes. Peter's given me the nod.'

He looks at the clock, at the heavy black phone and back at the clock. I hope he isn't going to do anything heroic like ringing a senior officer for advice.

'I'll be really quick,' I assure him, adding my best smile.

He picks a speck of sleep from the corner of his eye. 'I suppose so, then. Ten minutes, mind.'

He leads me through the back, via a basic kitchen to a room at the rear of the building. It has a solid timber door with a key in the lock.

'I'll have to lock you in,' the constable warns.

'Fine. Just don't forget me!'

He unlocks the door. 'Visitor for you.'

The room smells musty. I guess it would once have been a scullery or laundry. Felix Koller is lying on his side on a trestle bed against the far wall, his arms hugged around his body. There's one wooden chair with his raincoat draped over it and an empty mug beside his glasses on the floor. He sits up, winces as he hears the door slam and lock again and stares at me as if I'm an apparition. His eyes are amazingly big and round.

I shove his raincoat to one side and sit down. 'We haven't got long. My name's Daisy, I work at the Dolphin. Did you do it?'

He stutters, 'You mean the murder?'

'What else would I mean? I hardly came here because I thought you'd stolen the jam!'

'Jam?'

He reaches for his glasses, puts them on his nose and swings his legs to the side of the narrow bed. He's wearing a fleecy shirt and a moth-eaten brown cardigan with the buttons in the wrong holes. This is a bad sign, as if he's already given up hope.

'Did you kill Miss Laidlaw?'

'No!'

His accent is so slight, I hardly notice it. 'Good. Why were you in the bedroom at the hotel?'

'Lucinda asked me to meet her there.'

'When did she ask you?'

'She was out when I got up yesterday. I overslept — I was studying hard the previous night. I hope to be an architect. Lucinda left me a note on the kitchen table, asking me to meet her at the hotel at eleven fifteen. My watch was slow, so I was late and I didn't get there until eleven thirty.' He wrings his hands together. 'If only I'd checked my watch, she might not be dead!'

'There's not much point in thinking like that.'

'That's easy for you to say. I lost the note. I'm always losing things. Inspector Thaxted doesn't believe it exists.' He adds, perplexed, 'Why are you here?'

'I believe you're innocent.'

'Why?' He takes his glasses off and rubs them on his elbow. He has a sprinkle of freckles across the bridge of his nose.

'I just do. Answer my questions. Why were you staying with Miss Laidlaw?'

He has a hesitant way of speaking and an unworldly manner. If I spend too long in his company, I might end up shaking him. He and Thaxted share a certain fragility in appearance, but the inspector has a distinct core of grit.

'Lucinda was my mother's pen pal for many years. They had such a close friendship. I escaped to England in thirty-nine from Vienna. I was studying in London, but then I was interned. I had nowhere to go when the war ended. My parents were taken to Mauthausen and killed there.'

'Mauthausen — a concentration camp?' I'd seen a Pathé newsreel about Belsen at the cinema and I'd had to watch through my fingers.

'An extermination camp, yes.'

'I'm sorry.'

He inclines his head.

I have to swallow hard. 'So, did Lucinda get in touch with you?'

'She invited me to come and stay with her for as long as I needed.'

'Why did you run upstairs in the hotel?'

'I don't . . . that is, my room before in London was an attic. It was instinct when I saw Lucinda lying there. Upwards seemed safe.' He passes a hand across his eyes and rocks slightly. 'Poor Lucinda. Her poor head . . .'

'Did you touch anything?'

'No. I almost tripped over a stone figure on the floor. Like a big fish, and covered in blood.'

'That's something. You won't have left fingerprints.'

He makes a helpless gesture. He's a man whose face expresses every fleeting emotion. 'I'd found a place to be at peace, to study. Now . . . now they'll hang me.'

'Don't be so defeatist. What proof have they got?'

He gapes at me. 'Why have you come here? I saw you in the hotel.'

I'm about to tell him that I found Lucinda's note when I hear footsteps and angry voices. 'Here, shove this under your mattress. You left it in the café.' I take the book from my bag and hand it to Felix.

He gasps and pushes it out of sight as the door is unlocked and thrown open. Inspector Thaxted, leaning on his stick, with a crimson-faced constable hovering behind him.

'Come out of there at once,' Thaxted orders, turning on his heel.

I follow him while the constable locks up. Thaxted has an awkward, dragging limp and, like my bike, veers a little to the left. No squeak, though.

In the main office, he stands by the entrance, holding the door handle. Today's V-neck is cream and blue, which is an improvement. His hair is sticking up at the crown of his head and the creases at the corners of his eyes have deepened. I wonder what injury he sustained and how much it stops him sleeping.

He says, 'Think you're smart, don't you?'

'Yes, as you mention it.'

'Don't try my patience. I could lock you up.'

'It was a disappointing question. You'd do better asking me why I came here.'

He grimaces. 'You're a busybody.'

'That's what someone said to me about Lucinda Laidlaw.'

'Yes, and look what's happened to her.' He glances down, as if regretting the remark.

'Did Felix explain about why he ran to the top floor, about the attic he lived in before?'

'Yes, I had to listen to some Freudian rubbish about safety being upwards. I'll have to tell my shrink next time I see him.'

His tone makes me say, 'Do you see a therapist?'

'Be careful, Miss Moore.'

I blush because that was clumsy. 'OK, OK but don't you reckon that what Felix said has the ring of truth? It's simple, emotional, a panic reaction. He's been interned and his parents killed in a concentration camp. Being locked behind a door must be terrifying for him.'

Something passes across Thaxted's eyes that makes me guess I've struck home. 'You should go back to the Dolphin and see to the guests, carry out your *factotum* duties.'

Time to play my ace. 'But what about the note Miss Laidlaw left for Mr Koller? She was hardly inviting him to the hotel to murder her.'

Thaxted grinds his stick on the floor. 'Pack of lies. He can't tell us where it is and we can't find it.'

I slide the note from my bag and hand it to him.

He opens and scans it, says in a hostile tone, 'Where did you get this?'

'Mr Koller left a book in the café when he hurried out yesterday. I picked it up and I found the note in it last night.'

'You should have handed the book to the police.'

'I'm afraid it slipped my mind in the midst of all the turmoil. Mr Koller must have folded the note into the book and forgotten where he'd put it.'

'Where's this book now?'

I decide to confess on that score. 'I left it with him in the cell, to give him something to do. It's a history of Italian buildings — he's studying architecture.'

Thaxted closes his eyes for a moment, works his jaw. 'If you want to help this man — and for some reason you appear to be on a mission to do so — you'd do better to assist the police, not hinder us by withholding information.'

'Like you did from me?'

'Pardon?'

'You might have said that you're related to my employer's wife and you're aware of their living arrangements.'

'I'm not here to impart information to you, Miss Moore.'

'You will let Felix keep the book, won't you? It can't do any harm. He's had awful experiences. He's suffered terribly.'

I sense a softening in Thaxted. He must be a decent man if his mum's in the Peace Pledge Union. Maybe she'd come across Miss Laidlaw in pacifist circles.

He regroups, stiffens and says sternly, 'As have many people in recent years.'

'Yes, which is why we all need to be careful with each other.'

The inspector opens the door so gently, I can tell I've really riled him. 'Off you go and don't come back. Unless, of course, you trip over a more plausible murderer while you're sourcing deliveries.'

Stung, I stomp away. I do object to men dismissing me. At least Thaxted hasn't told me to find a husband.

CHAPTER SEVEN

Joan Dean asks for tea in the parlour when she arrives back from her rounds late afternoon. I offer to take it to her.

'You're getting stuck in suddenly,' Leslie says as I wait for the kettle to boil. He's scrubbing potatoes, up to his wrists in murky water. 'Where's Susan? She should be doing that.'

'Mrs Ward asked her to fetch some indigestion medicine from the chemist.'

Susan is pleased with her new stockings and was eager to give them an airing.

'She takes the mickey, with her "I wish I could be with my Harold." Treats us like personal staff, fetching and carrying for her all the time.'

'She's a reliable payer,' I point out.

'True enough.'

'Did her Harold wait on her hand and foot?'

'You bet. She used to send him out on errands half a dozen times a day. I reckon he turned up his toes out of sheer exhaustion.'

Leslie stops splashing water and splices a huge potato in half with a knife. His rolled-up sleeves expose his strong forearms. It wouldn't take long to nip up the stairs from the kitchen, bash someone over the head and return. He swivels, hefting another potato in one hand and I turn away quickly.

'Here, Daisy, have you got a sweetheart?'

'Not that I've noticed. Why?'

'My mate Jonty's scouting for a lady friend. He called by last week, remember? I could introduce you.'

I recall an unprepossessing, toothy youth with a cocky manner as I pour boiling water into the pot. 'I'll give it due consideration.'

'Hark at you! You'll be talking as posh as Mr Berrow soon.'

'I'm working on it.' I adopt my best BBC pronunciation. '*The rain in Spain stays mainly in the plain.* Have we got any sugar?'

'There's some left in that cupboard by the sink. Tell nurse to go easy.'

I take the tray through to the parlour. Nurse Dean is sitting in her navy uniform, her cap on the table, Gladstone bag by her armchair. She's taken off her black lace-up shoes and is massaging one foot.

'Hard day?' I ask.

'Bronchitis, bunions, boils and a bladder infection. All the Bs today.'

She has a turned-up nose, a dull complexion and a narrow smile. Her uniform clings to the contours of her hourglass figure, her bosom straining against the buttons. I've seen her whizzing along on her bike, her bag strapped to the back, her sturdy calves making light work of the road. Nurse Dean is attached to the local cottage hospital, but I've learned that she covers the town and several villages. She exudes animal energy and confidence.

I cross to the curtain and busy myself straightening it while she pours her tea.

'This is lovely. I've been dreaming about a decent cuppa. I get offered tea in lots of houses, but it's like dishwater. Have the police finished yet?'

'Yes, they've gone now, so you shouldn't trip over any more constables.'

'What a to-do! I heard they've caught the man who did it.'

'So they say. I suppose you'd come across Miss Laidlaw?'

She pleats her brow. 'I might have seen her around town, but not as far as I'm aware. I've not been here long, so I'm still finding my feet.'

'I don't suppose you could tell the police much, as you were out on your rounds yesterday.'

'I told the inspector, every day's a busy day. Lots of demobbed soldiers arriving home with aches and pains, chest problems and minor injuries. Plenty of headaches and neuralgia, but I'd say they're caused by mental stress. Not much I can do for those.'

'Sounds like you have a full list of appointments.'

'I certainly do. Hardly have time to breathe or get a snack. What's for dinner tonight? Please say it's not rabbit casserole again!'

'You're in luck, it's Woolton pie.' I finish teasing the curtains and move ornaments around the window ledge.

'Not so bad, and Leslie does good mashed potatoes. That Inspector Thaxted comes from Oxford, doesn't he?'

'That's right.'

'He's too thin, sickly and anaemic. I'd say he could do with iron tablets.'

'I believe he was injured in the war.'

Joan pouts her fleshy lips. 'I'm surprised at him having such a responsible job. A poorly policeman with a walking stick doesn't inspire much confidence. One of my patients told me Thaxted got shoe-horned back into the force because they were so short of candidates. He might find himself out of a job again once all the troops are home.'

I'm unsure why I want to defend the inspector, but I reply, 'I suppose it's his intelligence that matters, rather than physical strength.'

The nurse lifts a shoulder, unimpressed, pours more tea.

'Were all your calls yesterday morning around town?'

She raises her cup, fixes me in a glare. 'What's that to you?'

'Just wondered. You might have seen someone acting unusual near the hotel if you were visiting locally.'

She gives a mirthless laugh. 'Gosh, you sound like the police. I need to write up some notes now, if you don't mind. You can take the tray away with you.'

That's the second time today that I've been sent packing. I have a flashback to myself in the Whitehall office, coordinating crucial messages from all over Europe. I recall Churchill's fleeting visit to urge us on, that brief moment when his eyes lighted on mine and I straightened my spine.

I kick the door shut behind me with a slam, almost dropping the teapot.

* * *

I have a better time with Simeon Lancaster, who is an easy-going flirt with an inoffensive manner. He's in the bar after dinner with a brandy and he invites me to join him for a drink. I have brandy too. He puts the papers he's been reading into a folder and loosens his tie. He's fresh-faced with a shiny, bald pate and glints of gold in his teeth when he smiles.

'God save us from Woolton pie!' He shudders. 'Mashed root veg under mashed potato — it's like a form of torture. If the Nazis had had it as a weapon, they'd have won the war. I dream about beef wellington, lovely pink meat and crisp glazed pastry.' He burps loudly. 'Pardon!'

I'd seen him with a bottle of wine at dinner, and the broken veins in his nose suggest a seasoned drinker. He's lonely and out of his element in Fernfield. It's clear that he misses the city and he makes no secret of it. His desire for company, mixed with alcohol, makes him indiscreet, which I aim to encourage.

'You'll be long gone from the Dolphin by the time that's back on the menu,' I tell him. 'Can I get you another brandy? The one you've got is dangerously low.'

'Go on then, twist my arm.'

I pour him a fresh drink. The bar is shabby and window-less, a gloomy spot during the day, but comes into its own in the evening, when the fire and the lamp make it snug, a place where secrets might be whispered. I sit back down with my oaky brandy and wonder if Felix Koller is spending another miserable night in the police station. At least he'll have his book to read, if Thaxted has left it with him. I'd wager that he has. The inspector doesn't strike me as a small-minded man.

Lancaster says, 'Can you inform Vera that I'll be here for about another week?'

'Will do. Is it a complex piece of business at Granville Grange?'

'Indeed. There's a trust involved, some debts and impa-tient creditors. One of those big estates that's struggled in recent years. Hector Branch, the deceased owner, wasn't too canny financially and lousy at book-keeping. I'm having to be an accountant as well as a solicitor. Just as well I'm good at maths.' He leans closer, his fumy breath in my nostrils. 'In fact, Miss Laidlaw was a beneficiary, in a small way.'

'Really? Was she related to the family?'

'Distant link of some kind to the . . . dec . . . the deceased.' There are too many 'S' sounds there for him and he smiles at his own slurring.

'Inspector Thaxted will have been interested in that.'

'Expect so. He was going to visit the house.'

'Who owns it now?'

'Hector's son, Captain Clarence Branch.' He takes a pipe from his pocket, taps the bowl, lights up and crosses his legs.

I squash a cushion behind my back. 'I suppose you're putting in long days at the Grange, like yesterday, when you missed all the excitement here.'

'Certainly am. There's piles of paperwork to disentan-gle, and much as I like your little town and this quaint hotel, I'm longing to be back in London, where I have some hope of salmon or game pie at the Café Royal.' He expels a long plume of smoke. 'You're a Londoner too. Don't you miss it?'

'Now and again. I didn't have much to stay there for. Opportunities weren't throwing themselves at me.'

He tilts his head. 'Hope you're not offended, but you're like a fish out of water here. I mean, you've something about you, a city quickness.'

I see myself in his eyes, trapped in a backwater. 'I won't be here forever,' I say defensively.

'Just make sure the damp country air doesn't fog your brain. Then again, perhaps you'll marry a jolly farmer and raise robust children and chickens. There could be worse fates for a young woman.'

I shudder inwardly, unable to imagine one.

Lancaster hasn't noticed my unease, but continues to puff and muse. 'Have to say, this is such a tranquil place, I wasn't expecting a murder while I was here. I was going to call on Miss Laidlaw before I returned to London, to run over a few things with her. But, as they say, *memento mori*.'

'And that means?'

'Remember you must die.'

'Very cheery, I'm sure. Having a séance?' Dora bustles in, switching the main light on. 'You still here, Daisy? You're usually away by now. It's dark out there, and you going home alone. You need to be careful, there's all sorts back from the war and some of them aren't in their right minds, after things they've seen and done.'

Lancaster becomes philosophical. 'Interesting concept, *right mind*. Can any of us truly say we're in that state, given recent events in the world?'

'That's too deep for me, Mr Lancaster,' Dora laughs. 'It must be the brandy talking!'

* * *

I'm back home before JB. Tybalt and Oberon are waiting inside the door and twist around my legs. Oberon rarely mews but Tybalt makes up for him, miaowing piteously, as if he hasn't eaten for weeks. I serve them both a delicious helping of their rabbit pottage, light the fire in the sitting room and have a bath.

The house is silent. I'm not disposed to night terrors, but I can't help being aware of the darkness cloaking the lodge and that there's no one else nearby. My nearest neighbour is a woman who likes killing things. I sing 'Swinging on a Star' loudly to rouse my spirits.

After my bath, I don the dressing gown that JB gave me, saying it had been Joe's and therefore the factotum's rightful inheritance. It's almost ankle length on me, a beautiful green-and-maroon woven damask, with deep cuffs and pockets and a shawl collar. A delicious, spicy cologne wafts from it. It is on the large side, but once I've tightened the belt, it's fine. I love lounging around in its warm folds, feeling louche.

I'm brushing my hair when the phone rings. It's JB, sounding merry.

'Ah, Daisy, me old china plate, there you are! Any developments in the Laidlaw case?'

'I have more information. Where are you?'

'That's the thing, you see, I'm staying in London tonight, with Declan. We've made an evening of it and I'm at the studio tomorrow for a couple of hours, so I'm at his place.'

'OK.' I'm disappointed. I'd been anticipating a debrief.

'By the way, Declan has info about Peter Thaxted. He's up to speed on him more than me. I'll put him on.'

There's a crackle and Father Hickey says, 'Daisy me darlin' girl, is this old curmudgeon treatin' ye well?'

'He is. How are you?'

'Ah, I'm fine and dandy. I hear ye're mixed up in murder. I'm shocked by this Sodom and Gomorrah I've sent ye to. Yer poor mother must be turnin' in her grave.'

Especially as I sent her there. 'JB says you have details about Inspector Thaxted.'

He hiccups. 'Rosalind told me a while back there.'

'Who's Rosalind?'

His stage Irishman act is even more pronounced when he's drunk. 'Arra — in other words, the *kommandantin*. Sure, wasn't Peter in the police before the war. 'Twas machine gun bullets injured his leg, ripped right through and crushed the bone. Hence the limp. He was nearly a year in the hospital in Oxford, having surgery to piece it all back together. Anyways, didn't they decide to give him back his old job when he recovered. The poor crathur has to take pain killers. So, don't be givin' the man awful headaches as well.'

I hear him and JB sniggering, like two schoolboys. I'm jealous, longing to be in London, among the noise, lights and merry-making. 'In my defence, I'd have estimated I'm lightening his load, rather than adding to it.'

'He probably appreciates yer fine brain, Daisy. He told Rosalind he's surrounded by inexperienced, wet-behind-the-ears lads who couldn't catch a cold if they tried, let alone a criminal. Gotta go, I'm heatin' up soup here.'

JB is back on the line. 'How are Tybalt and Oberon?'

'Full of rabbit and stretched out by the fire.'

'Tremendous. What are you up to?'

'About to answer some of your fan mail.'

'The swooning thousands! It's wonderful to inspire such public passion.'

'Fan letters,' I hear him tell Father Hickey.

He cracks up and hoots, 'Get over yerself, Gary Cooper!'

'You two sound as if you're having a good time,' I say tartly.

'Ahem, indeed. See you tomorrow, shan't be late.'

I stack another log on the fire and pick up Joe Casey's photo. He's so young and hopeful. I tell him, 'Thanks for the dressing gown, hope you don't mind.'

I switch on the wireless and find a programme of film music, which is apt as I'm about to reply to JB's fans. I take the typewriter from the cupboard, undo the case and set it up on the table. A dozen or so letters are waiting in the manila folder. They're usually from women. I can never predict what I might find. Most are flowery and complimentary, others rambling or offering up tragic life events, a few offer criticism — men, mainly — and pointers for future roles, and sometimes there are strange ravings from fevered minds. The odd, thicker envelope may contain a script for JB's perusal, with a note along the lines of:

I do hope that you don't mind me sending this to you. I'd appreciate your opinion. It's a complex story of a warring family/long-lost lovers/a working-class chap made good/a surprising crime thriller/a tender romance.

If the script comes with a return envelope, it's sent straight back with a compliments slip stating:

Thank you for this, but I don't have time to read it and suggest you try an agent. Good luck!

If there's no envelope, it goes in the bin.

I use a standard, generic response to letters, with suitable additions and embellishments as the mood takes me. I like to make the job more amusing by mimicking the tone of some of the more annoying writers. With each reply, I enclose a studio portrait of JB, taken when he was somewhat younger. He's leaning slightly forward and to one side, chin resting on the flat of his hand. Moody and handsome. Pity it's black and white, so you don't get the flash of blue eyes.

I open the first letter.

Dear Mr Berrow,

I hope you don't mind me writing, but I wanted to tell you how much I enjoyed your recent performance in While the Sun Shines. It was very funny and gave us just the laugh we needed during bleak days! Your comic timing was spot on!

I hope to see you back on the stage before long. I loved your Rev. Ovington in Housemaster. You had me in stitches!

Yours sincerely,
Verity Ackroyd (Mrs)

I picture Verity in a tasteful suburban sitting room, waiting until her taciturn husband's gone to bed before she pens her fan letter and releases all those pent-up exclamation marks, which deserve to be returned in kind. Maybe it's the thrill of her week. I take a sheet of paper, already signed by JB, and insert it in the typewriter.

Dear Mrs Ackroyd,
Thank you so much for taking the time to write to me! I appreciate your very kind words and hope that you will continue to enjoy my work in the future.

I pause. Verity is a pleasant woman, genuine and not over the top, so I decide that she merits extra, cheery lines and exclamations.

I'm so pleased that you enjoyed the comedy. It's always lovely to receive praise! I hope you'll find that the future brings plenty to smile about!
With very best wishes,
Jeffrey Berrow

I check it through, entertaining a little fantasy about what the reply might be like if Ray Crampton was JB's factotum. He'd set out to educate and instruct, explaining that Verity was wasting her time on the indulgent, misleading fictions of capitalist impresarios and she should turn her attention to serious works by Brecht, Odets, Ibsen or George Bernard Shaw. He would warn, *Only the combined efforts of the proletariat, not comic delusions, will produce a fair and just society.*

I type the return envelope and stick the letter in with a photo, after which I stretch and decide on a small whisky. Tybalt is snoring softly and the theme to *Gone with the Wind* is playing. I haven't seen it, but JB has and condemned it as a luscious potboiler. I scan a couple more letters.

You were the best thing in Present Arms *but didn't rate the cheap scenery much.*

I'd love to see you play Malvolio, you'd be excellent.

I listened to the production of The Love Racket *but it wasn't up to your usual standard. Maybe you should try more dramatic parts if they get offered.*

That last one would offer me scope for a snide reply, but my mood has changed. Miss Laidlaw's death nagging at me. I take a sheet of paper and type quickly.

Laidlaw Case
Murder committed between 10.15 and 11.30. Plenty of suspects.
Leslie: in kitchen
Susan: kitchen and around
Dora: cleaning
Vera: in reception/around, popped out for change
Tim Jessop: in surgery, alone
Iris Jessop: shopping in Oxford, prob has alibi
Joan Dean: out on rounds
Simeon Lancaster: at Granville Grange
Amelia Ward: in her room
Felix Koller: seen running from room 1 at 11.30. Miss L had left him a note asking him to meet her there at 11.15.

It doesn't amount to much when I finish typing. I'm not sure that my list would impress Inspector Thaxted. I summon his strained, tired face. Does he worry that it suited his superiors to give him his job back when there was a shortage of candidates, but he might be replaced when fitter men return from the war, needing employment?

I leave the summary in the typewriter so that JB can read it when he gets back tomorrow, and put the guard in front of the dying fire. A guilty flashback to that other, traumatic night overwhelms me and my chest tightens. I'm only here in this comfortable house with JB, the cats and fan mail, the mysterious *kommandantin* lurking in the manor and the unexpected intricacies of the Dolphin, because I forgot a fireguard and sent my mother to her grave.

I slow my breathing and finish my whisky to steady myself.

The cats are fast asleep on the warm rug when I switch off the lights.

CHAPTER EIGHT

'That man left a note for you,' Vera tells me when I arrive at the Dolphin the next day. She's changed her hair, which was previously tied with a ribbon. Now it's styled in an asymmetrical, unflattering roll which perches like a wobbling sausage on the left side of her head.

'What man?'

'The man they arrested, the foreign chap. He's roaming the streets now, so I hope that inspector is on top of things.' She gives a little groan and holds her side.

'Are you ill?'

'No, just time of the month giving me jip.'

Dora emerges from the kitchen holding a fleece-covered hot-water bottle and presents it to Vera. 'Here you are, Vee, that'll help soothe things. Now, do you need anything else?'

'That's lovely, Dora, just the right temperature. You're an angel.'

Dora smiles at Vera, then at me. 'Us girls have to watch out for each other.' She lowers her voice. 'How are your monthlies, Daisy? Do you have trouble?'

'No, thankfully, just the odd twinge.'

'Skinny women never suffer so much, I've noticed. Me and Vera have some awful pains. I'll get you a cup of camomile tea in a minute, Vee.'

'Thanks, that always helps. Oh, before I forget, the police said we can take bookings again from next Monday, although we can't put anyone in Marlin for now. Ray's offered to clean the room once we get the all-clear. He doesn't want you or any of us girls having to touch it, Dora.'

'That's so good of him. He's a treasure, is our Ray.' Dora vanishes back to her polishing.

Ray is proving that he's an old-fashioned gent underneath the radical facade. Vera adjusts her hot-water bottle and hands me the envelope from Felix. I can see that she's dying to discover what the note's about, so I slip it in my pocket and wait until I'm in the toilet to read it.

12 Market Avenue

Dear Miss Moore,
The police have set me free as they have no evidence — or free insofar as I'm not in a cell.
The inspector had the note Lucinda wrote to me and told me you found it.
Could you come and see me? I would like to thank you in person. I will be at home, at Lucinda's, as I have nowhere else to go.
With immense gratitude,
Felix Koller.

I can't get away during the morning, because I'm covering reception for Vera, who has to take her mother to the cottage hospital for a chest X-ray. I deal with a few phone calls from prospective guests, place an order for new towels and check a town map to find Market Avenue. Vera's back just after one, so I take a break and cycle to see Felix Koller.

Miss Laidlaw's small detached house is called Woodlands and set back from the road, with a flower-filled garden at the front. In the wooden porch there's a tall wicker basket with a notice.

Please leave your food and clothing donations here. God bless you.
Thank you on behalf of all the people who are in need.
Lucinda.

I glance in and see tins of spam, jars of homemade jams and chutneys, knitted socks and scarves. I knock on the door and hear bolts rasping and several keys turning. Felix Koller is taking no chances with his security. When he finally opens the door there is a wonderful aroma of frying.

'Mr Koller, I got your note.'

'Felix, please.'

'Daisy.'

He takes me through and down steep steps to a higgledy-piggledy kitchen at the back. It's stacked from floor to ceiling with cardboard boxes labelled: Clothes, Coats, Shoes, Scarves, Hats, Socks, Food, Books, Games. The drop-leaf table is also covered in boxes.

Felix asks, 'Have you had lunch?'

'Not yet.'

'Then sit and have some with me, please. I'm making potato dumplings.'

He heaves the boxes from the table to the only free corner of the room, by the back door, and busies himself at the cooker. He's a different man today, more alert, in clean clothes, his hair damp from washing.

'I didn't expect to find you in such good spirits,' I tell him.

He turns to me with those huge eyes. 'I have my liberty again. I can lock the door and keep the world out. For now, I'm hopeful. I've learned to value each day of freedom.'

'How long were you interned for?'

'I was in a camp on the Isle of Man for almost three years. Lucinda campaigned on my behalf and sent constant letters to the Home Office. They finally listened and decided that a Jewish student of architecture was no great threat to national safety.'

I'm astonished that he says this without any sign of rancour. Anxious resignation sums him up. I cast an eye over the room while he attends to the food. There's a tapestry knitting bag on a counter with a grey balaclava in the making, beside jars of apple sauce, bottled plums, rhubarb chutney, a pile of pamphlets and books and a couple of large ring binders.

He brings plates of steaming food to the table, followed by two glasses of water. 'I'm so hungry. The food the police gave me was tasteless, like wet cardboard.'

He starts to wolf down his golden dumplings. When I take the first mouthful, I'm amazed. It's the best food I've had in a long time, herby and bursting with flavour.

'How do you get potatoes to taste so good?'

'Garlic, onions, marjoram, mustard. Lucinda has a veg-etable and herb garden at the back.' He puts his fork down, the first hunger pangs satisfied. 'Thank you. You found the note. That made all the difference because it proved that I wasn't lying about why I was at the hotel, although I believe that Inspector Thaxted still suspects me.'

'He'll have to, until he finds the culprit. You were at the scene and you ran.'

Felix drinks down most of his water, his prominent Adam's apple bobbing. 'Thaxted is an intelligent man. Another dumpling?'

'Please. You should give the recipe to Leslie, the cook at the hotel. I'm not sure he's ever used garlic.'

Felix smiles. 'British people suspect garlic. Like me, it's foreign and somewhat dubious.' He fetches the heavy frying pan and pops another herb-filled delight on my plate.

'Where did you live after you were released from internment?'

'I had a room in a house in Stoke Newington. That was bliss after the internment camp. My own door to lock! But the house was damaged in a bombing raid and I had to move into a hotel near Waterloo. It was terrible there. I was sharing a tiny attic room with three other men. It didn't do my nerves any good.'

'I understand all about unwanted company.' I give him a brief rundown on Hailsham House and the crowded dormitory.

'We've both made our escapes, then. The world has been in flight in one form or another for long years — from terror, hunger, fear.'

'We're the lucky ones.'

'I suppose. Lucinda was my luck, in the end. I was in touch with her, and when she heard about my attic, she said I must come here. I was happy to, but I kept very quiet. Lucinda explained that her neighbours are kind enough, but some are small-minded. She said they really only liked people who'd been born in the town — apparently they're called Fernies and very proud of this. I didn't go out too much. I studied, worked the garden, walked every day and called into the café now and again, although I don't like that monkey. I've had enough of being taunted in life. I kept my head down because I didn't want to invite any trouble.'

'But trouble found you.'

'Yes.' He finishes his food and slumps suddenly, a hand over his face. 'I see Lucinda, lying on the floor. Who could do such a thing? She was the kindest, loveliest lady, always helping others.' He gestures at the boxes. 'Every day, she was collecting for refugees and other victims of the war, writing letters for people like me. Always making something. She packed food parcels for the Red Cross and visited wounded soldiers in Oxford hospital — men who had no family, or none near enough to visit them.'

'I'm so sorry, you'll really miss her. You must have found it odd — that she asked you to meet her at the hotel.'

The afternoon is darkening, the kitchen suddenly suffused with shadows. In Whitehall, this was the weary time when we'd all start to droop and need a strong cuppa. One of my colleagues had a sister with a GI boyfriend, and occasionally he'd bring in Coca-Cola, chocolate or candy, which refuelled us late into the night. I fell on the chocolate as if it was manna from heaven. 'God bless Uncle Sam!' was the shout when American goodies appeared.

Felix rubs an eye. 'I assumed the meeting was something to do with Lucinda's work, perhaps collecting clothes or bedding that she needed a hand with. She was always out and about. I didn't give it much thought. When I went into the room, she was lying there . . .'

'Did you see anyone on your way in?'

'No, no one was around. I heard whistling from the kitchen, that's all.' He stacks our plates, scrapes herbs from a fork. 'Do you have family, Daisy?'

I explain about Dunkirk, my mother and the fire, editing my role in the latter. Will I ever tell anyone? I doubt it. My secret is a little pebble, like a gall stone, tucked hard and tight inside me.

'So much sadness,' Felix sighs.

I've had enough of pining and I intuit that, left to himself, Felix has a melancholic temperament. I'm sure that Lucinda geed him up, and I'll gladly take up the reins of doing that for her. I want to get on with finding this killer.

I lean my elbows on the table. 'Had Miss Laidlaw fallen out with anyone?'

'No. The police asked this too. She was too busy to have time to argue.'

'But some people might not have appreciated her pacifist leanings.'

'That's true. But surely that wouldn't be why someone killed her?'

I suppose that some people are bitter and dangerous enough to take a life over such an issue, but as I remarked to Vera, why wait until after the war to commit the crime?

Felix taps the table. 'Lucinda did tell me that she had words with Susan Bates, who works at the hotel.'

'Oh yes? What about?'

'It was a minor matter, so I said nothing to the police. Susan is so young. Lucinda caught her taking some things from the charity collection in the porch. This was soon after Susan came here from London, I believe. She told her off, but left it at that.'

'So this would have been a couple of years ago.'

'Yes. Lucinda sympathised with Susan, because she'd been through a great deal and lost everything.'

'Lucinda didn't suspect her of any more recent thefts?'

'She never mentioned that. Susan has a job and a home now, I'm sure she wouldn't steal from people who've been kind to her.'

Felix is incredibly tolerant, given how the world has battered him. I decide that the lachrymose waitress bears closer scrutiny, but I reply, 'There's no need to tell anyone else about Susan. Did Lucinda have any family?'

'A relative at Granville Grange, a Mr Branch. She saw him now and again. He died recently. She had a message to say that he was very ill, so she visited him the week before he passed away.'

'Will you be able to stay here now?'

'The inspector said it should be permissible. He's going to ask Miss Laidlaw's solicitor.'

I award Peter Thaxted a mental tick for a kind gesture.

Felix grips his head and pulls his fingers through his hair, a gesture I'll become familiar with. 'I'd completed two years of a degree in architecture in Vienna. Lucinda and I talked about me applying to Oxford when the war ended. I do hope I can stay here, at least for a little while. I'm fond of this house, and Lucinda is still all around me here. It's so quiet, and I've been working hard on the vegetable garden. Digging for victory!'

Grubby clouds are stacking and rain has started. I can see a couple of shirts blowing on the washing line. 'You'd better bring your clothes in and I should get back to work. Can I visit again?'

'I'd like that.'

I've just wheeled my bike to the road when I see Inspector Thaxted getting out of a car and fitting a trilby on his head. It's too big for him, sitting low on his brow, and obscures his face, lending him a slightly sinister air.

He beckons me over. 'What are you doing here?'

'Visiting Felix, at his request. I'm so pleased that you let him go.'

'For now.'

'Have you found any fingerprints on the stone dolphin?'

'Always so many questions with you, Miss Moore.'

I can be ingratiating when the mood suits and I need to curry favour with this man. He might be spindly, but you don't survive machine gun bullets and go back to work as a police inspector without resilience. 'Please, call me Daisy.'

'Miss Moore is fine.'

'Whichever you prefer. Thank you for letting Felix keep the book. I hoped you would. Will he be able to stay here?'

Thaxted tilts his head back and squints into the rain. A drop glints on the brim of his hat, and I watch, waiting for it to roll off. A scent of rotting vegetation rises in the damp air.

'I'm about to give Mr Koller good news, of a kind. Miss Laidlaw's solicitor has informed me that she's left him this house.'

'Goodness! That's wonderful!'

Thaxted wrinkles his eyes at me. 'Is it?'

'Yes, because he's a refugee, he has no other home and it shows that he meant a lot to her. He'll be amazed.'

The rain is coming down harder now, pinging off his hat and dripping down my face. My hair is slicking to my scalp. Neither of us moves.

'Maybe,' he says, drawing the word out slowly. 'There are two sides to every coin. You're assuming that he wasn't aware of the will. Inheritance is a tidy motive for murder, and as you've pointed out, Mr Koller is much in need of a home. It's a plight that many people find themselves in at present, so he's struck very lucky. Yes, most fortunate. Good day, Miss Moore.'

He tips his hat, turns and limps through the gate and up to the door of Woodlands. I wipe my wet face with my fingers and set off for the Dolphin. If Miss Laidlaw has left everything to Felix, he'll presumably receive her inheritance from Hector Branch as well.

He might now be in more of a pickle than he was before.

* * *

That afternoon, Leslie sets me to coring cooking apples and filling the centres with honey and cloves.

'Have you ever been to Granville Grange, Leslie?'

'I lived there with my uncle Benny for a while. He's got a cottage there, does all the general maintenance and gardening for the Branch family. I've been in the big house a few times. Old Mr Branch used to chat to me now and again. Nice enough chap.'

'Is it large? As big as Brize Manor?'

He stops chopping carrots and crunches a chunk, holding one out to me on the tip of his knife. 'At least twice the size! Knocks Brize Manor into a matchbox. Hector Branch died not long ago. He was weird as he got older, not all there up top.' Leslie twists a finger to his temple.

'What's his son Clarence like?'

'Acts as if he's God's gift to the universe. He came back from the war with a chest full of medals, so his head's even bigger now.' Leslie chucks a wedge of carrot in the air, catches it in his mouth. 'You're not Clarence's type. He goes for tall blondes.'

'That's a relief. I'd hate to have to turn him down.'

'Thought any more about Jonty? Can I give him the nod?'

'That's OK, Leslie. I'm not after a date at the moment.'

'Waiting for Mr Right, are we?'

'Something like that.' Am I? I've no idea. I've never met a man who kept my interest. My mother alleged that I'm too picky. Did that mean she settled for less than she wanted with my father? Perhaps that was the case, hence her bad humour. She did always give the impression of a woman who felt that she'd missed out.

I finish the apples, lick honey from my fingers and glance up to see JB standing in the doorway in a bottle-green trench coat and a scarlet scarf.

He waves to us. 'Baked apples! One of my favourites. Can we take two home, Leslie? I can't be bothered going out again tonight, the weather's so awful.'

'You're the boss, Mr Berrow. I'll pop a couple in a bowl for you.'

'Excellent. Daisy, it's pelting down out there, set in for the rest of the day now. I wondered if you might want a lift home. We can stick the bike in the back.'

'I'll just check that Vera doesn't need me for anything.'

Vera's at reception with clips wedged between her lips, peering in a cosmetic mirror. She's fiddling with the sausage roll on her head, which has drooped towards her ear.

'This style's too much trouble, if you ask me.'

'I liked the more natural waves you had before.'

She eyes my springy locks. 'Is that what you call yours — natural?'

'No, I call mine unique.' I've been cutting my own hair for several years, chopping it in short layers. 'Is it OK if I get a lift with JB?'

'No skin off my nose. It's filthy out there, Noah's Ark weather.'

JB's spacious Austin chugs us home through the dusk, the wipers working hard. Blinding rain lashes the car from low-slung damson clouds. It hammers on the roof and bounces off the bonnet. The world outside is out of focus, lost in veils of water.

'The Gods are angry.' JB rubs condensation from the fogged windscreen. 'Either that, or one of them's left the bath plug in.'

He smells familiar, of London smoke and dust. I'm moved by a ripple of homesickness as I gaze out at the sodden, forlorn fields. This time six months ago, I might stop in a café when I left work, have a bite to eat before the blackout, watch the world go by. I'd been at the centre of things. Now

I'm stuck in what Father Hickey calls 'the back of beyont', surrounded by dripping trees and hedges.

I peek at JB. 'Did you have a hangover this morning?'

'Not at all. Declan made me a big fry up that set me up for the day. I've been home already, by the way. I saw your crime summary.' He drives sedately, humming now and again, his hands light on the wheel.

'I have an update.' I fill JB in on the events of the day, but keep quiet about Susan for now. If all she got up to was pilfering from the charity box, I don't want to get her into trouble with JB or the Fernies. 'One minute, Felix was in the clear, now he's got a motive.'

JB does his Jimmy Cagney impression. 'Yeah, baby, the cops'll be on his tail.'

'Inspector Thaxted was pleased about the inheritance.'

'Stands to reason. Any policeman likes a clear suspect.'

'You sound knowledgeable.'

'I played Sam Spade in *The Maltese Falcon* last year. Taught me everything I needed about detection. You still reckon Mr Koller is innocent?'

'Yes, and I'm sure he had no idea about Miss Laidlaw's will.'

'Sounds a very cosy scene — you, Felix and the dumplings. Perhaps you find romance in his tale of persecution, endurance and courage,' JB says craftily.

'I admire him. Don't you?'

'Certainly. As long as he's not a murderer.'

JB hums some more, slows and stops. A couple of fat-bottomed sheep are ambling across the road, their stocky white shapes blurry in the downpour. One of them stands and stares at us. JB toots his horn and they break into a run and skitter away.

'Have you considered,' he says, 'that apart from giving him a motive for murder, inheriting Miss Laidlaw's house might be something of a poisoned chalice for your friend Felix?'

'You mean he might not be welcome in the neighbour-hood — not a Fernie? It did cross my mind.'

'Yes. It's one thing to have a foreigner staying temporarily in a parochial town like Fernfield, quite another to accept him as a permanent neighbour. Susan faced prejudice when she first arrived, and she's a native. Some people were convinced she was a female version of the Artful Dodger, bound to steal anything that wasn't nailed down.'

They weren't completely wrong about that. A glum mood envelops me. JB hums again and slows for yet more dithering sheep. Do they belong to a jolly farmer seeking a wife who'll raise children and chickens?

I can barely see out of the streaming waterfall on the windscreen now.

I decide that I hate the countryside.

CHAPTER NINE

Later, outside of cheese on toast and baked apple and with a whisky in my hand, I'm much soothed. The fire is rustling with licks of flame, and Tybalt is lying before it while Oberon snoozes on a cushion. JB has a cigar going and I'm warming my feet on the fender.

We're running through some lines from *The School for Scandal*, with me playing various characters to JB's Backbite.

'*The young lady's penchant is obvious.*' He leans back in his chair and closes his eyes as he recites his dialogue.

'But, Benjamin,' I reply as a passable Crabtree, '*you mustn't give up the pursuit for that. Follow her, and put her into good humour. Repeat her some of your verses.*'

'*Mr Surface I did not mean to hurt you—*' JB is getting into the swing of things now — '*but depend on't your brother is utterly undone.*'

'*O Lud! aye — undone — as ever man was — can't raise a guinea—*' I break off. 'What's a wainscot, JB?'

'Wooden panelling along a wall. What makes you ask?'

'It was mentioned a couple of pages back.'

'Ah, yes. There's some at the manor, especially in the library.' He pulls on his small cigar, which is the colour of leathery skin, resembling a little finger. He adds wistfully,

'The library is lost on the *kommandantin*. She never reads if she can help it.'

'Do you miss living at the manor?'

He smiles at me, but there's a hint of regret. 'Not at all. I do hanker for the library, although I can borrow books by appointment.'

'How long did you live there?'

'Too long.' He pauses, taps his cigar into an ashtray, where it throws out a tiny circle of sparks. 'You were missing London this evening, Daisy.'

'I was. Sometimes, it feels very remote and isolated around here.'

'Fernfield and the countryside can be a hard pill to swallow after London, especially in today's kind of bleak weather. I found that. It took me quite a while to adapt and I'm glad I have my regular excursions to the smoke.'

'Did you move when you married?'

'I did. I was living in a flat off Fulham Broadway. The *kommandantin* owned Brize Manor and I found it irresistible.' There's a touch of nostalgia in his voice, along with self-mockery.

'How did you meet?'

'She was a deb, gracing an after-theatre party in the West End. We bonded over Hanky-Pankys.' He sees my bafflement. 'They're cocktails. We married the following year and I moved in at the manor. I had notions of myself as the local squire.'

He might have fallen in love with the house as much as his wife. I pull my feet back from the fender, where they're getting too hot. 'I expect I'll get used to living here, JB,' I tell him, relaxed by the whisky.

'Here's an idea. Once Miss Laidlaw's murderer has been caught, you could pop down to London with me sometimes. Sit in on rehearsals, get a lungful of the city. Yes, how about that?'

I'm cheered. 'Sounds good to me.'

He rubs his hands together. 'Splendid. That'll do for my lines tonight. Let's have some music.'

He leans across and switches on the wireless. Ella Fitzgerald sings 'Cheek to Cheek'. JB crosses his legs and swings a foot in time to her velvety voice. 'So, Daisy, what are we going to do tomorrow to further our investigation?'

I like that *we*. 'I was planning to call at Granville Grange. Lucinda had an inheritance from Hector Branch and she visited him just before he died. Leslie's uncle works there. I'd like a chat with him, see if I can find out more about her connection to the family. I doubt I'd get into the house itself.'

'Hector Branch — what a buffoon that man was. A clear example of centuries of inbreeding.'

'The Branch family married their own?'

'Oh yes. Not uncommon for the gentry to be more than kissing cousins over the generations. Charles Darwin was the grandson of first cousins and married one himself. Might explain why he took an interest in natural selection.' He sniggers. 'As Declan has it, "The family that lays together stays together." He reckons there was a fair sprinkling of incest in rural Ireland at one time. Proximity with six in a bed and all that.'

I digest this. 'Does Clarence Branch have buffoon tendencies?'

'Probably, although his father married a Scottish woman, so he's benefited from fresh blood. He doesn't have the slack mouth — remarkably attractive for that family, in fact. He had a good war, as they say.'

'So Leslie told me.'

JB is tapping his chin, a sign that he's pensive. 'I have a free day tomorrow. Why don't we drive over to Granville Grange? I can visit to offer my condolences and we might get some information. You'll undoubtedly see examples of wainscot there too.'

'I like that plan. What if Captain Branch knows the terms of Lucinda's will? He might have been expecting to inherit from her.'

'Good question. Perhaps we'll get some clue when we call on him. I'll phone Vera in the morning, tell her you're not going to be in. I need to speak to Leslie anyway, about some bunnies the *kommandantin* has for him.'

'He's been trying to fix me up with his pal, Jonty.'

'Doesn't sound a promising name.'

'Jonty isn't a promising prospect, either. I declined.'

JB throws the stub of his cigar in the fire, where it flares and hisses. 'Anyway, you're far too busy with me, Tybalt and Oberon to have time for courting.'

'Am I?'

'Certainly. Not to mention your ongoing investigation. Do you suspect any of the hotel staff?'

'Haven't found any reason to, so far.' Although I'm keeping Susan in mind. Maybe her emotional outbursts are a sign of guilt.

JB raises an eyebrow, says mischievously, 'I have a bet on with Declan, that you'll solve the murder before Thaxted.'

I'm tickled by this. 'What's the prize?'

'Supper at Rules in Covent Garden. And if you do solve it first, you're included in the meal.'

'I'm disappointed that Father Hickey doesn't have more faith in me,' I remark, with mock regret.

'Ah now, he has every faith. But someone had to wager the opposite and Thaxted went to Cambridge, so it could be argued that he has an edge.'

'I suppose it beats leaving school for the biscuit factory.'

'But then again, Thaxted didn't work in *Whitehall* during the war.' JB widens his gleaming blue eyes meaningfully.

Oberon sidles from his chair, stalks to the door and paws at it.

'And with that,' JB declares, 'we'll call it a night.'

* * *

The next morning, we drive through Fernfield and north for about five miles. The sun is out in a racing sky and there's a chilly breeze. Bronze leaves swirl around the roads, which are free of sheep. I've told JB how I sing 'North Country Maid', adapting it to my bicycle squeak, and he's been teaching me 'John Barleycorn'. It's robust and bloodthirsty, making my northern maid sound wan in comparison. We belt it out as we sweep along.

There were three men came out of the West,
Their fortunes for to try,
And these three men made a solemn vow,
John Barleycorn must die,
They've ploughed, they've sown, they've harrowed him in,
Threw clods upon his head,
And these three men made a solemn vow,
John Barleycorn was dead.'

'Declan and myself do a jolly good harmony version,' JB informs me. 'We'll sing it for you sometime. Now, we're almost there, so get ready to doff your cap and mind your Ps and Qs.'

My jaw drops when I see Granville Grange. Huge, blue-and-gold wrought-iron gates topped by scrolls and crests stand open, leading to a wide avenue. We pass a gatehouse with mullioned windows. JB points and tells me that's where Leslie's uncle lives.

'The army considered requisitioning this place during the war, but it would have needed too much work.'

The house is Jacobean style, made of grey stone, with corner towers and an entrance courtyard which has a large rectangular pond at its centre. Huge urns filled with tattered foliage stand like weary sentinels to either side of the front door. I'm beginning to understand the pecking order of these country dwellings: grange, manor, lodge, gatehouse.

'It's amazing,' I breathe.

'Well, yes — until you see the rotting windows and missing roof tiles up close. You're heading for genteel decay. All fur coat and no knickers, as they might well say in Walthamstow. I wouldn't be surprised if Branch sells the place. I'd be tempted to, if I were him. Of course, he might be planning to marry and produce a dynasty of little Branches. Too awful to contemplate.'

JB pulls the bell on the massive front door. I'm expecting an aged retainer to answer, but a man dressed in fawn jodhpurs and a burgundy riding jacket opens it. He has a spry, military bearing and carries a folded newspaper.

'Yes?'

'Captain Branch.' JB holds out a hand. 'Jeffrey Berrow. We met at a dinner dance in Oxford, before the war. I live at Brize Lodge.'

'Brize Lodge.' Branch repeats the name as if he's trying to pronounce it in an unfamiliar language.

'I knew your father slightly. I came to offer my condolences.'

'I see.' Branch grimaces, his eyes sliding to me and away again. He bats the paper against his thigh.

'This is Miss Moore. She's my assistant.'

Branch's nose is too small for his wide face and his skin has a shiny patina. I realise that I've seen him before. He was in the bar of the Dolphin one evening with a haughty, golden-haired female friend. Branch told Susan off for spilling some of his gin-and-tonic. I can see that he's debating whether or not to invite us in. In the end, custom has its way, even if it lacks manners.

'Well. I was about to head out for a hack. You'd better come in, I suppose.'

He turns on his heel and strides ahead, his boots ringing on the chequered floor. JB wiggles his eyebrows at me, ushers me in and closes the door. We follow Branch across a vast, echoing expanse of hall. I have a vague impression of stuffed animals in cases, hunting trophies and oddments of heraldry.

We join Branch in a huge sitting room with a tiny log fire burning in a vast marble fireplace. There's more smoke than flame drifting from the damp wood and the room is freezing. Two sagging sofas have been pulled up to the fireplace, leaving brighter patches of carpet where they once stood.

'Do sit down,' Branch says charmlessly. He has a high-pitched, lazy voice.

We sit on one of the lumpy sofas while he perches on the arm of another. A weighty, ancient dog is lying to one side of the fire. He raises his head, casts a rheumy eye on us, then sinks back down with a little groan.

Branch nudges the dog with his foot and laughs without humour. 'Toby's like Dad was, on his way out. The vet reckons we should put him down. Neither use nor ornament, are you, Toby?'

I get the impression that Captain Branch felt the same way about his father, and wouldn't have minded assisting him on his way out of the world. I'm glad that JB is wearing an aromatic aftershave today, as the dog emits an odour of stagnant water.

'I'm so sorry for your loss,' JB offers.

'Thanks. Well, it was expected. Dad had been ill. A blessing, really. Out of his misery now.'

'So I understand. Still, it's difficult to come back to.'

Tap goes the paper against Branch's knee. 'Yes. And now this business with Lucinda on top of everything else. Just what I needed. Life's all solicitors and bureaucracy. There's a bloody nuisance of a lawyer, Lancaster, in the library right now, sweating over papers and bothering me with questions I can't answer. What's the point of keeping a dog and barking yourself? I tell you, I'd rather be commanding a company in battle any day than dealing with all of this.'

If Branch is grieving, he's hiding it well. He hasn't noticed me since we came in. Staff don't merit attention. I listen to the chit chat, taking in the gloomy hunting scenes on the walls, the damp stains and paper peeling around the windows, the faded, torn carpets and the general air of frowstiness. It beats me why people would willingly live in such discomfort. No wonder Simeon Lancaster is so disconsolate and in need of strong drink when he's spent a day here.

The dog farts loudly and flicks his tail, as if to distribute the stink. He then glowers at us, daring us to comment. We all freeze as the foetid pong ripens the air.

'I'll order some tea,' Branch says, rising and pulling a bell handle.

A tiny, oldish woman appears almost immediately, as if she's been hovering outside the door. She's dressed in a shapeless skirt and blouse and her greying hair is tucked under a striped woollen beret.

Branch waves the paper in her direction. 'Martha — tea, please, and any edible biscuits you've got. And give the solicitor a cup, keep him on his toes.'

'Yes, sir.' Martha has a country burr and a slight lisp.

I grasp my opportunity to escape the farting dog and glean information. 'I'll give you a hand.'

Branch ignores me and barks, 'Make sure the milk's not off,' as I exit after Martha.

She moves fast, trotting along in furry carpet slippers. It must be a way of keeping warm. We travel along cold, tiled corridors, one of which has wooden panelling on the lower walls, and I make a mental note to tell JB that I've spotted a wainscot.

The kitchen is cavernous and only slightly warmer than the rest of the house. Blackened cast iron pots and pans hang from timber beams, and a kettle puffs noisily on a range which is flanked by two chairs. I'm struck by a dreadful stench, infinitely worse than Toby's fart, like something rotting. I approach the big pine table and spot the source. A half-plucked pheasant is lying on it in a pool of pinkish-brown blood. Next to it is a bowl containing the glistening giblets. My stomach heaves. I put my hand in front of my face and back away, swallowing. I cross to the other side of the kitchen, as far away from it as possible.

Martha shakes the kettle, bangs it back on the range and comes closer to scrutinise me with watery eyes. 'Who are you, then?'

'Daisy Moore. I work for Mr Berrow, the gentleman I came with. I help out at the Dolphin hotel in Fernfield.'

'Oh. Took you for a boy, the way you're got up. I don't hold with females wearing trousers.'

'I got used to them in the war.'

'Bloody war. Turned everything upside down. My two nephews killed and then poor old Mr Branch dying.'

'You're right, the war was rotten. My dad died at Dunkirk.'

I've struck a chord — the community of the bereaved. Martha forgives me my trousers, touches my arm quickly, then skips away to the range. '*He* survived and came back like a bad penny,' she mutters.

'You mean Captain Branch?'

'Him, yes.' She takes a pin out of her beret and pushes it under the front to scratch her scalp.

The terrible smell is in my nostrils and I'm sure I can taste it. 'Do you mind if I have some water?'

'Help yourself.'

I take a glass from the greasy wooden draining board and open the rusting tap. There's a clanking and then the water gushes, cold and cleansing. I lean against the sink and sip it slowly. 'Have you worked here long?'

Martha pauses while splashing water from the kettle into a brown earthenware teapot. 'Forty-five years.' She laughs. 'I've fallen apart with the house. Here, out of the way, I want to rinse this.'

She bobs across to the sink, her slippers scuffing the flagged floor, and empties the water from the teapot. I watch the thin, light brown stream and am reminded again of the bleeding pheasant.

'Yes, a long time,' she continues. 'I tended to Mr Branch in his final illness. I wouldn't be surprised if *he* gives me my cards now. Won't be easy, stirring my stumps at my age.' She opens a tea caddy and spoons out black leaves.

'I heard that Miss Laidlaw came to see Mr Branch before he died.'

'Nice woman, although daft with some of her notions about world peace and sharing everything we've got. Not human nature, is it? Terrible shame what's happened to her.'

'You've heard, then.'

'Benny Mathis told me.'

'I work with Leslie. Is that his uncle?'

'He is.' She shakes the teapot, peers in at the leaves. 'I'll add a spoon extra for the pot. They're tricky, those

Mathis boys. Wouldn't trust that Benny as far as I could throw him.'

'How do you mean?'

'Benny's a poacher and I worry about what he's up to on the black market. He'd have been pleased if Hitler's lot had won the war.'

'He's a Nazi sympathiser?'

'I suppose you could say that. Some of the things I've heard him come out with . . .' She shakes her head. 'Leslie was a tearaway at school. He got expelled one time. Right old hoo-hah, there was.'

'Was this when Miss Laidlaw was the head teacher?'

'That's it.'

I'm dizzy and nauseous. It's hard to blot out the smell of offal and I can't stay here much longer. I drink more water and pinch my nose. 'How was Miss Laidlaw when she visited Mr Branch?'

Martha vanishes into a larder and comes out with a jug of milk. She sniffs it. 'As if I'd give him milk that's turned! What was it you were saying?'

'I suppose Miss Laidlaw was upset when she called round.'

'Indeed, because Mr Branch was dying. They weren't close but even so . . . She stayed for an hour or so. I didn't see much of her because we had a burst pipe in the scullery and I was mopping up water for the plumber. Now, I've got some shortbread somewhere.'

There's a buzzing in my ears and cold sweat on my brow. I have to get fresh air or I'll heave. 'I won't have tea, thanks. Can you tell Captain Branch and Mr Berrow that I've a headache and I've popped out for a stroll? I won't be long.'

Martha shakes her head and pours boiling water in the pot. 'You youngsters! Please yourself. You can go out the side door.'

* * *

I stand by one of the urns in the courtyard, bend down with my hands on my knees and take deep breaths. Slowly, my ears quieten and the nausea recedes. I straighten up and continue to breathe for a few minutes. Glancing down, I note that the rim of the urn has broken away, leaving a jagged edge.

I walk quickly down the avenue, away from noxious smells. The BO in a crowded bomb shelter had never been much fun, but it was perfume compared to that house. As I near the gatehouse, I see a man outside the open door, rolling a cigarette. He has the same bullet-shaped skull as Leslie, covered with combed-over hair, but he carries a lot more bulk, with bull-like shoulders.

'Mr Mathis?'

'Hello sweetheart, that's me. Benny to my friends, of whom there are too many to name. And you are?'

'Daisy Moore. I work with Leslie at the Dolphin.'

'He's mentioned you, said you come from London.' Benny eyes me up and down. 'You visiting here?'

'I came with Mr Berrow. He wanted to give Captain Branch his condolences.'

Benny's shoulders quiver with laughter. 'The captain won't have much use for those. Couldn't wait for the old man to kick the bucket. Made no secret of it.'

'Martha indicated as much.'

'Martha Prentice? Old mouldering Martha is worried she's for the high jump.'

Benny has a scathing manner. I dislike his heavy presence and take a step back. He leers, aware of my discomfort.

'Are you worried that Captain Branch will sell up?'

'Worried? I don't let things like that bother me, sweetheart. I've always got irons in the fire. The cap'n has inherited a pile of problems as well as a pile.' He gestures behind him at his home. 'This place is falling apart, like everything else on the estate. Woodworm, dry rot, damp. You name it, we've got it. Doesn't do my bronchials any good.' Benny taps his chest, tweaks the end of his cigarette, licks the paper and lights it.

'Martha was telling me that Lucinda Laidlaw visited Mr Branch shortly before he died.'

'Stupid old biddy. I heard she got herself murdered. How sad, too bad.'

'You didn't like her?'

'Can't say I had much time for her, with her love of conchies and refugees. Talk about a bleeding heart.'

From where I'm standing, at an angle to the door, I can see into the hallway and the photo of Oswald Mosley on the wall. The leader of the British Union of Fascists is wearing his uniform of black boiler suit with shiny belt. 'You've got different views?'

'Oh, yes. Very different.' He winks. 'I'll tell you about them sometime if you like, but I'd have to get on better terms with you first.'

'Sounds intriguing. When did you last see Miss Laidlaw?'

He fingers a shred of tobacco from his bottom lip. 'I was working on the lawnmower that day she visited, and she stopped by me on her way out. She was right peaky.'

'Upset about Mr Branch, I suppose.'

Benny leans a hip against a dripping water butt. Everything around here is crumbling, leaking, disintegrating. 'More than that, I reckon. She struck me as right funny, said something about maybe she shouldn't have come, Mr Branch had told her something disturbing.' Benny draws deeply on his cigarette, hardly breathing out any smoke. There's a *plink* as the butt drips more water.

'I wonder what he said to her?'

'Dunno. She wittered on, something about an awful lie. That was it. I wasn't that interested. She hurried off, white as a snowdrop. Mind you, old Mr Branch was raving towards the end. Whatever he told her, he was probably recalling something that happened years back.'

Perhaps, but this nugget of news makes the nausea worthwhile. 'Do you recall when that was?'

'July time, sweetheart. Mr Branch died not long after. You're a nosy one, just like Leslie told me.'

'He says I'm nosy?'

'Curious, like. And you'll have heard the saying, "curiosity killed the cat".'

'I have, but the complete saying ends, "but satisfaction brought it back".'

'Eh?'

'The saying means the opposite of what most people believe. It's not a warning against curiosity, it's saying that people should be inquiring.' *Put that in your cigarette and smoke it, sweetheart.*

He ogles me. 'You're a smart one and no mistake. I'd say you could teach me a thing or two if we spent time together. Want a cuppa? I'm just about to make a brew. Or we could have something stronger, if you're in the mood. Or to *put* you in the mood.'

I want to ask him about Leslie's expulsion from school but he'll probably insist I accompany him inside, and I have a growing desire to escape from him. I imagine a lair full of fascist insignia. 'No thanks. I'd better head back. Mr Berrow will be wondering where I've got to.'

'That's a shame. Just call by any time, Miss Curiosity. Any friend of Leslie's is a friend of mine.'

CHAPTER TEN

'I was hoping you were finding out something useful to compensate for my agony,' JB says as we drive back. 'I'd rather have hot needles poked in my eyes than take tea with that ghastly Branch man again.'

I've explained about the kitchen, the bloodied pheasant and my visit to Benny Mathis. 'Useful, maybe, but how do I find out what this disturbing lie was? It must be something to do with the Branch family, surely . . .' I duck down suddenly as I see a black car driving towards us.

'What are you doing, Daisy? Not nauseous again?'

'That's Inspector Thaxted. He must be on his way to Granville Grange. I don't want him to see me.'

'Why ever not? You're allowed on the public highway.'

'He'll realise I've been to the house. I'm already in his bad books.'

JB chuckles. 'Branch will probably tell him about us anyway.'

'He might not refer to me. I was beneath his notice.'

'You can get back up now, the dreaded inspector's long gone.'

I get up slowly, checking out the rear window. I half expect to see that Peter Thaxted has turned round and is pursuing us. I must be light-headed after my encounter with Martha and her pheasant entrails. I straighten my twisted coat. 'Martha also told me that Miss Laidlaw expelled Leslie Mathis from school. She said there was a hoo-ha about it.'

'Leslie would hardly have murdered his old head teacher all these years later. You should go back to Felix Koller. He might recall something about Lucinda's visit to Hector. If she was that upset, she'd surely have mentioned it to him.'

'We could call on him now. I'd like you to meet him.'

'I'm game. I can gauge if he's as innocent as you make out.'

'I do hate being called sweetheart. Benny Mathis is a horrible lecher.'

'I suppose he lives a solitary kind of life, gets overexcited when he meets a young woman.'

I shudder. 'He makes Leslie's mate Jonty positively attractive. He's a fascist sympathiser too. I saw a photo of Oswald Mosley on his wall, arm raised and spouting venom.'

'With Mosley out of internment, the blackshirts will be crawling back out of the woodwork soon, I expect. Mosley and Hitler — men with silly moustaches and hearts of pure evil.'

Felix is arriving home with a bag of shopping when we reach Woodlands. We all stand on the path beside beautiful ochre chrysanthemums as I introduce JB.

Felix twitches his head to his left. 'Let's go inside.'

I follow his glance and see a net curtain moving next door. He fishes out his heavy set of keys, undoes locks and shows us into a cosy sitting room at the front of the house.

'I'll make some tea,' he says, lighting the fire he's laid in the grate.

JB stands when he's left the room, hands in pockets, swivelling around on one heel. 'Very quaint.'

I sink into one of the worn leather armchairs. The wallpaper is yellow and brown, traced with ivy leaves. There's a writing bureau, bookshelves, two standard lamps, an oval mirror over the mantelpiece and scores of pottery donkeys, some with panniers.

JB examines a couple. 'I'm surprised there aren't donkeys on the wallpaper.'

'Don't be a snob. At least this room warms up fast, unlike those vast acres of gloom at Granville Grange.'

He laughs and sits down. 'I am a snob sometimes. Living at Brize Manor spoiled me.'

'Did you have servants?'

'A cook and several maids, plus the redoubtable Mrs Milligan. Life was entirely comfortable, yet unbearable.'

I'm about to question this enigmatic statement when Felix returns with a tray of tea, and a plate of honey and ginger biscuits. He's fretful again today and his hand shakes a little as he lifts the teapot. 'Inspector Thaxted came to see me after you left yesterday.'

'I met him on my way out and he told me about your inheritance.' I take two biscuits, hungry now my nausea has worn off.

'Good and bad news for you.' JB is sitting back and watching him.

Felix crouches forward in his chair. 'I had absolutely no idea that Lucinda had made me her heir. I told the inspector as much, but I'm not sure he believed me and he pointed out that it makes me a suspect again. He told me that she made the will in 1941, while I was interned.'

'Did he say if she'd had a prior will, and if so who her beneficiary was?' I ask.

Felix hands us both cups of tea. 'No, he didn't mention that. I'm so stunned. I couldn't sleep last night. Lucinda's solicitor has asked to see me after the funeral. The inspector said I might find myself a rich man.'

'What will you do with this inheritance?' JB asks in a deceptively mild voice.

Felix pushes his hands down on his knees, steadying himself. 'I have no idea. My mind's in a stupor. I wish Lucinda had told me.'

'You don't have to make any decisions just yet,' I say.

He sips his tea, unconvinced. 'It's just . . . overwhelming.'

I take a third biscuit. 'These are delicious. Did you make them?'

'Me? No, Lucinda did.' He tears up and blinks.

JB stirs his tea. 'Felix, when Lucinda went to visit Hector Branch, just before he died, how was she when she came home?'

Felix does his hair-tugging trick. 'She was very tired and didn't say much, just that Mr Branch was ill and hadn't got long to live. She went to lie down . . . yes, yes, she did, because she asked me to wake her at three o'clock so that she could go to Oxford for a hospital visit later that day.'

'And did she say anything else about Mr Branch?' JB asks.

'We had tea before she went to Oxford. She talked a little about the visit but she was distracted. It must have been hard for her to see this dying man.'

'We've heard that he was quite confused,' I say.

Felix pushes his glasses up his nose. 'But you see, Lucinda said that she found him surprisingly lucid that day. They spoke for a while. At one point, she observed that some people had no qualms about lying, but then she went on to discuss the garden, asked me to dig out the remaining spinach. I recall her saying that about lying, because I had to look up "qualms", a word I hadn't come across before.'

I pour us all more tea and pass the biscuits round so that I can have another. It's lovely and warm in the room now and I'm full of honey bliss. The war has been tough for people like me, with a sweet tooth. 'Lucinda didn't say who this liar was?'

Felix shrugs. 'That's all I can remember.'

I have an idea. 'Did Lucinda keep a diary?'

'Yes, she sat in that chair you're in and wrote in it every night.'

I exchange glances with JB. 'Could we see it?'

'The inspector took it away yesterday.'

'Oh.' I crunch my biscuit. Of course he did.

Felix cradles his face in his hands. 'Why are you asking about this? Did Lucinda hear something that caused her death?'

'She might have,' JB tells him.

'I see. I do miss her. If something was worrying her, she should have told me.' He clicks his fingers. 'Is that the reason why she asked me to meet her in the Dolphin — was it about this person who'd lied?'

'Could be,' I tell him. 'Maybe she was going to meet them and wanted you there to back her up.'

'But why at the hotel?' JB asks. 'Why not meet here?'

'There are too many questions.' Felix sighs. 'And another question is, who will arrange Lucinda's funeral? This is worrying me.'

'Ah, I have news about that.' JB slides me a sidelong glance. 'I haven't had time to tell you yet, Daisy. When I was talking to Captain Branch on my own, he said reluctantly that he supposed he'd have to organise it. He added sharpish that the payment would have to come out of Lucinda's estate and he'd make sure the bill went to her solicitor. I got the impression he's not aware of your inheritance yet, Felix. He might fire some shots across your bow if he was expecting to be Lucinda's beneficiary.'

Felix is horrified. 'I hadn't considered that. It could cause a lot of trouble!' He drops his head back and groans.

He's an innocent abroad, despite his grim life experiences. I pull a face at JB, who adopts his best avuncular tone. I wonder which character he's summoning. I gather from the warmth in his voice that he's decided that Felix is genuine, and not a killer.

'Listen, Felix, it might not come to that. The law's the law, and you're entitled to the inheritance Lucinda left you. You need to be aware of possible problems from Branch, but in the end, you're her beneficiary. You just have to tough things out for now. You've already done that in your life, so you need to "screw your courage to the sticking place". Those are Lady Macbeth's words, not mine, by the way.'

'Yes, chin up, shoulders back,' I add, echoing Peregrine Bowles when he was chivvying us during a long shift. 'You've got friends in me and JB. We're on your side.'

'You're so kind,' Felix says. 'How can I ever repay you?'

'We'll take some of these biscuits with us,' JB tells him. 'They'll keep Daisy quiet. I'm surprised she has a tooth in her head, with her craving for sugar.'

At the door, I turn to Felix. It's not good for him to hide in the house on his own too much. 'Would you like to meet me in the Napolina tomorrow around one for a coffee? If you can stand the monkey, that is.'

'Thanks, I'd like that.'

In the car, JB turns to me. 'Chin up, shoulders back. Where on earth did that come from?'

'Someone I used to work with. Given the circumstances, it was more apt than quoting a woman who's urging her husband to commit murder.'

'True. I hadn't thought of it like that. It was the first quote that popped into my head. I once played Macduff in Leeds. Have you studied Shakespeare then, Daisy?'

'Not as such. We had a book called *Tales from Shakespeare* at school. I didn't find it very interesting, but I did like Lady Macbeth.' She'd struck me as a woman who'd have worn trousers if she could. 'What do you make of Felix?'

JB hums a little tune. He's teasing me, making me wait. I peer out of the side window and watch the hedges reel by until he gives in.

'I agree with you, Daisy. He's a genuine, honest sort of chap.'

'It's very annoying that Thaxted has Lucinda's diary. I want to discover more about Leslie's expulsion from school, but I'd prefer not to approach him directly. I'll ask Ray. Leslie might have told him something about it while they were working together.'

'Hah! You'll have to be prepared for instruction on the post-war capitalist conspiracy.'

'It'll be suffering for the greater good.'

* * *

JB drops me off in Fernfield and I call at the bakery. It's early afternoon, with almost everything sold, so a quiet time. Ray is sitting behind the counter in his white floury apron, drinking a mug of tea and reading the *Daily Worker*. When he greets me, I realise that his lugubrious countenance is similar to that of Toby, the malodorous dog.

'Didn't expect you around today, Daisy. Vera said you were busy with Mr Berrow.'

'I've been helping him, just finished.'

'Haven't got much if you're here to buy. There's some cheese straws I made with spare flour.'

I am still hungry and a savoury snack is appealing. 'Please, I haven't had any lunch. Can I have a couple?'

I lean against the counter and eat them out of the bag, catching the flakes in it. 'I bumped into Martha Prentice earlier. She's an interesting woman.' I'm angling to avoid any mention of Granville Grange, in case I get a diatribe about bourgeois entitlement. Faint hope.

Ray's mouth turns down. 'You mean she's slave labour at the Grange. Branch will sell it from under her and she'll be out on her ear after years of service. It's disgusting.'

'Absolutely, it shouldn't be allowed. Martha mentioned that Leslie was expelled from school and there was a lot of trouble with the head, Miss Laidlaw.'

The change of subject throws him nicely. 'He was going on about that the other morning. Said there was quite a to-do. I suppose her death reminded him of it.'

'What did Leslie tell you?'

Ray swallows tea and fiddles with the pencil behind his ear.

'I'm not sure now, I was in the middle of a batch, so the oven was noisy. Broke windows, I reckon. Maybe worse. Yes, that's it, he swore at the teacher and Miss Laidlaw sent him packing. His mum stormed into the school and demanded she sort it out.' Ray folds his arms, dislodging cloudy puffs of flour. 'Leslie said he went back to school, so it must have been resolved.'

I can tell that he's about to ask me why I'm interested, so I head him off. 'Anything of note in the *Daily Worker*?'

'This French collaborator, Laval, has been sentenced to death. Firing squad.' He adds with relish, 'Good riddance to him.'

'Do you shoot, Ray?'

'Me? No. Funny question!'

'It's just that you're keen on people being shot.'

'Ah, I see.' He fixes me with a serious frown. 'In context, that's all, if it's necessary to the march of international social-ism. As V.I. Lenin said, "The capitalists will sell us the rope with which we will hang them." Things will come full circle.'

'That's all right then, if it's Lenin's instruction. I'd best get on. Your cheese straws are very good.'

But Ray has a head of steam going now. 'Don't forget, "bread for all, and roses too". That's what life will be like come the revolution.'

'I can hardly wait, as long as I can avoid guns and rope — otherwise, the bread and roses won't be much comfort.'

I exit the shop with my last section of cheese straw. All in all, I've got off quite lightly.

CHAPTER ELEVEN

The next day, I decide to see if I can earn myself some brownie points with Inspector Thaxted. I call at the police station late morning to find an unfamiliar constable on the desk. He asks me to wait and carries on filling in a ledger. Everyone needs their moments of petty tyranny, so I sit patiently with my newspaper. He's a heavy breather and I listen to the in-and-out of his lungs in the silence.

While I'm occupying the time by completing a cryptic crossword, another policeman appears from the back of the station and stands at reception, removing his bicycle clips. He takes no notice of me but bends down to his colleague. They whisper, but not so softly that I can't hear.

'Thaxted back yet?'

'Nope. He's gone for a lunch break by the river.'

'Hope he doesn't jump in.'

'Fat chance. If he did, I wouldn't get wet to save him. Careful when you see him.'

'Tetchy today?'

'And some. Probably his leg giving him jip. He tore a strip off me for not getting the rota up to date.'

'Ta for the warning. Maybe he forgot to bring his pills with him.'

'What's he take?'

'Dunno, but he's on them throughout the day. Wish they improved his temper.'

'I'll be glad when this case is wrapped up and he pisses off back to Oxford.'

'And so say all of us. I'll make a brew.'

When he's clumped to the kitchen, the reception constable decides to give me some of his time.

'Yes, miss?'

'I was hoping to see Inspector Thaxted.'

'He's just stepped out for a sandwich.'

'Will he be long?'

'Can't really say.'

'I'll catch him later, then.'

The constable nods and returns to his ledger and his breathing, drawing vertical columns with a wooden ruler.

It's a lovely autumn day, mild and sunny, glowing with russets and golds. I walk to the river and along the leaf-strewn path, taking off my coat and tying it around my waist. I spot Peter Thaxted sitting on a bench in the distance, and slow down as I see that he's kneading his injured leg with both hands, digging his fingers into the calf. I wait and watch fish flash, rippling the water. Are they swimming down to London, on their way to the sea? I imagine them, navigating through the bridges, past St Paul's, the Palace of Westminster and the Tower of London and on to the Thames estuary and the North Sea. My heart is sore.

When I turn to the bench again, Thaxted is leaning back, staring up at the sky, his lips moving.

I scuff leaves and cough as I approach. 'Hello, Inspector Thaxted.'

His trilby is next to him, alongside a sandwich box and his walking stick. It strikes me as a lonesome scene. Does he make his own lunch, or does his mother do it? What did he have in his sandwich — potted meat, fish paste, egg or the dreaded spam? I hope whatever it was, he enjoyed it and it's made him less tetchy.

'Miss Moore, hello.' He squints a little in the sun, the skin around his eyes like crinkled tissue paper.

'Do you mind if I join you for a minute?'

'Be my guest.'

He doesn't move, so I walk to the other side of the bench. We sit in an awkward silence. I sneak a glance at him. He seems jaded, staring at the river, a muscle working in his jaw.

I clear my throat. 'I was just staring at the sky and realising how lovely it is that it's empty, and that we no longer have to scan for enemy aircraft.'

'I imagine you had to be very alert in London.'

'Yes, but everyone got used to it.'

'Oh, you can get used to anything.'

Is he referring to his leg? 'I suppose you can. I expect I'll get used to living around here. Just now, I envied the fish, swimming to London.'

He shifts around slightly, wincing and appraising me. 'You feel out of place in Fernfield?'

'Sometimes. When it's pouring and everything's forlorn, and I could be trapped at the end of the world.'

'Hm. I couldn't live in a place like this, or in the sticks. Brize Lodge is quite isolated. I'm glad to get back to Oxford in the evening.' A long pause, then he adds lightly, 'I imagine you never felt trapped in Whitehall.'

I stay quiet for a while. He's tilted his head back again, his eyes closed. I've been finding out about him, but the grapevine can work both ways. I gather that he's been busy too. He or his mother would only have had to phone the *kommandantin* to get some background on me. Or perhaps he has contacts in London. I'm gratified that he's bothered.

'I did enjoy working in Whitehall, it was rewarding.'

'So I understand. Now, what have you come to barter? I assume your invasion of my lunch break is no accident.' His amber gaze turns on me.

'Miss Laidlaw expelled Leslie Mathis from school. It caused quite a stir.'

'Who told you that?'

'Martha Prentice, and I also asked Ray Crampton about it.'

'Ah yes, your little jaunt to Granville Grange yesterday. Have you spoken to Mr Mathis about the incident?'

'No. It would have been years ago. Not much of a motive to kill Lucinda.'

'True.' He's lost in thought.

'Did Miss Laidlaw change her will when she made Felix her beneficiary?'

'I can't disclose that. But it's not relevant.'

I sense a little shift in his attitude to me. I'm not a mere factotum after all. 'Did Lucinda's diary offer anything interesting?'

'Possibly.'

'I can't detect much bartering,' I complain. 'It's one-way traffic for information at the moment.'

He snaps, 'That's because I'm a detective, the war's over, Whitehall is behind you and you're a hotel worker.'

So much for my fleeting moment of gratification. 'No need to be so restrained, Inspector.'

He folds his arms. 'And no need for the sarcasm. As far as I'm aware, no one has *asked* you to meddle in Miss Laidlaw's murder.'

We relapse into silence. He grips his leg again and his lips move.

I decide that I have little to lose and venture further. 'Are you distracting yourself?'

'Pardon?'

'Are you repeating something to distract you from the pain in your leg? Something like, "This will pass." I worked with a man who'd been injured in a bomb blast and he'd repeat that to himself. He said it helped. Mind over matter, tricking yourself.'

Thaxted shakes his head. 'You're inexorable.'

'Is that a compliment?'

'I'm not sure.'

We exchange a glance, then silence descends again.

After a while he says, 'I repeat, "All is well" or just "Calmness".'

'Does it help?'

'Sometimes. Not today. The mind isn't always obedient.'

I shield my eyes from the sun and try a direct appeal. 'I'm not setting out to irritate you. Asking questions about Miss Laidlaw is helping me resist brain rot.'

He rubs his jaw. 'Why on earth didn't you stay around Whitehall? Surely there would have been a job for someone with your abilities post-war. The government must have tons of work that needs doing.'

'Not for the likes of me, or any of the other women I worked alongside. I was dropped like a hot potato, told to vanish and find a husband, start a family.'

'Ah,' he says softly. 'That must have been a blow.'

'Yes. I did get a sort of offer from Benny Mathis yesterday, but I managed to resist. If I tell you something else, will you let me in a bit more on what you've found out?'

He makes a side-to-side motion with his hand. 'Try me.'

I explain what I learned from Benny and Felix about Lucinda's visit to Hector. 'She was upset because someone was lying and it sounded as if it would have been a family matter. She might have recorded it in her diary.'

'Not as far as I can see.' He picks up his stick and rolls it between his hands. 'On July ninth, the day she visited Mr Branch, she's written, "check staff" and underlined it.'

'That's all?'

'Yes.'

'It has to be significant, doesn't it? What staff?'

'That's to be determined.'

'What about alibis — Mr Lancaster and Nurse Dean?'

He takes his time answering me. 'Mr Lancaster is accounted for at the time of the murder. Nurse Dean was on calls around town and cycling between visits. No one we've spoken to saw her back at the Dolphin during the morning.'

'Was Miss Laidlaw her patient?'

'No. Miss Laidlaw hadn't sought medical attention for more than six years. She was a healthy woman when someone ended her life.'

'Did you find any fingerprints on the stone dolphin or in the room?'

'None on the dolphin and otherwise only Miss Laidlaw's and Miss Sullivan's.'

'I do appreciate you talking to me like this.'

He turns to me with a sombre face. 'Don't get accustomed to it. I was overcome by a momentary impulse, which I'll no doubt regret, to prevent your brain shrivelling.' He picks up his trilby, runs bony fingers around the rim. 'If you want a lift, I'll drive to the hotel now and speak to Leslie Mathis about his school days.'

'Don't mention that I told you about that incident. I have to work with him.'

'I'll manage to keep that confidential. Are you accepting a lift?'

I check my watch. 'I can't. I'm meeting Felix in the Napolina in ten minutes.'

'You've become friends very quickly.'

'He's on his own and quite isolated now Lucinda's dead. I find him interesting. He's been through a lot in life.'

'I see. You said he didn't like the nut-throwing monkey in the Napolina.'

'He doesn't, but it's the only café in town, so we're not spoiled for choice.'

Thaxted grins. 'I had a cup of tea in there yesterday. The owner kept Rindi under control. Perhaps he was worried I might charge the monkey with breach of the peace.'

He puts his hat on, tucks his sandwich box in his coat pocket and gets up slowly, leaning on his stick. He gasps and then mutters under his breath as he straightens.

'I'll contact you if I hear anything else that might be useful,' I say.

'I'm sure you will, Miss Moore, I'm sure you will.'

I catch a hint of cordiality in his voice and take that as a good omen.

* * *

I reach the Napolina five minutes late, but Felix isn't there. I need something hot to eat. The only cooked dish is mock duck. I've seen it on plenty of menus but never tried it, so decide to give it a go. I order that with a pot of tea. Rindi is nowhere to be seen.

I ask Jock, 'Where's that naughty monkey?'

'Upstairs with my granddaughter. She loves playing with him. They throw nuts at each other. By the way, I couldn't be bothered shaping a mock duck on top of the dish, but it's tasty enough.'

I sit by the window with my tea. When the food arrives in an enamel bowl, it's layers of sausage meat with apple, onion and sage. Stuffing, basically. I can't understand why anyone would bother shaping it like a duck, but the war made people obsessed with sham dishes: potato piglets, mock goose, poor knight's fritters. The food's not bad and very filling. Simeon Lancaster would take fright at it.

Jock stops by to ask if it's OK.

'Fine, thanks. But now the war's over, you could just call it sausage layer or sausage meat savoury and forget the duck.'

'Aye, I suppose I could.'

I keep glancing out of the window but there's no sign of Felix. It's half past one. I get another tea, accepting Jock's offer of sticky toffee fudge to go with it. Felix still hasn't arrived when I've finished. Perhaps he's forgotten, taken up with worrying about murder and his inheritance, or maybe he's talking to Lucinda's solicitor. I should have asked for his phone number.

There's a niggle of worry in my head and I decide to go to Market Avenue. The sun has vanished, the sky has a mauve, menacing hue and the air is chillier. I button my coat and walk fast to the house. There's no answer when I knock, so I try again, louder and once more for luck. I spy through the filmy net of the front window but the sitting room is empty, the fire unlit. When I try the side gate, it's locked.

I tear a piece off my newspaper and lean on the window ledge to scribble a note.

Dear Felix,
Did you forget about meeting me in the Napolina today? Ring me at the Dolphin when you get this.
Daisy.

I put it through the letterbox and set off for the hotel, the mock duck sitting like a rock in my stomach.

CHAPTER TWELVE

When I get back to the Dolphin, I hear that Susan has come down with flu.

'That girl is more trouble than she's worth and a right attention-seeking little madam,' Vera complains. 'She was sneezing all over the place earlier. I packed her off to bed. Can you help Leslie prepare dinner and serve tonight? That inspector was back here, asking him questions, so we're all behind.'

'What did Inspector Thaxted want?'

Vera has abandoned her sausage roll hairstyle and her waves are tucked back with tortoiseshell grips. 'Don't ask me. Leslie was fed up after he'd gone. Surely the police should leave us alone now to get on with our work.'

Listening to Vera, you'd believe the Dolphin was heaving with guests. 'Maybe we should ask Nurse Dean to check on Susan when she comes in.'

'It's only flu, not pneumonia! Start sending a nurse in and she'll milk it and stay in bed for a week. I gave her some aspirin, that'll sort her out. Are you going to stand there all day, or could you manage to give Leslie a hand?'

'I'll do that. I've asked Felix Koller to ring me here. Can you give me a shout when he does, and tell Dora I'm expecting a call when she arrives?'

'Koller? The police still suspect him, don't they?'

'I'm not sure, Vera. I don't.'

She gives a heavy sigh, mutters something about personal calls and answers the phone. I wait to see if it's Felix, but she starts to discuss a coal delivery.

In the kitchen, Leslie is spooning oatmeal into a bowl with unnecessary force. He has a face like thunder.

'Vera says you need a hand.'

'You can do the cabbage.' He gestures with his head to where it's lying on the draining board.

'What's for dinner?'

'Trench meat pudding.'

'Always makes me think of trench foot.'

'You're so sharp, Daisy, I'm amazed you don't cut yourself.'

I glance at his rigid back. Has he found out that I told Thaxted about his expulsion? 'I hear the inspector came to see you again.'

'You hear right.' He starts to wrestle a block of suet as if it's his enemy. 'Bloody nerve, coming and asking me about when I was at school.'

'That's going back a long way.' I cut off the woody stalk of the huge cabbage, separate the leaves and start washing the mud from them.

'I said to him, what, are you going to arrest me for something I did when I was ten? He was going on about how I might have resented Miss Laidlaw.'

'Did you? One of my teachers once told me that I was too opinionated and I'd never amount to anything. I'd spit in her eye if I met her now.' My sudden spark of anger towards Miss Eakins startles me. I haven't recalled her for a long time. Strange, how the past can suddenly ambush you. It grates on me that if I did bump into Miss Eakins, I wouldn't be able to tell her about my war work and relish her astonishment.

Leslie snorts and half-turns. 'Your teacher was right about you being opinionated. I bet you were hard work. You wouldn't bash her head in if you saw her, though.'

'No. I suppose that's what you told the inspector.'

'I did. He can believe me or not. He limped off like Hopalong Cassidy and I hope he bloody stays out of my way. Get a move on with the cabbage, I need the sink.'

The rest of the afternoon and evening fly by with kitchen work and serving. Leslie remains taciturn. The trench meat pudding proves popular with everyone except Mr Lancaster, who asks if he can have a chop instead.

'Bloody finicky Londoners,' Leslie grumbles, hefting the frying pan.

Around eight o'clock, I check with Dora. No one has phoned for me. I take Susan a cup of tea in her room on the top floor. Her bedside lamp is on and she's half sitting, coughing and blowing her nose.

'Hello, how are you? I brought you a cuppa.'

'Ta. I'm ever so hot and I've an awful headache.'

She's flushed and sweaty, her hair sticking to her forehead, and the room smells ripe.

'Do you want me to open the window?'

'Oh no! My mum always said to keep the window shut when you're poorly.'

'Have you got aspirin?'

'Yeah, I'll take some more with the tea.' She coughs loudly. 'Vera's cross with me. I didn't get the flu on purpose!'

'Her bark's worse than her bite.'

'I can't stand her. She's a right bitch, always sarky to me. Her old man goes on about helping refugees and big houses standing empty, but like they say, charity begins at home.' She blows her nose again, long and loud.

There's an edge of craftiness to Susan. I've been considering her as a child but she is, after all, a streetwise Stepney girl. I sit on the edge of the bed. 'Speaking of charity, I believe that you and Miss Laidlaw had a run-in over the collection in her porch.'

She replies through the hanky, 'What d'you mean?'

'She caught you helping yourself.'

Susan tosses the hanky aside. 'Old cow. She said she wouldn't tell no one. And she's the one who went on about trust!'

'What happened?'

'Blimey, it was just a scarf and a few bits, other people's cast-offs.' She scowls. 'Anyone would reckon I'd raided the bank! Who told you?'

'It doesn't matter. Miss Laidlaw gave you a telling off?'

'Yeah. I had to listen to a load of stuff about honesty and Miss Laid-down-the-law made me promise not to do it again.'

'And have you kept to your promise?'

She lowers her head and rubs her eyes. 'Yeah. I never nicked nothing from her again. Yuck, I don't feel too good.'

Do I believe her? I'm unsure, but I'm not going to get anything more from her now. 'Is there anything else you need before I go?'

'No. Ta for coming up.'

'I'll ask Dora to pop in before she goes. You like her, don't you?'

'Yeah, she's alright, too much almost, fussing and fidget-ing around like a mother hen.'

Susan's a hard girl to please. In reception, Dora agrees to see her before she leaves and confirms that there's been no phone call for me. She's in a jolly mood, enjoying being in charge, her knitting to hand for when things are quiet. JB mentioned that she's single and lives alone, hence her will-ingness to do evening work. I've gathered that she likes to be wanted and never objects to extra duties.

Outside, I fetch my bike and stand by the kerb, fretting about Felix and not sure what to make of his silence. I cycle to Market Avenue. It's a cold night, clear and starry, with a nipping wind. A fuzzy halo circles the moon. The house is in darkness, the downstairs curtains still pulled across and the fire unlit. There's no response when I knock on the door. I crouch and peek through the letterbox. My note is still lying on the floor.

I get back on my bike and cycle to the police station, which is closed. There's a phone box across the road. I find the number for Oxford police station and call it. I'm told that Inspector Thaxted won't be available until the morning, so I ring off, not sure what to do. Felix is a grown man. Maybe he's gone to Oxford or London, needing to get away from this small town and the Fernies for a while.

I ride back to Brize Lodge, hoping that JB will be there to advise me. He appears in the gubbins room with a finger to his lips. I'm aware of the kitchen clock ticking.

He steps close to me and murmurs, 'The *kommandantin* is within. Steady the buffs!'

I take off my coat and straighten my sweater, fighting down a flutter of anxiety. 'Lead on.'

She's standing by the fireplace, one knee crooked forwards, a hand resting on the mantelpiece in ownership pose. Her flared tartan dress is belted and accompanied by a single string of pearls. On her feet are elegant T-bar shoes with a low heel.

'Rosalind, this is Daisy.'

'Hello,' I say, more shrilly than I'd intended.

She looks me up and down much as Benny Mathis did and then nods. I've passed muster. 'Good evening, Daisy,' she says in a neutral voice. 'You're fresh-cheeked from your cycling.'

She has a very posh accent, several notches up from JB's. Her hair is drawn back in a tight bun at the nape of her neck and secured in a black net. She has a lean, fit body, and her face is thin, with a slightly hooked nose. All that tramping her estate while she kills things must keep her in good shape.

'Shall we sit down?' JB asks. 'No extra charge for the chairs. Tot of whisky?'

'With a splash of soda for me,' the *kommandantin* says, folding her skirt neatly under her as she sits in my usual chair.

'Please,' I tell him.

Oberon is asleep on the spare armchair and I scoop him onto my lap and sit down. He turns around clockwise three times, smacking my face with his raised tail, before he settles on me again.

'Declan told me you were a cat person. That went in your favour,' Rosalind tells me with a smile that doesn't quite stretch her lips.

'Thank you. It wouldn't have with my mother. She disliked my cat.'

She ignores this. 'And have you settled here?'

'Yes, thanks. I'm anxious tonight, though.'

She sips her whisky and soda. It occurs to me that her presence might be useful, given her family connection to Peter Thaxted.

'What's up, Daisy?' JB asks.

I explain about Felix. 'He didn't phone me, and when I went back to the house this evening there was no sign of him. I realise that he could have gone somewhere, but it's odd.'

Rosalind asks, 'Does this chap Felix Koller have friends in the area?'

'None that he's mentioned. In fact, he's kept a low profile since he moved here. The police station in Fernfield was closed. I tried calling Inspector Thaxted at the Oxford station, but they said he wouldn't be there until tomorrow morning.'

'It is worrying,' JB says. 'Felix is fragile and hardly the type who'd fail to turn up when he says he will, especially as you've been a support to him. What to do?' He taps his chin. 'Rosalind, you're just the stout party for this sort of situation. You must have a home number for Peter. Could you ring and ask his opinion?'

He's very gallant with her, a light flirtatiousness in his tone. I recall Vera's remark that he realises which side his bread's buttered. Glancing at his wife, I see from her pleased smile that she likes it.

'Well . . . it is late,' she says, 'almost ten o'clock. One doesn't wish to set the cat among the pigeons.'

JB selects a cigar. 'I expect a policeman like Peter is used to late-night phone calls.'

'I am worried about Felix,' I stress.

'Accepted,' she says with a sniff, 'but on the other hand, he is a young man and perhaps he's sought company. One doesn't wish to embarrass him.'

I rub my fingers through Oberon's fur. 'There has been a murder, and he's connected to the victim.'

'All the more reason not to add to the existing drama, I would have thought,' Rosalind fires back.

She probably regards murder as a social *faux pas*. I back off and cast a beseeching glance at JB.

He picks up the baton and says to her sweetly, 'I'm sure Peter wouldn't mind, Rosalind. He respects you, and if something unfortunate has happened to Felix, it gives him a head start.' He raises his glass to her and drinks.

She seizes the poker, prods the fire with short jabs. 'These logs have dried well, they give out good heat. I'll get Winters to bring you another load at the end of the week.' She fingers her pearls. 'Oh, very well, I'll call Peter. I won't let the phone ring for too long. It really is a very unsocial hour for such a communication.'

She rises smoothly and goes out to the hall, where the phone sits in a narrow alcove. JB crosses his fingers at me. I stroke Oberon's ears to quieten my nerves. He twitches in his sleep.

After a short pause, the *kommandantin* speaks. 'Good evening, Peter. It's Rosalind here. I'm so sorry to disturb you at this late hour . . . Oh, good, I'm glad, but it must be an inconvenience . . . I'm at Brize Lodge at present and there appears to be some concern about a chap called Felix Koller . . . Yes, Miss Daisy Moore arrived home a little while ago and she's worried . . . Well, she believes he's missing . . . I see. Wait a moment, Peter.'

She walks back in. 'Peter has asked to speak to you, Miss Moore.'

I lift Oberon and place him on the chair, brushing his hairs from my trousers, and hurry to the phone. 'Hello, it's Daisy.'

'What's this about Felix Koller?'

I recount my story to him. 'I'm sorry to disturb you, but I am worried about him.'

His voice is low and weary. 'Did you knock at any neighbours and ask if they'd seen him?'

I lean against the wall, rubbing the patterned paper. 'No. I didn't like to, as it was getting late.'

'It would have been an obvious thing to do.'

'To you, maybe, but Felix told me that the neighbours aren't exactly friendly. Lucinda had cautioned him they were best avoided and that, basically, they don't like anyone who wasn't born in Fernfield. They're called Fernies.'

A sigh. 'I'm sure they are. Well, I don't see that anything can be done tonight. He might have gone on a jaunt somewhere. I have his phone number. I'll ring it now and ask him to call you if he answers.'

A jaunt doesn't sound at all like Felix. On the other hand, I've barely made his acquaintance and I might have egg on my face tomorrow. 'OK, thanks. I'll call at the house again first thing in the morning if I haven't heard from him.'

'Are there spare keys anywhere?'

'I doubt it. Felix pays great attention to security.'

'Understandable. If Mr Koller hasn't surfaced, I'll meet you at the house at nine sharp tomorrow morning. That way, if he opens the door and is baffled by these alarms, you can explain yourself. Good night.'

I'm left holding a buzzing receiver. I replace it and go back to the sitting room. 'Inspector Thaxted is going to try phoning Felix now, and if he's there, he'll ask him to call me. If he isn't, the inspector is going to meet me at the house in the morning.'

'Good. That's eminently sensible, as I would expect of Peter.' The *kommandantin* gets up. 'Jeffrey, you may walk me home. Good night, Miss Moore.'

'Shan't be long,' JB tells me. 'Put some cocoa on, I'd love a mug when I get back.'

In the kitchen, I put milk to warm in a pan and give Tybalt and Oberon fresh water. All the time, I'm listening for the phone. I'm not expecting it to ring, and it doesn't.

CHAPTER THIRTEEN

I reach Woodlands at half eight the next morning. I barely slept, and when I did I had awful dreams about the fire that destroyed our house, with Felix mingled in there as a shadowy figure. I twisted and turned so much that Tybalt demanded to be let out of my bedroom at 3 a.m.

I can tell that Felix hasn't been back and my note is still on the hall floor, but I knock anyway. Then I sit on the porch step in a lukewarm sun until Inspector Thaxted arrives with the red-cheeked constable who'd let me into Felix's cell. He gives me an accusing stare. Another man is with them, a locksmith.

'Not home?' Thaxted asks.

'No, and I've knocked.'

'I rang him at seven this morning again. OK. Locks, please, Mr Evans.'

I step aside and stand by a prickly pyracantha that climbs up one side of the porch. Its tawny berries gleam in the light. The locksmith gets to work while the constable observes, as if he's learning the skill.

'You can't come in, in case there's been a crime,' Thaxted warns me. 'You might as well go to the hotel and I'll contact you there. Has Mr Koller ever mentioned where he walks?'

'Not specifically, just that he went for a walk daily. What will you do once you've searched the house?'

'If he's not ill or dead in there, start a wider search around town, contact hospitals.'

'Can I help?'

'Not just now. Off you go and let me get on.'

Thaxted turns away as the locksmith shoves the door open and he leads the way into the house, bending to pick up my note. I stand for a moment, scanning the empty hall. The constable smirks and waves goodbye before slamming the door on me.

* * *

Leslie's in a better mood this morning and asks if I'll take a breakfast tray up to Mrs Ward. 'Dora would, but she's seeing to Sue. She loves fussing around people. Pity she's never married, she'd make a lovely mum.'

'Can't you matchmake for her?'

'She was engaged to a local chap, but he was killed early in the war.' Leslie has a faraway expression. 'She told me that's it, there'll be no one else for her now. Sad, really, being left with such an empty life. Anyway, she'll be smothering Sue in kindness.'

'How is Susan?'

'Dora says she's poorly, but her temperature's down and she's over the worst of it. Hope she hasn't given her bug to the rest of us.'

No, I mutter to myself, cranky from worry and lack of sleep. *Wouldn't want the Fernies being infected by wals.*

I climb the stairs with Mrs Ward's usual breakfast: sausage, egg, tomato, fried bread and a pot of tea. Not what Dr Jessop would recommend. On the way, I meet Ray coming out of Marlin, a bucket in his hand containing pinkish water.

'That's that finished,' he says. 'Clean as a new pin now, even the carpet. Took some elbow grease.'

'Thanks for doing that, Ray. Not a nice job.'

'What has to be done, has to be done,' he comments, heading downstairs.

Is that a quote from Lenin? It sounds vaguely doctrinal.

Mrs Ward is in her chair, legs propped up, and she asks me to wheel across the tray that sits over her when she eats. I oblige and set her meal before her. She has a thick layer of orange powder on her face and some of it has caked around her nostrils.

'Sit and have a chat while I eat,' she commands, attacking her meal with relish. 'What's going on in the world?'

I perch on the window ledge. 'The Nuremberg trials will begin next month, women have just been allowed to vote in France for the first time, the Japanese have surrendered Taiwan and the police are still searching for Miss Laidlaw's murderer.'

She spears tomato. 'Maybe they won't find him.'

'That's always a possibility.'

'I heard that the police came back to talk to Leslie yesterday.'

'It was something to do with him being expelled from school.'

'I remember that. He smashed some windows. Leslie turned out alright in the end, but those Mathis boys were tough nuts.'

'I heard that Leslie's mum had it out with Miss Laidlaw at the time.'

Mrs Ward pours tea and adds milk. 'Built like a tank, Nancy Mathis was, with flaming cheeks. She worked at Granville Grange for a while until she had Leslie. She was always plump, but she ballooned after the baby. Her husband was killed in a tractor accident, so she had a lot on her plate. She went storming into the school after Leslie was expelled. He was her one and only, the apple of her eye. Lucinda let Leslie back after a fortnight of argy-bargy and his mum dropped dead just days later, massive heart attack. Went down in the greengrocer's, like a tree falling. She was only thirty-six. Lots of people said it was the strain of what had happened with the boy. This egg's overdone.'

I watch as she dips her fried bread in the congealing yolk. Fat glistens on her chins. I stifle a yawn and rub my eyes.

'Young girl like you shouldn't be tired at this hour of the morning. Stayed up late?'

'Yep. Did Leslie hold a grudge about what happened to his mum?'

'Leslie? Doubt it, he's not the type, a sunny sort usually.'

'Who took him in when his mum died?'

'Benny, his uncle. Now, *he* was the one who held the grudge, if you ask me. Benny was ever so close to Nancy. She was his big sister and she'd always indulged him. He was really cut up after she died and he used to say that Lucinda had blood on her hands.'

There's a tap on the door and Vera puts her head round. 'Morning, Mrs Ward. There's a phone call for you, Daisy.'

I run downstairs, hoping for good news. It's a constable at the police station.

'Inspector Thaxted asked me to phone you, miss. There's no sign of Mr Koller, no evidence of any disturbance or of where he might be. We've started a search.'

'Thanks for telling me.'

I sink back on Vera's stool and bite the side of my thumb. When she appears, I stand and move aside. She turns back the sleeves on her cardigan, revealing a pretty silver bracelet, embellished with crystals.

'That's a lovely trinket, Vera.'

She smiles, runs a finger over it. 'Ray bought it for me last month. It's too nice to wear to work, really, but I do love it.' She gestures upstairs. 'If Mrs Ward keeps eating like that, she'll burst.'

'Eating's her only pleasure in life. She might as well go happy.'

Vera examines me. 'What's up with you? You look like you've lost a pound and found a sixpence.'

'Felix Koller is missing. The police are searching for him.'

'Is he indeed?' Vera nods with satisfaction. 'Well, we all know what that means.'

'Do we?' But I can guess what's coming.

'He did it, didn't he? He's the killer. Now he's taken off. Probably miles away by now. He might even have run back to wherever it is he came from.'

'He escaped from Vienna. I doubt he'd want to go back there, it's in chaos.'

'Home's home though, isn't it?'

'I'm not sure that Austria would appeal to a Jewish person right now.'

'That inspector should never have released him, then there wouldn't be this problem.' She frowns at me. 'How come the police are phoning you about him?'

'I was supposed to meet him in the café yesterday and he didn't turn up. That's when I started to worry about him.'

'You do get your fingers in lots of pies, Daisy. Now, if you're not too busy, can you clear the dining room and then cover reception for half an hour while I check the laundry bills?'

'I just need to ring Mr Berrow first. I said I'd update him about Felix.'

'If you must. Some of us have got a hotel to run!'

I call JB and tell him the news. He says "*nil desperandum*", which doesn't soothe me. I clear the dining room of dirty crockery and re-lay the tables, hoping that Susan isn't going to be ill for too long. While I sort clean cutlery, I mull over what Mrs Ward told me. Is it significant that Leslie's mother once worked at Granville Grange? It means the Mathis family had another close connection there. Perhaps Miss Laidlaw told Benny more about her meeting with Hector Branch than he'd let on.

Just after three o'clock, Peter Thaxted phones me. 'We found Felix Koller a couple of hours ago. He's been taken to hospital in Oxford, the Radcliffe. He's in a bad way, I'm afraid. Badly beaten.'

I'm angry rather than upset. 'Where was he?'

'In bushes by a stretch of the river, about half a mile north of Fernfield.'

'Is he going to pull through?'

'I can't say. The bushes gave him some protection from the cold, at least. I'm sure you can go and see him, if you want.'

'Is this attack connected to Miss Laidlaw's murder?'

'I intend to find out. I have to go. I'm sorry.'

It's raining heavily now. Vera's sniffy when I tell her what's happened, and that I want to visit Felix.

'I don't see why you have to go running off to Oxford at the drop of a hat. This Felix Koller's a stranger to you!'

'He hasn't got anyone now that Miss Laidlaw's dead. I'll be back as soon as I can.' I play my trump card. 'Mr Berrow would want me to go. Could you ring him with the news?'

'It's all most peculiar, that's all I can say. I can't work out what the world's coming to, what with a murder here and now this man getting attacked.'

Then she switches mood, in that way she has, and dithers around me, pointing out that it's pouring again and I'll drown if I cycle to Oxford. She tells me that there's a bus at half three that passes the hospital, so I board it at the stop outside the chemist and ask the driver to tell me when to get off for the Radcliffe. The window is clouded with condensation. I wipe it with my glove and stare out as the bus lurches along sopping country lanes. It stops randomly to let people on and off and the driver has interminable conversations each time, ranging over how long rationing will continue, how people are supposed to manage on three clothing coupons a month, and the proposal for a National Health Service. I'm impatient to get to Felix and press my foot on the floor, as if I could will the bus to accelerate. I try not to imagine him clinging on to life.

When I find the ward Felix is in, a nurse tells me to take a seat while she fetches Sister Mason.

'But how is Felix?'

'As well as can be expected.'

I wait on a bench, aware that my feet are damp, courtesy of stepping down from the bus into a wide puddle.

Sister Mason's shoes rapidly tap the linoleum as she takes me to her office. She is small and alert, with a dimpled chin. 'Now, who are you exactly, Miss Moore? Would you like to slip your coat off? It's very wet.'

I shrug my coat off and drape it over the back of my chair. 'I met Felix a couple of days ago. He's been living in Fernfield with his friend, Miss Laidlaw, who was murdered recently at the Dolphin hotel. I work there. Will he be OK?'

'We hope so. He's stable for now. You're not family, then?'

'Felix doesn't have any family. He's Jewish, from Austria. He escaped to England and was interned before being released. His parents were murdered in a concentration camp and he doesn't have any friends in Fernfield, apart from me. I reported him as missing to Inspector Thaxted of Oxford police.'

'The poor man, so many terrible events in his young life and now this,' Sister Mason laments.

Her sympathy brings tears to my eyes and I blink them away. 'He's frail, but he's courageous.'

'May I take your phone number and address?'

I give her the numbers at the hotel and Brize Lodge.

'I was shocked to hear about dear Lucinda Laidlaw,' Sister Mason says. 'I met her through her work here, at the hospital. A fine woman.'

'Was that when she visited patients?'

'Yes, that's right. She spent time with wounded men and liaised with their families, helped them write letters home, that sort of thing. She did a great deal for the Oxford Committee for Famine Relief as well. They raised money to send food to occupied countries during the war. Lucinda was tireless in her efforts. I spoke to her here just last month and she was starting to focus on the Save Europe Now campaign.'

'I haven't heard of that. What is it?'

'It's in its infancy, but gathering support. It's lobbying the government to allow food parcels to Germany. The population there are suffering terribly. I've written in support of it. The campaign is asking people to send a postcard, agreeing to give up some of their own rations to feed Germans. Why did we fight a war if we then sit back and allow people — innocent children — to starve? I'm so glad that Lucinda told me about it.'

'From what I've heard about her, she was a very selfless woman.'

'She was indeed.' Sister Mason smiles at me. 'Isn't it wonderful to be able to speak of the war in the past tense? Although I fear that the aftermath may be almost as bad in many ways, given the madness in the world. Now, I must tend to my patients. Would you like a cup of tea?'

'Yes please, but when can I see Felix?'

'In a little while. The doctor's with him now. He's sedated, so he won't be aware that you're here. He was very cold and he has extensive bruising and several fractures. He's fortunate that they found him when they did. If it had been much longer . . . Be warned, he's alarming at first sight.'

'I understand. Thanks.'

'You can wait in here until I give you the nod.'

In a while, after I've drunk my tea, a nurse comes and leads me to where Felix is at the end of the ward, enclosed by curtains. His left arm is bandaged, his face a terrible mass of bruises and lacerations. There are stitches from behind his right ear to his temple. I take his right hand and press it, say his name.

I sit with him for about twenty minutes. He doesn't stir. Then Sister Mason says it's time to go, but I can come back and visit tomorrow.

'Can you say when he'll wake up?'

'Later this evening, hopefully. Then the police will want to talk to him. He might have seen who did this to him.'

She walks me to the ward door and takes a leaflet from her pocket.

'You might like one of these. Lucinda gave me some that last time I saw her. It's about the postcard scheme.'

The bus back to Fernfield is crowded with people heading home from work. I sit squashed up against a window, next to a big man with a haversack, reading the leaflet Sister Mason gave me.

SAVE EUROPE NOW CAMPAIGN

The German people are starving.
German children are starving.
At present, the British government is not allowing food relief to Germany.
We fought a just war. Is this just?
We do not believe that German civilians should be penalised in this way. We have faith in our shared humanity.
Romans 12:20: 'If thine enemy hunger, feed him; if he thirst, give him to drink. Be not overcome of evil, but overcome evil with good.'
If you wish to make your voice heard, please send a postcard to the government, agreeing to share your weekly ration with our German brothers and sisters.

I note that the man next to me is canting his neck to read the leaflet. 'What's your opinion of this?'

'Not much,' he sneers. 'Suppose it's handed out by those pacifists and conchies who wanted us to lie down under the Hun. Send that lot our grub after what they did? No thanks!'

'Children, though? They're not to blame.'

'True, but we've got our own kids to feed. They should have thought about that before they all followed Adolf, shouldn't they? I'm not taking food off my kids' plates and putting it on theirs. They lost the war, love, now they have to live with it. Far as I'm concerned, fewer Jerries in the world can only be a good thing.'

He gets off soon and I watch the miles slip by. The bus is warm with bodies and breathing, the engine hums steadily. My eyes are gritty and heavy, lack of sleep catching up with me. I close them, thinking. A lot of people would react angrily to the leaflet, just as my fellow passenger had done. People's hearts have been hardened by fear, bombs, death and long years of deprivation. Lucinda must surely have encountered some hostility when she handed her message out. Enough to make someone violent?

I jolt awake as the driver shouts, 'Fernfield!' and climb down from the bus into the dark and cold. The lights of the Dolphin shine a welcome in the distance.

CHAPTER FOURTEEN

The next day, I'm up early and ring the hospital immediately. The nurse on the ward tells me that Mr Koller is awake and speaking to the police. JB has already left for London, as recording of *The School for Scandal* is starting this morning. I eat a solitary breakfast, celebrate Felix's improvement with an extra-strong cup of tea, feed the cats and leave JB a note before I depart for the hotel. Thick mist drifts clammily across the roads, creating a dreamlike landscape. I pull my scarf up around my face and cycle carefully in and out of dense patches, wary of wandering sheep.

Susan is still unwell, with a bad cough, so I see to the breakfast service. Dr Jessop comes down a little later than usual and joins his wife at their table. He's frowning, and asks if Nurse Dean is around, but I tell him she's already gone out. He harrumphs and orders egg on toast.

I clear away after breakfast, all the while contemplating the Mathis family and their association with Granville Grange. I want to talk to Martha again. I promise to be back at the Dolphin in the afternoon to help Leslie, before cycling to Granville Grange late morning. It's turned much colder now the mist has cleared and my breath puffs out before me.

I ride quickly past the gatehouse, not wanting to encounter Benny Mathis, but there's no sign of him. I carry on up the avenue, past the crumbling urns and around to the kitchen door. I knock, praying that there won't be any dismembered fowl today. Martha lets me in with a cheery greeting. She's in the same clothes, with an extra-bright blue cardigan.

'It was perishing early this morning,' she says. 'I hate that white mist, it gives me the creeps and it sneaks through every nook and cranny of this place. What brings you here again?'

To my relief, she's making treacle tart, rolling pastry out on a marble board.

'I needed exercise and I wanted to have another chat with you, so I cycled this way.'

'Exercise! Don't they work you hard enough at the hotel?'

'Obviously not.'

She laughs. 'Well, you're healthier than last time, I'll say that. Bit of rosy apple in your cheeks today. I suppose we could have a cuppa. His highness is in Oxford, so he won't be ringing the bell.'

'I could make it, if you want to get on with your pastry.'

'No, thank you very much! I'm the only one who rules in this kitchen. Sit over there by the range.'

She wipes her hands on a tea towel and puts the kettle on. I sit in a chair beside the range, glad of the heat. Even so, it's not warm enough to take my coat off. Martha brews up and turns a chair around to sit near me.

'I hope I'm not holding you up,' I say.

'Not at all. It's good to have company. I was used to Mr Branch needing me. I'd be up and down to him all day long. Since he's gone, the days are endless. I rattle around here and take that solicitor cups of tea.'

'Captain Branch isn't home much?'

'No, thank goodness! Always out riding or womanising or doing deals, that one. He eats what I put in front of him with barely a thank you.' She proffers a plate. 'Slice of parkin?

I had some oatmeal and I found a sprinkle of mixed spice in the back of the cupboard, so I made it yesterday.'

We sit by the humming range, eating the spicy cake with our tea. Martha's a rapid eater and has finished hers before I've had more than a couple of bites. I'm impressed — I'm usually the first in a room to demolish a sugary treat.

She slurps her tea, smacks her lips and wiggles in her chair. 'How are you getting on at the Dolphin? Is Vera being a pain?'

I've begun to comprehend the connected web that operates in and around Fernfield, so I reply cautiously. 'We get on OK, thanks.'

'She can be contrary, our Vera, but that's because she's so broody and nothing's happening.'

'That's a shame.'

Martha reaches for another wedge of cake. 'Don't stand on ceremony — help yourself to more of this if you want. I was talking to Vera's mum last week and, according to her, Ray's lacking in that department. Not got the firepower, apparently.'

'Oh dear.'

'Oh dear, indeed. I mean to say, you have to sow if you want to reap, don't you?'

Martha sniggers and slips a round, dark-green tin from her skirt pocket. She twists the lid, takes a pinch of snuff from it and sniffs vigorously. Does she mean that Ray is impotent? Perhaps, even in bed, he's distracted by worries about the development of the Marxist dialectic in post-war Britain. Vera's attempts at a new hairstyle might be a way of trying to catch his attention, pep him up. And perhaps his gift of a bracelet is a way of making amends for disappointments on other fronts.

Martha waves the tin at me before she puts it back in her pocket. 'You could say Ray's not up to snuff!'

I can't help being sorry for Ray, having his bedroom performance bandied about like this. Who else might Vera's mother and Martha have told? Maybe all the Fernies know and are eyeing Ray up and assessing his firepower when they buy their loaves and cheese straws.

'Let's hope a baby Crampton arrives soon,' I say. 'By the way, I learned that Nancy Mathis worked here before she had Leslie.'

'That's right, she was a cleaner. A bloody good one too. That girl had muscles. The silver shone when she'd polished it.' Martha sneezes gustily and blows her nose on a grimy hanky. 'That's better, always good to have a clear out! Nancy left just before she got married. The cleaners after her were all useless. Mr Branch left finding them to me and I never could get anyone to match Nancy.'

'Did Leslie come and live here with Benny after his mum died?'

'Oh no, Benny was a farm labourer then, lived in a cottage at Easton Farm. He got the job here about sixteen years back. Mr Branch needed a new groundsman and he wanted Benny, said he was a solid worker. Another cuppa?'

'Please. Was Mr Branch a widower for a long time?'

'Ages, dear. Mrs B. died along with their second baby, a little girl she was. Clarence was only five.' Martha lifts the teapot, with its knitted cosy, and pours. 'There you go, that'll put hairs on your chest.'

'Thanks. When Miss Laidlaw came to see Mr Branch just before he died, he told her something that worried her.'

'Oh, yes?'

'Apparently, he was making sense when she saw him and he said something about a lie. Did he say anything to you? You were caring for him.'

Martha draws herself up in her chair, indignant. 'Yes, I was, missy, and he was away with the fairies. He had no idea what he was talking about. One minute he mistook me for the dead Mrs Branch, next he reckoned I was his mum, some days he'd no idea who I was. The poor old chap couldn't remember his own name sometimes.' She folds her arms. 'You ask that Nurse Dean if you don't believe me, she used to call in to see him. Spent ages with him some days. I used to worry she'd moved in! I reckon I was better at dealing with him than she was. He was agitated sometimes when she'd been in with him. Anyway, if you don't believe me, she can tell you I'm not making it up about him being soft in the head.'

The cosy atmosphere of chatting by the range has vanished. 'I didn't mean to offend you.'

'Well . . . the police were here asking about Mr Branch and now you. Let the poor old man rest in peace. He might have owned this big house and acres of land, but he didn't have much of a life, what with his wife and baby dying and a son that never had much time for him, even when he'd gone gaga. The captain was back here, flogging his dad's stuff off before the old man was cold in his coffin.'

'Sorry, it must be very intrusive.'

'Oh, don't get yourself waxed up. Truth is, I miss Mr Branch. He was always kind to me, and it was awful seeing the way he was before he died. Tell you what, hope I collapse over the rolling pin and that's it, lights out.' She sets her mouth tight, rises and carries the teapot to the sink.

I feel rotten for quizzing her. She's old and grieving, and faces losing her way of life and her home in the near future. 'Thanks for the tea and the chat, Martha.'

'That's alright. Now, I've a treacle tart to be getting on with, if you don't mind,' she says gruffly.

I'm cycling back down the avenue when I see Mr Lancaster striding towards me, buttoned into a black wool coat.

'Afternoon, Daisy. I was stretching my legs.'

'I called to chat to Martha. How's your work going?'

'Getting there. It's a complicated business and Captain Branch isn't the most patient of men. Expects me to wave a magic wand or find thousands down the back of a sofa.' He tightens his scarf around his neck. 'I heard about Mr Koller. How is he?'

'When I rang the hospital this morning, he was awake and speaking to the police.'

Lancaster gestures back down the avenue. 'There was a police car at the gatehouse just now. I suppose they're still asking questions about Miss Laidlaw as well as Mr Koller.'

He says cheerio and strides on. When I reach the gatehouse, I see the constable who was busy with his ledger the other day, standing by a police car.

I stop my bike beside him. 'Are you visiting Mr Mathis?'

'He's kindly helping us with our enquiries. On your way, miss, if you don't mind.' He taps my front mudguard. 'I reckon this tyre could do with air.'

As I head out of the gate, a car is slowing to turn in. Captain Branch stares forbiddingly at me through the windscreen before he accelerates up the drive.

* * *

I won't be able to visit Felix, because of hotel duties. When I ring the ward, a nurse says that he's a little better and that she'll give him my good wishes and tell him I'll see him tomorrow. I'm not sure if I should mention to Leslie that his uncle Benny is helping the police. I decide to leave well alone. Benny will get in touch with Leslie if he wants.

In the lull before serving dinner, I drop by Susan's room with a fresh jug of water. I can hear her coughing as I near her door. She's sitting up, propped against pillows, completely washed out. I sit on the end of her bed and ask how she is.

'I'm better. Can't stop sleeping, though.'

'Have you still got a temperature?'

'Not so much. Only at night. Dr Jessop popped in to see me. He's ever so nice. Told me to keep on the aspirin and he gave me cough syrup.' She pulls a face. 'It's disgusting.'

'My mum used to say, "The worse it tastes, the better you'll feel." I'm not sure it's true.'

Susan sniffs loudly and pushes her straggling hair back. 'Do you miss your mum?'

'I miss her annoying me.'

'I miss my mum so much. She always called me her sweet Sue.' She covers her eyes and shudders.

I'm not much good in this kind of situation. 'Here, have a drink of fresh water and I'll get you a cuppa, if you'd like one.'

She coughs again and drinks some water. 'Ta. I don't want any tea. Daisy, I . . .'

I wait, but she's fiddling with the sheet, pleating the edge between her fingers. 'Yes, Susan?'

'I'm worried, like.' She has her head down, muttering.

'Can I help?'

'I dunno. I've been lying here fretting about it.'

'You can try me. Is it about you and Miss Laidlaw?'

'Not me, no.' She speaks in a sudden rush. 'It's just something I heard and I suppose I should've told the inspector, but I was worried I'd get in trouble. Captain Branch comes in here, and I reckon he could be really mean if he heard I'd said anything about him. He's ever so snappy with me.'

'Does it concern Miss Laidlaw?'

She nods and blows her nose, then has a coughing fit.

'Have another drop of water and then tell me what's on your mind.'

She gulps some down. 'I was coming out of the newsagent not long ago and I saw Miss Laidlaw and Captain Branch standing by his car. They was arguing — well, he was. He was ever so angry and he tore up a piece of paper and stamped on it.'

'What about Miss Laidlaw?'

'Her voice was low, like she was trying to keep things a bit more even. I couldn't really hear her. He was barking at her, something about peace-loving cowards and defeatists, and then he got in his car and drove away.'

'What did she do?'

'She bent down and picked up the pieces of paper, put them in her bag and walked off. She was shaking her head, like she was sad.' Susan demonstrates, which sets off another coughing bout. She sinks back against the pillows. 'Should I have said something to the inspector?'

'It's never too late. Would you like me to tell him?'

'Would you do that? Will he be cross?' she says with relief.

'I'm sure he won't. Leave it with me. Don't worry about it, OK?'

'OK. Ta. I might sleep again now.'

'Best thing when you're poorly.'

I phone the police station from reception, and when I'm told he's busy I leave a message saying that I have information for Inspector Thaxted.

Then I get on with the stimulating task of serving sausage and mash with root veg and cabbage, followed by apple pie.

* * *

I'm preparing to head home at about eight thirty when the inspector arrives. As I exit the kitchen, I see him limping towards me, his bony knuckles gripping his stick. He shrugs his coat off, hangs it with his trilby on a hook by reception and greets Dora.

'I've come to see Miss Moore. I could do with a drink and, in fact, something to eat, if it's not too late.'

Dora, who's keener on rules than on hospitality, says, 'Oh, now, dinner's finished, Inspector, and Leslie's gone home.'

He raises an eyebrow at me. 'Not even a sandwich for a hungry officer of the law?'

'I'm sure I can find something in the kitchen,' I tell him. 'The parlour is empty, we can sit in there.' I nod to Dora. 'Leave it to me.'

She raises her knitting and clicks away with her needles. 'Just don't mess with any of Leslie's stuff, he doesn't like it.'

I draw the curtains in the parlour while Peter Thaxted sinks into a chair, loosens his tie and unbuttons his suit jacket.

'Did you see Felix today?' I ask. 'How was he?'

'We spoke to him for ten minutes. He's very weak, but they're optimistic that he'll pull through.' A flicker of pain crosses his face. 'Can I have that drink and some water?'

'I'll get them now. There's some sausage, mash and veg left from dinner, shall I fetch you a plate?'

'No sausage, thanks. I'm a vegetarian.'

'Gosh. I've never met a vegetarian before.'

'I'm broadening your life experience, you see. The mash and veg will be fine, with some cheese if you have it, and a glass of whisky would be wonderful.'

In the kitchen, I put some mash and vegetables to heat up in a frying pan and cut a wedge of cheese in the pantry. While the food is warming, I fill a jug with water and fetch two glasses of whisky from the bar. Back in the kitchen, I slice the cheese on top of the vegetables and brown the dish under the grill. Then I put everything on a tray and head for the parlour.

'Make sure he pays for that food. We're not running a soup kitchen,' Dora calls to me.

Thaxted is reading his notebook when I arrive with the tray. I'd love to be able to see what's in it. He tucks it into his inside pocket and sits forward, palming white tablets into his mouth from his other hand and sipping water.

'Thank you, this is just what I need,' he says politely, putting the tray on his lap. His voice is fainter than usual, as if his throat is parched.

'Cheers!' I sip whisky. 'I saw police outside Benny Mathis's house today. Did you get anywhere with him?'

'You're like a deity, Miss Moore, omnipresent and all-seeing.'

I'm not sure what he means, so I nod wisely and press on. 'Did Benny tell you anything?'

Thaxted is eating neatly, crouching over the plate. A lock of his snowy hair falls across his forehead. He holds his whisky up to the light, swirling it in the glass, and drinks some before replying. 'We arrested Benny Mathis for the attack on Felix Koller. I'm going for attempted murder. A pedestrian gave us information about seeing a man fitting Mathis's description along that stretch of the river, around the time of the attack yesterday morning. Mr Koller also managed to recall enough to identify him. Mathis is being held in Oxford.'

'Did he say why he did it?'

'Not a great deal, but he's a man smouldering with pent-up rage. I imagine that having to keep his fascist sympathies under wraps in recent times has been a strain. His account amounted to foreigners and Jews have got it coming and there's no place for them here. He denied being a member of the British Union of Fascists, but he's certainly a strong supporter. They'll be flexing their muscles again soon.'

'That's what JB said. Mathis has a photo of Mosley in his hallway.'

'So I noticed.'

'Do you believe he murdered Miss Laidlaw?'

Thaxted takes another mouthful of food. 'He denied it, and the postman saw him working at Granville Grange around eleven on the morning of the murder, so he has an alibi.'

'When will Leslie hear about this?'

'A constable's going to his home around now. It'll be all over town tomorrow.'

'Leslie will be terribly upset. His uncle brought him up after his mother died.'

'Yes, it will be difficult.' He finishes the food and licks his fork. 'Leslie's not a bad cook.'

'The grilling of the cheese was the genius touch, however.'

Thaxted smiles. 'Self-praise is no praise. You have information for me.'

I run through my details about Nancy Mathis having worked at Granville Grange, and Susan's story concerning the argument between Captain Branch and Miss Laidlaw.

Thaxted adds a splash of water to his whisky and rubs his leg. 'Why didn't that silly girl tell me about this when I spoke to her?'

'She's easily scared and she worried it might get her into trouble with the captain. He drinks in here sometimes and he's been snappy with her.'

'Susan Bates should have been more worried about getting into trouble with the police.'

'She's told you now. She's got bad flu, so don't alarm her,' I say hastily.

He stares at me. 'I'm not a brute!'

'Don't vegetarians have a reputation for being non-violent? Before the war, there used to be a man waving a placard around Piccadilly. It said, *Meat inflames the brain and the blood. We will achieve world peace through vegetarianism.*'

Thaxted sits back and stares at me. 'I can never guess where a conversation might stray with you. Sadly, the placard man was inaccurate. Hitler was a vegetarian later in life.'

'Ah, that's news to me.'

His mouth twitches. 'They didn't discuss it in Whitehall?'

I pretend to consider this. 'Not as far as I can recall. I don't suppose it was regarded as that important. Maybe vegetables have more inflammatory qualities than we realise. Turnips might cloud our reason, carrots might incite rage.'

'Who can say? Nature can be dangerous territory.'

We both drink our whisky.

'Did Miss Laidlaw's pacifism kill her?' Thaxted murmurs.

'I've been wondering about that.' I recount my conversation with Sister Mason and hand him the Save Europe Now leaflet. 'Captain Branch was probably tearing up one of these during his argument with Miss Laidlaw.'

Thaxted rests an elbow on one knee while he reads it. 'I've seen this before. My mother has been handing them out. She's mentioned that she's encountered hostility, some of it pretty vocal.'

'Emotions are running high, especially now that people are seeing films about concentration camps and mass extermination. I spoke to a man on the bus about the leaflet. He was scathing, had no sympathy for starving Germans. What if someone got so angry that they lashed out at Miss Laidlaw?'

The inspector cradles his whisky and frowns, ridges of fine lines bracketing his mouth. 'Her murder was planned, not an angry outburst. Someone got her to come to room one at eleven fifteen. Her note to Felix Koller indicates that she might have been apprehensive about the meeting, and wanted the reassurance of his presence. Unfortunately, he was late so she was alone with her killer.'

'The murderer did plan it, but that doesn't mean it wasn't someone who objected to her charitable actions for Germans or her pacifist views in general.'

'You could be right. How did the murderer know that room one would be empty?'

'Anyone who worked at the hotel or was staying here would be aware. Ditto, friends and family of theirs. Also, it wouldn't be difficult to establish that the hotel is usually quiet at that time of day. That could amount to quite a lot of people.'

'It was a convenient place to use. Out of sight, behind a closed door and a quick exit straight down the stairs.'

I finish my whisky. 'Martha Prentice knows more than she's telling. She got upset when I asked her about Mr Branch's health in his final weeks.'

'I'll be interviewing her and Captain Branch again. Thank you for your help, Miss Moore, and for the food and drink. What do I owe?'

The inspector's attitude to me has certainly altered in the last few days — unexpectedly tolerant. I'm flabbergasted to hear him thanking me. I'm about to comment on it, but check myself. If I do, he might make a scathing response. 'Dora will tell you, you can pay at reception. Do I gather that you won't object if I carry on asking questions?'

He stands and steadies himself with his stick. 'I can't stop you and it does keep you ticking. I suppose I can't stand by and allow your brain to deteriorate.'

Dora has nipped to the loo, so before I go home, I ring through to Vera and tell her about Benny Mathis.

'Leslie's just been round to explain. He's in a right state. He can't work tomorrow because he wants to see Benny,' she says huffily. 'That's the bakery and the hotel up the creek. What a palaver. I suppose Susan is still malingering?'

'She's not well enough to work.'

'I'll get Dora to cook, then. She's stepped in before and she loves being in the kitchen. I'll pitch in with whatever else needs doing.'

'I'll serve breakfast tomorrow and then I'd like to visit Felix in hospital. I'll only be a couple of hours.'

'Yes, if you must. Visits to prisoners, visits to patients . . . you might as well take up charity work. What's the world coming to with all this mayhem? I thought things would be calmer when the war ended!'

I hear Ray in the background, shouting something about inequality and social disintegration.

'Oh, do shut up, Ray,' Vera snaps. 'I don't need a dollop of bloody Marx tonight as well as all this other stuff. Is Dora there, Daisy? Tell her to pop in here when she's finished. I need to tell her about Leslie.'

I say goodnight, guessing that there's not much chance of a baby Crampton any time soon.

CHAPTER FIFTEEN

JB is in bed when I get back to Brize Lodge, the fire burning down to a glowing ash. I feed the cats and spend five minutes scratching under their chins. My eyes are gritty with tiredness, but before I can sleep I want to update myself and JB on the case. I get the typewriter out and review.

Laidlaw Case
Leslie: Could have motive. LL had expelled him from school & his mum died, some said from shock. No alibi.
Captain Branch: Could have motive. Argued with LL about food for Germany. Alibi?
Martha Prentice: Keeping something back.
Nancy Mathis: Worked at Granville Grange. Relevant?
H Branch told LL something about a lie when she visited him & she noted that she should check staff records.
Was LL murdered because of pacifism/support for starving Germans?

I write an additional note to JB, telling him that Benny Mathis has been arrested, and check that the guard is firmly in place before the fire. Then I crash into bed with Tybalt and Oberon lying on either side of me, pinning me below the blankets.

I have confused dreams involving smoke, flames and Charlie Chaplin as Adolf Hitler, eating mashed vegetables.

* * *

Felix is awake when I visit him the next morning. His face is a palette of black and mauve and there's now a plaster on his left arm.

'I'm lucky to be alive. He meant to kill me.'

'You're right. Mathis is a heavyweight compared to you. Are you in a lot of pain?'

'Not so much. They've given me drugs.'

'How did it happen?'

'He came up behind me and dragged me into the bushes. He was swearing about filthy foreigners. That word, *wals*. I saw his face and then I don't recall much more.'

'Just as well. I'm so sorry.'

He squirms, moving his legs restlessly. 'I don't want to stay in Fernfield now.'

'Don't let someone like Mathis frighten you away. Get better and then take stock. Do you want anything from the house? I could collect it for you.'

'Not yet. When I can read, some books, please. You'll find them all in my room at Lucinda's. Did that Mathis man kill her?'

'No. He has an alibi. Still no news on that.'

He turns his head carefully. 'There is something you could do, if you have time. The clothes and food in the porch and the kitchen need to be taken to St Clement's vicarage tomorrow, for collection and distribution. It's important to carry on Lucinda's work. Could you manage that?'

'Leave it with me. I'll ask JB to lend a hand.'

'Thank you. So kind. The house keys are in the drawer here.'

I find them and turn to say goodbye, but he's fallen asleep.

Sister Mason waves to me from her office as I'm leaving the ward, and comes to the door. 'Felix is on the mend, amazingly,' she says. 'He has a strong will.'

'He's needed it.'

'I'm glad I caught you. There's a patient at the other end of this corridor who's been asking about Lucinda. She used to visit him and help him with letters home to his dad in Newcastle. And she was trying to locate any trace of his brother, who was missing in action. He asked if you'd stop by to see him.'

'Why does he want to talk to me? I never met Lucinda and I'm not familiar with her work.'

She moves closer, lowers her voice. 'He's poorly and he doesn't have any visitors. His father is disabled and can't travel. He's been in here four months and likely to be several more. He's had a lot of surgery. It would give him a boost if you'd say hello.'

I can't help remembering Vera's comment that I might as well take up charity work. Well, I did burn my house down. I have a lot of amends to make. 'I'll drop by and speak to him.'

'Thank you, I could tell that you're a good person. His name's Robert Etherington. We've told him we'll find someone else to help with letters home, so there's no need to get involved with that. Just to advise you, he has difficulty with speech from a jaw wound and also a degree of mental impairment because of his injuries. We have given him a notepad and paper, but he can't always communicate well.'

I admire Sister Mason's persuasive skills as I walk to the other end of the corridor with a degree of dread. I'm not frightened of Robert Etherington's injuries, but I've no idea what this man might hope I can do for him. I find him sitting in a high-backed chair next to his bed, wearing pyjamas and a tatty plaid dressing gown that's on the tight side. I expect a lady almoner found it for him in a cupboard of dead men's clothes. He has a patch over his left eye and his mouth and jaw are misaligned and drooping.

'Hello, I'm Daisy Moore. I didn't meet Lucinda Laidlaw, but I have met her friend and lodger, Mr Koller.'

Etherington turns his one, bloodshot eye on me. He nods and says, 'Sit,' indistinctly, pointing to a chair at the end of his bed. The rug placed across his knees slides to one side and that's when I see that his right leg is missing.

I pull the chair up near him. 'I'm sorry about Lucinda, Mr Etherington.'

He makes a guttural noise. 'Murdered.'

I move a little closer, as it's hard to make out his words. 'That's right, someone killed her.'

He starts to say something, stops, swallows and manages: 'Wonderful.'

'She was wonderful? Yes, she did help lots of people.'

He taps his chest. 'Helped me. Brother.'

'Your brother who's missing? Did Lucinda have any news of him?'

He shakes his head, stutters, 'Girlfriend.'

'Sorry, whose girlfriend?'

An impatient sound, then he reaches for the notepad on his bedside table and writes slowly. It's painful to watch him, stopping and starting. After a few minutes he holds out the pad to me and I read his scrawl.

Percy girlfriend. Not right. Lucinda made note.

He's staring at me intently and it's as if I'm at sea without a rudder or compass. 'Who's Percy?'

'Brother.'

'Your missing brother?'

He nods but waves a hand and points at the notepad. 'She not right. Lucinda.' He makes a writing motion. 'Lucinda.'

I switch between him and the notepad, seeking inspiration. 'Lucinda wrote something down about Percy's girlfriend, who's not right.'

He nods and presses his sleeve against his mouth. 'Shouldn't . . . pretending.'

I've no idea what this man is trying to tell me and I'm not sure which of us is more frustrated. 'Where did Lucinda write this?'

He shapes a large square, makes a page turning motion. 'Bind . . . binder.'

'She wrote it in a binder.'

He nods, seizes the notepad and writes in capitals. *PLEASE FIND.*

'I'll try. I can't promise anything. I'll keep you informed. I'll see if Lucinda recorded anything about your brother as well.'

He nods at me and tries to smile, managing an alarming grimace.

'Hello, Robert, are you ready for your physio? Get all those muscles stretched.' A woman in a white uniform has arrived, pushing a wheelchair.

I'm glad of the excuse to escape, which makes me a complete heel. I hurry from the hospital's confines, glad to be fit and well and out under a washed blue sky.

* * *

Vera is in a surprisingly upbeat mood, dressed in an apron and with a scarf tied around her head. Her face is glowing.

'I did some cleaning. It always makes me perk up, for some reason.' She beckons me closer. 'I heard Dr Jessop in the parlour with Nurse Dean earlier. He was giving her a right telling off about something. She was really fed up afterwards. Took off on that bike of hers as if the devil was at her back.'

'What was it about?'

'I'm not sure. I heard him shout, "basic routines". He sounded very annoyed and he's usually such a mild man. Mind, there's something going on at the cottage hospital as well. It was bothering him the day I took Mum there. He was going around with an officious chap with a clipboard. Now, can you take a tray of tea up to Mrs Ward and check on Susan. I haven't had time to pop in.'

Susan has had a wash and combed her hair. She says she's a lot better and she wants to come back to work tomorrow. I'm cheered at the prospect of escaping dining-room duties.

Mrs Ward is dozing in her chair when I take her tea in. She's pale, her skin doughy and dry.

'Can you pour it for me, dear? I'm as weak as a kitten today.'

'I hope you haven't caught Susan's flu, Mrs Ward.'

'Oh no, dear. My leg's infected, that's what's knocking me back. Dr Jessop examined it this morning and he wasn't best pleased.'

'You can't help getting an infection.'

'He wasn't annoyed with *me*. He was asking about Nurse Dean and when she last checked it. I did say to him that she's rough. Anyway, he cleaned and dressed it himself and he's given me something to take. He said he'll pop back this evening to see how I'm doing.'

This must be why the doctor was cross with Joan Dean. It reminds me of something that Martha Prentice said and I'd forgotten — that Nurse Dean visited Hector Branch when he was ill, and spent a lot of time with him.

When Joan arrives back from work and asks for her tea in the parlour, I make sure I take it to her. She's yawning as I bring it in and clearly not in the best of moods.

'Hard day with all your patients?'

'I should say. I'm bushed, I could sleep for a week. This flu that Susan's had is going round. That's all I need on top of the usual ailments.'

'At least she's better and should be up and about tomorrow.' I opt for flattery to soften her edges. 'Hope you don't catch it, we can't have you being sick. Fernfield would struggle to manage without Nurse Dean, you're very well respected.' I sound horribly sycophantic but it goes down well with Joan.

She pauses, teacup in hand. 'Oh, really?'

I sit opposite her. 'Yes, lots of people are very positive about you. Martha Prentice at Granville Grange was singing your praises just the other day. She said you were such a help with Hector Branch before he died.'

'That's kind of her. He was a poorly old gentleman, very muddled.'

'Well, she really appreciated the time you took with him.'

'He was no trouble, to be honest.' She smiles to herself. 'No, it was a pleasure to call on him, it wasn't really like work.'

That doesn't ring true. 'Will you be popping in to see Mrs Ward tonight? Apparently her leg is playing up. She wasn't too good earlier,' I say innocently.

Joan's colour rises and she turns away, fiddling with her teaspoon. 'I understand that Dr Jessop is going to deal with her for now. Happens sometimes. Best for the doctor to monitor if there are any complications.' She gives a toss of the head and adds with a touch of defiance, 'I expect he'll discuss the options for any treatment needed with me.'

That's the first time I've heard that a doctor would consult a nurse. 'He and his wife are moving back to their house in a couple of days. The work's almost finished.'

She brightens, knocks her tea back. 'That's good. Better for Mrs Jessop to be at home in her condition. Could you fetch me another brew? That hardly touched the sides.'

In the kitchen, Dora is singing along to the wireless and cooking up a storm with a game casserole. She wipes her brow and tells me that Leslie's all cut up about his uncle, but he'll be back at work tomorrow. She tastes from her wooden spoon. 'That Mr Koller would be wise to move somewhere else. Pity Miss Laidlaw ever brought him here.'

'Why's that?'

'Like Leslie said, if he'd never come here, this wouldn't have happened and Benny wouldn't be facing jail.'

I'm speechless for a moment. 'Or putting it another way, if Benny hadn't attacked him, Felix Koller wouldn't be lying in a hospital bed. Benny's lucky he's not facing a murder charge.'

Dora stirs the casserole roughly. 'We don't need *wals* coming here and bothering people. It only leads to trouble.'

I'm so insulted, I have to hold my fists tight to stop myself trembling. 'You'd better get used to it, Dora. There are going to be plenty more people needing a place to live, and Fernfield is so attractive at first glance, until you meet the inhabitants.'

'What d'you mean by that?' She turns around, her tiny mouth compressed. 'This is a lovely town.'

'Maybe, as long as your face fits.'

'People that don't like us can lump it.' Dora clangs a lid on the saucepan and marches to the pantry.

I thump the kettle down. I'd like to go straight to Brize Lodge, pack my bag and head back to London. But I'd miss JB, Tybalt and Oberon, I can't abandon Felix and there's a murder to solve.

* * *

JB listens to my complaints about Fernies and *wals* over cocoa. He puffs a cigar and turns his mild gaze on me. 'You'll find prejudice everywhere, me old china, even in big cities. My neighbour in Fulham was obnoxiously antisemitic. It's just more noticeable in Fernfield. There are plenty of people around here who don't hold those views.'

'Maybe.' I stroke Oberon with my bare foot.

'Everything's up in the air at the moment, people are unsettled and unsure. Declan says, "Sure and begorrah, isn't the poor old world in a fierce ree-raw." That means troubled, by the way.'

I have to smile at his accent as much as the quotation.

'And behold, Daisy's gloom dissipates! Down to brass tacks — I read your update on the murder. Any developments?'

'I met Inspector Thaxted and told him about Captain Branch's argument with Lucinda. He's a vegetarian.'

'Captain Branch is?'

'No, Peter Thaxted.'

'Oh yes, so's his mother. It's all part of the pacifist philosophy — opposition to cruelty and violence. I wonder what's cockney rhyming slang for a vegetarian?'

'Uncle Reg — veg.' I explain about the placard man at Piccadilly. 'People used to refer to Uncle Reg and call him that as they passed by.'

'Ha! How did you find out that Peter's an Uncle Reg?'

'He had some dinner at the Dolphin last night while we swapped notes.'

JB twiddles his cigar. 'It sounds as if you and he are a little more friendly.'

'I presume he's decided that I'm not just an interfering busybody. JB, there's something off about Nurse Dean.'

'I'm all ears.'

I tell him about Mrs Ward's leg, Dr Jessop's anger, and Martha's comment about the nurse's visits to Hector Branch. 'It sounds vague, but she's a curious mixture of aggressive and defensive.'

'You're right, it does sound vague. I imagine that doctors and nurses often fall out, and I suppose those two are still learning each other's methods.' He blows a smoke ring. 'I wonder if Captain Branch is our killer? All that violence and misery he'd have seen on active service — it must change a man and he might have believed that Miss Laidlaw was denying everything he'd fought for.'

'Thaxted is interviewing him again.' JB's comments have put me in mind of Robert Etherington. I recall seeing ring binders stacked in the kitchen at Woodlands. 'Can you help me with taking charity contributions from Lucinda's house to St Clement's tomorrow? There's quite a lot. Felix is concerned that it gets distributed.'

'I happen to be free tomorrow, so I will chauffeur you.' He turns up the wireless. 'Moonlight Serenade' is playing. 'Now, shall we foxtrot?'

CHAPTER SIXTEEN

Lucinda's house is chilly when I let myself in the next day. Felix has stacked all the donation boxes in the sitting room. I count eleven of them. There's a one-bar electric fire in the hall. I take it to the kitchen and plug it in, where it throws out a tiny glow. The sky outside is dark and lowering over one of those days that never quite emerges from the night before. I switch on the light, pull the curtains back fully and bring the two ring binders to the table. The green one is labelled REFUGEES & POWs, the red one, HOSPITAL.

The green binder demonstrates that Felix wasn't the only person Lucinda wrote letters about. There are dozens to the Home Office, supporting internees and other displaced people. Every charitable collection is documented and pages of records show parcels collected and donated to the Red Cross for prisoners of war.

I leaf through the HOSPITAL binder, which has card separators marked A to Z and is fat with pages in Lucinda's writing. She has maintained a record of every patient she has visited and helped, noting dates of letters sent and requests the patient has made with outcomes. There are handwritten copies of letters she has sent to the Red Cross, seeking information about missing relatives and friends, with a comment in capitals at the top of each one: STILL SEARCHING, FOUND, NO TRACE, DEAD.

I've kept my coat on, but even so, I shiver and pull the electric fire as near as the lead will allow. I turn to the Es and locate Robert Etherington. Lucinda has visited him weekly for months, writing each time to his father, noting when she has read a reply to him and taking him slippers, tobacco and toiletries. The letter about his missing brother, Percy Etherington, who was fighting in the Ardennes is marked STILL SEARCHING. Behind this letter is a sheet of paper with a note dated 2 August 1945.

It is so hard to understand Robert at times and he gets terribly frustrated. He does have problems with his memory and organising his ideas. Today, he was agitated and clearly wished to communicate something. If I understood correctly, he believed that he had seen his brother Percy's girlfriend in the hospital that morning. Robert couldn't remember her name, or explain where he'd spotted her. He kept insisting that she's not right, but I've no idea what he meant. He was so distressed — I have to try and help him. I'll see if I can trace this girlfriend, as it would also be a link for Robert to his missing brother. Presumably, she isn't aware that Robert is a patient in the hospital. I asked a couple of nurses on his ward if they knew anything about her. They just said that Robert was having a bad day, he was tired after X-rays and a first fitting for a prosthetic leg. One of them implied he'd probably imagined seeing someone. I will ask Robert's father if he has any information about Percy's girlfriend.

There's a copy of a letter to Robert's father attached to this note, asking for information and a brief reply.

34 Alma Terrace
Newcastle

Dear Miss Laidlaw,
I hope this finds you well. I can't tell you anything about Percy having a girlfriend. He didn't have one here at home. Maybe he'd met someone when he was in training camp, or on weekend leave. Robert

never mentioned anyone to me. Both my boys served in the Royal Northumberland Fusiliers.

Thank you for helping Robert and trying to find out about Percy for us.

Yours Faithfully,
Thomas Etherington.

There's no other information. I presume this must mean that Lucinda didn't get anywhere. It's hard to see how she could have found a nameless woman who Robert Etherington might have been mistaken about. I sit back and contemplate Lucinda's activities. She must have spent days on all this work, ferrying food and clothing, copying letters by hand, doggedly ploughing on while receiving insults and hostility from some of the community. It makes me feel humbled and annoyed with myself for complaining about this town and the weather.

JB arrives as I'm making a note of Thomas Etherington's address. He's natty in a conker-brown herringbone overcoat, a tangerine cravat and brogues.

'Gosh,' he says when he surveys all the boxes, 'Lucinda was a busy woman. I'm glad I'm strong today. We should just about get them all in.'

I help him carry the boxes to his car. At St Clement's vicarage, the vicar thanks us effusively.

'We will miss dear Lucinda terribly. It's her funeral tomorrow. Just a simple service. Captain Branch didn't want any fuss.'

I bet he didn't. I expect he's ordered the cheapest coffin too. Although I didn't meet Lucinda, I should be there, for Felix's sake. 'I'd like to attend. What time is it?'

'Eleven a.m., and you're most welcome.'

In the car, I turn to JB. 'Felix will be terribly upset that he can't be at Lucinda's funeral. He probably hasn't been told when it is.'

'You can call the hospital from home later, so that he can be there in spirit. Funerals are damned depressing occasions, as far as I'm concerned. Long faces and soggy sandwiches and then everyone buggers off, glad that the grim reaper hasn't made it to their door just yet.'

'I gather you won't be coming.'

'I'm recording tomorrow, so that lets me nicely off the hook. I expect the *kommandantin* will be there. She likes a funeral — it gives her an opportunity to play the *grande dame* and patronise the yokels.'

I'm thirsty after our exertions. I suggest a coffee in the Napolina and JB agrees dubiously.

'I've never been there. Not sure it's my kind of place. The trouble and strife alleges that it lowers the tone of the town.'

'You haven't lived if you've never had a monkey throw nuts at you, and you needn't tell her you've been there.'

It's warm and cheery in the café, which is busy on this raw, gloomy day. On the way to the counter, I see Inspector Thaxted, sitting on his own with a pot of tea, and I nudge JB. Thaxted is reading a newspaper and hasn't noticed us. 'Tico', a popular samba song, is playing, and JB executes a few steps. We order coffee and JB eyes Rindi, who's sitting meekly on Jock's shoulder with his chin tucked down.

'Your monkey appears quite well-behaved,' JB tells Jock, 'although I've heard bad reports about him.'

'He's the cabaret around here. He had a busy morning, so he's taking a break now. I expect there'll be mischief later.' Jock leans against the counter. 'Rindi tends to make a beeline for people if they're nervous of him.'

'If he comes anywhere near me, he'll regret it,' JB says firmly. He then turns and saunters over to Thaxted's table.

'Peter! Good to see you!'

Thaxted smiles and nods to me when I follow over.

'Mind if we sit with you?' JB asks.

'Be my guests.'

JB pulls out a chair for me and one for himself. 'Double trouble, interrupting your tea.'

'I can't believe that Miss Moore would cause trouble.' Thaxted widens his eyes.

'Not intentionally,' I tell him.

JB undoes his coat. 'We've just been engaged in good works, delivering food and clothing to the poor and needy.'

Thaxted is taken aback. 'I didn't have you down as do-gooders. Not your usual field of endeavour, Jeffrey.'

'It was stuff that Miss Laidlaw had collected,' I explain. 'Felix asked if I could get it to St Clement's for distribution.'

Thaxted extends his injured leg and swivels the ankle. 'How is Mr Koller?'

'Doing OK. I said I'll take him some books as soon as he can sit up and read.'

JB nudges his chair in and asks, a little too loudly, 'So, Peter, are you near to finding out who spilled blood on the carpet in my hotel?'

Heads turn at the tables nearby and Thaxted glares at him.

'Please keep your voice down, Jeffrey. I can't discuss police business with you, and certainly not in here.'

'You're happy to discuss it with Daisy,' JB says in an exaggerated whisper.

Thaxted shakes his head at me ruefully, as if I'm a traitor.

'JB has helped me,' I say. 'I bounce ideas off him.'

'Clearly. Quite the Holmes and Watson.'

'Daisy types case summaries, keeps me up to speed,' JB adds. 'She's very organised.'

Thaxted rubs his forehead. 'An ideal quality in a facto-tum. Case summaries sound so important. Maybe you should drop copies into the station for me to give me pointers.'

I'd kick JB under the table if he wasn't my employer. 'It's my way of ordering my thoughts, Inspector, that's all.'

Thaxted shakes his head. 'No, modesty doesn't suit you. In fact, it's faintly alarming.'

'Can't you give us some kind of heads-up?' JB pleads.

Thaxted cups his chin as if considering this. 'No. Have *you* any information for me, Jeffrey?'

'Well . . . no. But as the hotel owner, and with the great-est respect, I have an interest in the case.'

'Granted, but I can't comment.'

JB tastes his coffee. 'Ghastly,' he pronounces, pulling a face. 'The music's much better.' Then *sotto voce*, he adds, 'But see here, Peter, any news of the captain? Daisy told me about the *argument*.'

'Sadly, and with the greatest respect, nothing I can share with you.'

JB grins. 'Touché, old chap.'

It's dawning on me that these two are old sparring partners, and enjoying the game of cat and mouse. I'm somewhat miffed, as if I've been left out of the plot. I had been going to tell JB and Thaxted about Susan's petty pilfering and the mysterious woman at the hospital, but now I decide to keep the information to myself.

Thaxted and JB start talking about family members I've never heard of, so I tune out and watch Rindi as he climbs on Jock's head, from which vantage point he beadily surveys the customers. I avoid his eye. A moment later, a nut hits the back of JB's head and he pauses mid-sentence. Thaxted laughs, a rusty sound like a door creaking.

'Come on then, JB, me old china,' I say, upping my cockney credentials, 'put your money where your mouth is and make that monkey regret it.'

* * *

St Clement's is a twelfth-century church with a tall spire, set on a hill above the Thames and with a graveyard in its grounds. Access is through a moss-covered lychgate and up steep steps. An information leaflet tells me that lancet windows were added in the thirteenth century, with later additions of a Gothic arcade and chapel. None of this means much to me, and it's a shame that Felix isn't with me to explain the architectural history. I can appreciate that it's a restful, lovely place, with a great deal of stained glass, mosaics of the saints and a silver chandelier over the altar. It is, however, freezing, with no visible heating, and this might explain why the vicar keeps the funeral service to twenty minutes, rattling through the prayers at speed.

There are around thirty mourners. Simeon Lancaster is at the end of a row, next to Iris Jessop, and Vera has come with Ray, leaving Dora in charge at the Dolphin. Captain Branch is in the left-hand front pew in military uniform, accompanied by the blonde woman who'd been with him in the bar at the hotel. She's wearing a dark grey coat with huge lapels and a fur stole. The *kommandantin* is in the front pew to the right, erect and dignified, sporting a broad black hat with a veil pulled down over the brim.

We listen to two readings from the Bible, punctuated by frequent coughs from the congregation, including, '*I am the resurrection and the life, saith the Lord; he that believeth in me, though he were dead, yet shall he live: and whosoever liveth and believeth in me shall never die.*' I've always been impressed that this neatly covers all bets. Father Hickey read it at my mother's funeral. The vicar states that Lucinda was a kind, gentle and charitable woman, a stalwart of the parish, and reads from his Bible again. '*Whoever sows generously will also reap generously.*' Unfortunately, that reminds me of Martha's comment about Ray's bedroom abilities, and I have to cover my mouth. At the end we sing 'Amazing Grace' accompanied by a wheezing organ.

Lucinda is buried at the edge of the cemetery. She has a fine view of the Thames. The sun is out and a robin is busy in the laurel hedge nearby. I notice that Rosalind is watching me. She inclines her head graciously, her hat dipping.

When the interment is finished, people start to wander back towards the lychgate. Ray and Vera walk with me.

'The toffs are a mean, penny-pinching lot, and no mistake,' Ray complains. 'There's no funeral refreshments organised.'

'I must say, it's a bit off,' Vera agrees. 'I've never heard of such a thing. It's not right at all.'

'Captain Branch doesn't care about proper traditions,' Ray adds. 'He'd have preferred to stick the old lady in the grounds at Granville Grange and spare the funeral expense.

If Benny Mathis hadn't got himself banged up, Branch would probably have got him to dig the hole.'

We stop at the wall by the gate, hovering in that way that people do when a funeral is over but it doesn't seem quite right to leave.

Vera takes Ray's arm. 'All right, that'll do, we don't want people to hear you and take offence.'

'I'm only saying what a lot of folk are thinking.'

'Even so. Coming back to the Dolphin, Daisy?'

I've been watching an encounter further up in the graveyard that I want to check. 'I'll be there in ten minutes.'

When they've moved away, I skirt past the vicar and Captain Branch's companion, who are talking to the *kommandantin*, and walk around the edge of the graves. Captain Branch and Nurse Dean are standing by a large stone angel, next to a stately yew tree. She's close up to him, wagging a finger. I didn't see her in the church and she's in her work uniform. The sun strikes off the medals on Captain Branch's chest. It appears to be a heated exchange, although I'm not close enough to hear them. He makes a dismissive gesture with his hand and strides away from her towards the lychgate. I shrink back behind a tall gravestone as she stares after him with a face like thunder. Then she turns onto a path that runs to the other side of the church and stomps along it in her sturdy black lace-ups. I follow her at a distance, crunching through leaf fall, and watch her exit through another gate. When I reach it and get a view of the road, I see her cycling away fast.

I can't make out this disagreement. When I return to the lychgate, Branch is speaking to the vicar, apparently composed. His companion is snuggling into her stole and gazing up at him adoringly. Rosalind is departing in her car, a navy-blue sedan, sitting very upright behind the wheel. I expect she had deportment lessons as a child and practised balancing books on her head.

I walk back to the Dolphin deep in thought and spot Iris Jessop a few yards in front of me, standing at the bus stop outside the chemist. She has one gloved hand resting on her bump, and her shopping basket hooked over her other arm.

'Are you off to Oxford?' I ask.

'Yes, and I can't wait to enjoy the heating on the bus. It was freezing in the church! Lovely service, though.'

'Was Nurse Dean there?'

Iris shakes her head. 'No.'

'I suppose she's busy with the living. It must be quite a challenge for her, getting around a new area.'

'Yes, I'm sure. It takes a while and she's new to the role.'

'She wasn't a district nurse before she came here?'

'No, she was in a sanatorium in Kent — Sittingbourne — so it's quite a change for her, being out and about in the community.' Iris shades her eyes and peers up the road. 'This bus is late and I must get to the drapers in Oxford. We're having new curtains at long last, and I want to get them ordered before Tim decides we can't afford them after all. He keeps going on about how much the rewiring has cost, but we had to have it done, it was dangerous. It means we're having to redecorate as well and it all adds up, but I want it just right for when the baby comes.'

Another woman arrives at the stop and they start chatting about pregnancy, so I move on. At the hotel, the staff are gathered in the parlour, where Vera has broken open a bottle of sherry.

'Here, Daisy, have a warming glass. The Dolphin does things properly. We're toasting Miss Laidlaw's memory, even if her family isn't!'

I'm touched by the gesture and click glasses with Vera.

Susan coughs, downs her drink and pats her chest. 'I've never had sherry before, except in trifle.'

Leslie is quiet. He's been muted since seeing his uncle, keeping his head down.

Dora pours herself a second glass and raises it to the company. 'Here's to peace and being allowed to get back to normal, just like we were before the bloody war!'

We all drink, although I predict that Dora's going to be disappointed if she expects life to revert to its familiar pre-war rhythms.

CHAPTER SEVENTEEN

Felix is improving and sitting up. His bruises are less lurid. I've brought him some books from home and apples from the tree at Brize Lodge.

'I regret that I wasn't at Lucinda's funeral. Did it go well?'

'Yes, and she has a lovely grave, with a river view. You can visit her there when you get home.'

'I might be discharged in another week or so. Are people . . . are they talking about me much?'

'Not that I'm aware of. People have short memories, Felix. They're more taken up with shortages, jobs for troops coming home and when their relatives will get demobilised.' Simeon Lancaster has told me that divorce applications are already increasing and he predicted that there'll be plenty more, with men returning as strangers and some finding that their wives have been having affairs in their absence.

He absorbs this. 'Thank you for the books. At least if I can study, I'm making some use of this lying around.'

'Reading one-handed isn't much fun.'

'Better than not reading at all. Luckily, my glasses more or less survived the attack, although the frames are bent. One of the nurses taped up the arms for me. Just as well, as I can barely see my hand in front of my face without them.'

When I've spent a while with Felix, I head to Robert Etherington's ward. He's in the day room, leafing through a car magazine. Two men are playing dominoes at a small table and another is standing by a window, drawing shapes in the misted glass.

Robert waves to me and moves his mouth in a shape that I now understand is a smile, not a scowl. His hair has grown a little, curling around his ears.

'Hello, Robert. I brought some cigarettes for you. They're called Spanish Shawl and I expect they're not much good, but they're all I could find.'

He studies them, slips them in his dressing-gown pocket and raises a thumb.

'I haven't got any news for you about your brother. Is someone else coming to write your letters home?'

'New lady.'

'I'm glad.' I tell him about Lucinda's funeral and the hymns we sang.

'Good.' He's low in mood and not very interested in my presence, but I've had an idea so I persist.

'I'm still trying to find out about the woman you mentioned, Percy's girlfriend. Were you and Percy in the same regiments?'

Robert shakes his head and holds up two fingers. 'Percy battalion.'

'Percy was in the second battalion of the Royal Northumberland Fusiliers?'

'Right.'

'Can you tell me the names of any of Percy's friends in the second battalion — if I could contact them, they might know his girlfriend's name and her whereabouts.'

There's a spark of interest in his good eye again. He massages his jaw and takes out one of the Spanish Shawl cigarettes, lighting up. The packet states that they're perfumed with amber, but it smells awful, like charred meat.

One of the men at the table calls out, 'Cripes, who's thrown a dog in the fire?'

'Sorry,' I tell him. 'They were the only cigarettes available in the newsagent.'

They laugh and chorus, 'Spanish Shawl.'

They switch to playing cards and the man by the window joins them. Robert takes his notepad from his pocket and laboriously writes a name for me.

Frank Tattersall. 'Percy friend.'

'Thanks. I'll see if I can do anything with this. I don't suppose you've seen the woman again around the hospital?'

'No.' He taps the arm of his chair. 'Not right!'

'OK. Sorry about the cigarettes.'

He leans back and closes his eyes, the Spanish Shawl dangling from the corner of his sagging mouth.

* * *

Vera's had to take her mother to another medical appointment, so I'm covering reception and making use of a handy phone to call the headquarters of the Royal Northumberland Fusiliers. I explain that I'd like information about the second battalion, and after a lot of clicking sounds I'm put through to a young-sounding man.

I announce vaguely that I'm linked to the Red Cross — a lie, but I tell myself it's a justified one in the circumstances. 'I'm trying to help a severely wounded man called Robert Etherington, who was in your regiment. His brother, Percy Etherington, was in your second battalion and he's missing. Robert would like me to see if I can contact Frank Tattersall, who was a friend of Percy's and in the same battalion.'

'I can check for you. The second are back now. It might not be good news, like.'

His accent is almost impenetrable. 'I understand. Also, maybe you could see if there's any update on Percy.'

'Not sure about that, but I'll try. You'll have to wait.'

'That's very kind of you.'

While I'm waiting, I'm tempted to peek in Vera's make-up bag, which she's left in one of the desk's pigeon holes. It contains an almost used-up compact of Max Factor powder, a stub of Red Majesty lipstick, a black brow pencil, a little tin of Vaseline and a mirror. The Vaseline explains how she gets that gleam on her lips. There's also a folded-up article from a magazine, which is an agony aunt's advice column with the headline, *Problems between the Sheets*. 'Helping Hannah' has proffered guidance about letting a man take the lead in the bedroom. I'm wondering if Vera wrote the letter and I'm longing to read more, but the phone crackles into life, so I zip the bag up and replace it.

'Hello, miss. Well, this is a matter of good news and bad, so I'll give you the good first. I'm glad to say that Frank Tattersall made it back safe and sound and he's home now with his mam and dad.'

'That's a relief. Can you give me his address so that I can write to him?'

My helper reels off an address in Gateshead, then pauses and says more slowly, 'I'm afraid that Percy Etherington has now been recorded as dead. We've just written to his dad.'

'I'm sorry to hear that, it will be a terrible blow.'

'Aye, it will that.'

'Thanks so much for your help, I appreciate it.'

I put the receiver down. Should I tell Robert Etherington what I've learned? I sit, weighing it up, and decide that his father should be allowed to pass on the news. I'll give it a couple of days and check if Robert's been informed. In the meantime, I might be able to make progress with Frank Tattersall, regarding the mystery of Percy's girlfriend. I take a sheet of headed notepaper from the drawer and write to Frank, explaining the situation. I add JB's phone number under the hotel's, cheekily reassuring Frank that he can ring me and reverse charges.

* * *

I'm on my bike, squeaking back to Brize Lodge as dusk is gathering. There's a smear of evening mist, with a crescent moon climbing the sky. I'm a mile or so out of town, and just getting into my stride with 'North Country Maid' when a car overtakes and pulls in on the verge a little way ahead. Its lights are doused and a man gets out, slams the door hard and puts up a leather-gauntleted hand to me. Captain Branch, dressed in a khaki military greatcoat, his trousers tucked into riding boots. My lamp beam picks out his face. He's not happy as he strides towards me. His coat gives him a bulky, forbidding shape.

'Miss Moore,' he says in his high tones, 'I want a word with you.'

I put my feet on the tarmac. 'Hello, Captain Branch.'

He folds his arms, taps a glove on a bicep. 'I don't recall inviting you to my home.'

I act innocent. 'Mr Berrow asked me to accompany him when he visited.'

'I'm not referring to that occasion, as you're very well aware.'

'Oh?'

He stamps a boot on the ground. 'I'm talking about your recent solo visit, when you were asking Martha Prentice impertinent questions.'

The mist is growing thicker and more vaporous, closing in on us, stroking my cheeks with wraithlike fingers. Branch is standing very near.

'Martha kindly offered me a cup of tea.'

'I don't like people coming to my house and badgering my staff.'

'That wasn't my intention. We just had a chat.' Poor Martha — the captain must have interrogated her after he saw me leaving the grounds.

'Don't play games with me. You were asking about my father, Lucinda and the Mathis family. Martha's a foolish old woman and a gossip. Your visit upset and worried her. My family and its employees are none of your business. Stay away from Granville Grange.'

'Or what?'

He grabs my handlebars. 'Or you might find yourself out of a job. Your sort isn't wanted around here. You'll find yourself back in whatever London slum you crawled from.'

I'm alarmed. It's a lonely spot, cold and dark, and the heat of his anger is radiating through the chilly murk. He might be a murderer. On the other hand, I'm not impressed by his tin-pot general act. I bet his men mimicked his high voice and nicknamed him *Soprano* or some similar insult.

'Walthamstow isn't a slum, Captain Branch. My home was certainly better heated than yours.' *Especially the night I crisped it.*

'Don't test my patience, my girl. Learn some manners and mind your own business. I gather that you've befriended that parasite Koller who was leeching off Lucinda, and you've been spreading tales about her and me. I won't warn you again.'

I place my foot on the pedal, ready to push off. He notices and his grip tightens on the frame.

'Don't threaten me. I can talk to anyone I want to.'

'Not in my home. And you'd better keep your busy tongue in check. If you don't, you'll regret it.'

I can't resist. 'What were you arguing with Nurse Dean about at Miss Laidlaw's funeral? You were very angry.'

He's wrong-footed and blinks at me. 'What are you talking about now?'

'You were arguing in the cemetery, quite a ding-dong. Was it something to do with her visits to your dad before he died?' I can see from the tension in his face that I've struck home, so I throw in: 'I believe they had long conversations.'

He snarls, 'Whoever's told you that, it's absolute nonsense.'

'Tut, Captain — arguing with Lucinda in the street and with the nurse among the graves. Rowing publicly with ladies. Not very good form for an officer — although I'd draw the line at gentleman. You're so angry, you must have something to hide.'

His hold on the bike has loosened while he digests this. I twist the wheel sharply, unbalancing him and ride away as fast as I can. I worry what I'll do if he comes after me. He could run me off the road, leave me dead in a ditch. I work up speed, waiting for a car engine behind me, but there's only an owl hooting and a faint lowing of cattle. I keep going though, working up a head of steam, pockets of mist drifting in front of me.

Overall, that was a useful, if alarming encounter. Branch was unnerved when I mentioned Joan Dean and her visits to his father. Definitely a thread to pull on.

I'm hugely relieved when I see the lights of Brize Lodge shimmering in the gloom. I'm not going to mention my strange encounter to JB — I don't want him insisting that I need to be ferried in a car for now, and I refuse to let the captain cramp my style. I dismount from my bike and wheel it into the gubbins room. I rest against it as it dawns on me that Hector Branch might have had a number of lucid moments. What if he'd divulged the story about a lie to Joan Dean as well as Lucinda?

CHAPTER EIGHTEEN

I wake in the night, wanting a drink of water, but Tybalt is lying across my legs and I don't want to disturb him. So I stare at the ceiling, pondering Hector Branch and summing up what I've found out about him.

The old man must have realised that he was dying. Maybe he had an urge to get something off his chest. He'd upset Lucinda with his tale of an awful lie. It would be reasonable to suppose that this lie was connected to his family, otherwise why would he need to reveal it? Martha told me that Hector was always confused, but Felix reported that Lucinda found him lucid on the visit when he divulged the lie. Then Nurse Dean had appeared at his bedside and chatted to him. She spent a long time with him on some visits, after which he was agitated.

Hector's guard was down and he was passing in and out of confused and more rational states. (At this point, I picture pockets of mist clearing and then re-forming.) He might even have reckoned that Nurse Dean was Lucinda and repeated his story to her. If that was the case, then Joan Dean would have heard something that Hector Branch had needed to disclose, possibly something that would reflect on the family. I recall Captain Branch's hostility the night before, and I'm sure I'm right.

I need to find out what Lucinda meant by *check staff*. I wriggle, but Tybalt doesn't stir. Really, I could do with talking to Martha again, but I don't want to get her into trouble or encourage the captain to report me for trespass. I'll try Leslie, if I can catch him in the right mood. It might be difficult, as I am aligned with Felix, who in his eyes is the cause of Benny's incarceration.

I manage to turn drowsily on my side without annoying my sleeping friend.

* * *

Leslie always appreciates an offer of help, so the next day I make myself useful in the kitchen with bread-and-apple pudding. He's not talkative, wrapped up in himself, with a gloomy manner. No matter what I make of Benny, he was Leslie's father figure for many years as well as his uncle. I'm thankful that I haven't detected any personal animosity as I cut stale bread into triangles.

'I was chatting to Martha Prentice again. She was telling me that your mum was a housekeeper at Granville Grange.'

'Years back, that was, before I was born.' Leslie checks his recipe book. 'Mum liked it there, the way she talked about it.'

'Why did she leave?'

'Got married, had me.'

'This enough bread?'

He glances over. 'Should be fine. Spread honey on it and slice the apples nice and thin.'

'Martha spoke very fondly of your mum. I suppose you make friends when you work together in a place like that.'

'Expect so. There were quite a few people working there then, from what Mum used to say.'

'Did she keep in touch with any of them?'

Leslie weighs flour. 'There's Bet Leyland — Aunty Bet. Not my real aunty, but one of mum's friends. Bet always remembers my birthday, gives me something. She's knocking on now, but she still does for the vicar.'

'Am I cutting these apples thinly enough?'

He comes over. 'Not bad. Make sure you use the bruised ones first.' After a pause, he adds awkwardly, 'How's your foreign friend?'

'Felix? He'll be OK.'

Leslie sighs. 'I dunno, the country's in a right old state. Reckon it's going to take a long time to sort things out. Anyway, I'm glad he's on the mend.'

I suppose that's the nearest I'll get to Leslie saying sorry, so I nod and carry on with slicing apples.

* * *

Joan Dean is exiting the library as I pass by, carrying a couple of books which she stacks in the basket on the front of her bike. She's buoyant today and gives me a cheerful grin. 'Out and about, Daisy?'

'It's such a lovely day, mild like spring.'

'Certainly makes my job easier when it's like this. The patients are cheerier too.'

'Is Mrs Ward better?'

'Oh, Dr Jessop's dealing with her for now,' she replies airily. 'We agreed on a temporary change of treatment plan. She's not the easiest of patients and she could do a lot more to help herself.'

I nod understandingly. 'Did you make it to Miss Laidlaw's funeral? It was a lovely service.'

'I was working, but I saw everyone outside while I was doing my rounds. It was a good crowd.'

I click my fingers. 'Oh yes, I saw you having a chat with Captain Branch. So sad for him, losing two family members in the one year. I suppose he takes some comfort from the fact that you nursed his dad.'

There's the briefest of pauses before she responds. 'He did thank me for the care I gave old Mr Branch. I told him, it's all part of the service. I'm sure he has a lot to do now, sorting out Granville Grange.'

'Mr Lancaster is helping him.'

Joan tightens her coat belt. 'Oh yes, that's right. Well, the day's wasting and I have to see a man about his ingrowing toenail.'

'It must be so different from working with TB patients. You were in Sittingbourne before you came here, weren't you?'

Her expression hardens slightly. 'That's right. Who told you that?'

'Mrs Jessop mentioned it. Quite a change for you.'

'We all have to adapt to changes now the war's over. I must be off. No rest for the wicked!'

I watch her cycle away, briskly ringing her bell to alert a pedestrian. Her library choices interest me and I reflect on them as I walk to the vicarage, where I hope to track down Bet Leyland. I could do with an excuse for my visit, so on the way I stop at Woodlands, pleased to see that some new donations have been left in the porch.

The vicarage is a substantial, handsome house, double-fronted, with bay windows. A slender woman in her early sixties, with fine features and a turban around her hair, opens the door. I realise that I glimpsed her at Miss Laidlaw's funeral. She's holding a floor mop and she smells of lavender and soap. I introduce myself and explain that I've brought some donations from Miss Laidlaw's house.

'The Rev's not here at present,' she tells me, 'but do bring them in, he's always glad to receive any items.'

'Thanks. Shall I carry them through?'

'You can just put them down there, by the coat rack. You from London?'

'That's right.' I'm half expecting some remark about incomers, but she nods.

'My great gran was from Leyton.'

'That's not far from where I was born.' I put the bag down and turn to her with a smile. 'Are you Leslie's Aunty Bet, by any chance?'

'That's right, dear. Are you a friend of his?'

'I work at the Dolphin and sometimes I help him in the kitchen.'

She laughs, her thin face lighting up. 'I always crack up when I hear of Leslie cooking. He and Benny used to live on shepherd's pie. Benny'd make a big one on Monday and they'd eat it for the rest of the week.'

'Leslie has more of a repertoire now. He's down about his uncle at the moment.'

Bet leans on the mop. She has lovely nails, oval and neat. They must take some maintenance, especially after house cleaning. Mine are always nibbled and ragged.

'He's taken it hard about Benny,' she agrees. 'It's a terrible shock, but that uncle of his has always sailed close to the wind. Never more than a hair's breadth from trouble.'

'It must be very difficult for Leslie. He can't have had an easy life, with his mum dying when he was young.'

'Oh, that was dreadful. Poor Nancy. Gone, just like that.'

'Leslie told me that you were friends from Granville Grange.'

'That's right, dear. We worked together and I stayed on for a while after she left. Those were good times, with Nancy at the Grange. We had some laughs. She was always on the go and such a bonny woman. She lost her looks and put on a lot of weight after Leslie.' Bet has spotted a cobweb and reaches up with the mop to clear it. 'This old place is much too big for the vicar on his own. It attracts dust and clutter. I always hoped he'd marry, the house could do with a woman's touch. But he's a dry old stick now, don't suppose anyone would have him.'

Bet is sociable, but I can tell that I'm not going to be offered tea or a sit-down chat. Perhaps the vicar wouldn't approve of his charlady socialising on his time.

'I suppose you knew Hector Branch quite well.'

'He was a nice man. A daft brush, even back then, but always had a smile and a kind word.'

'He was fond of his relative, Miss Laidlaw. Did she visit him when you worked there?'

'I don't recall seeing her. I met her through the parish and all the work she did. Mind, she'd left me a note asking if she could have a chat with me not long before she died. I was over in Abingdon visiting my sister, so I never did get a chance to see what she wanted. I expect it was about donations and such.'

I scent that I'm on a trail here. Surely Lucinda's note must have been connected to checking with staff who'd been at Granville Grange. I want to ask Bet more about this, but she's doubled back to Hector Branch.

'Mr Branch was never on top of things, not like Miss Laidlaw. He could have done with some of her efficiency. I'm not surprised the Grange got in such a state.' She sighs. 'I'm not on top of things myself at the moment.'

'Are you unwell?' She's pinched around the mouth.

'Oh no, it's not my health, dear. I'm struggling with getting my widow's pension. My hubby Stan died in June and there's some mix-up with forms. I can't really make head nor tail of it. Stan used to deal with all the form filling and such. I was about to ask Leslie to lend me a hand, but he's got enough on his plate now, with what's happened to Benny.' She gives another, deeper sigh.

I grab my chance of getting my feet under Bet's table and learning more about Granville Grange. 'I could help you with it, if you like.'

'You, dear? Oh no, I couldn't impose.'

'Really, it would be no trouble. I used to work in a government department, so I understand how they operate.'

She bites her lip. 'Well . . . if you're sure.'

'We Londoners have to help each other.' That gets a laugh, so I say, 'I could pop by later today, if you give me your address.'

'That's ever so kind of you. I'll be home by four.'

I point over her head. 'There's another cobweb up there, near the light shade.'

Armed with Bet's address, I head back to the hotel, happy with the day's work so far. Lucinda was at the centre of something and I'm determined to find out what that was and why it killed her. It would give me huge satisfaction to get there before Inspector Thaxted. I'm longing to find out about his interview with Captain Branch, and whether he has an alibi for the murder. I glance at the police station as I pass by, but I decide to keep a low profile for now.

* * *

There's an ambulance outside the Dolphin. Two men are carrying Mrs Ward down the stairs, no mean feat, and they're bracing themselves. She's complaining at every bump, and as she disappears into the back of the ambulance, I can hear her wailing that she wishes she was with her Harry.

Vera's standing by the door, pulling her cardigan across her chest and puffing her cheeks out with relief. 'Thank goodness they got her down, I was worried they'd get stuck on the stairs or drop her.'

'What's up?'

'It's her leg. Dr Jessop arranged for her to go to the cottage hospital after he examined it this morning. He was worried about the infection she's got, and said he wanted her to have more medical care. Mind you, at least Dora will have a chance to give her room a good clean and an airing. It's been getting like a hospital ward up there.' She raises an eyebrow at me. 'You're like the cat that's got the cream.'

'I might have had a taste.'

'According to Ray, we'll all be bathing in it, come the revolution,' she responds drily.

Ray appears down the stairs behind her, carrying his toolbox. 'What's that, Vera?'

'Oh, just chatting. Have you fixed that window?'

'It'll do for now. I need to buy a new catch. I'll pop into the hardware shop later and see if they've got one.'

I spend a couple of hours on busy work, then set off on my bike to Bet's house. It's an end-of-terrace on the northern edge of town, with cabbage and sprouts planted in the front garden. The door leads straight into a tiny sitting room where a bright fire is burning in the grate. Bet has tea ready on a tray, and letters and forms spread out on a low table. She's wearing a drab brown dress, given a splash of colour with scarlet buttons, and a purple apron tied at the waist.

'That painting's familiar.' I nod at a watercolour of a lush dell with picnicking fairies which hangs over the mantelpiece.

'I won it in a Christmas raffle. Mrs Berrow painted it. I wish I had her talent. Have you met her?'

'Yes, she came to Brize Lodge. I met her there with Mr Berrow.'

'They get on better now that they live in separate houses. Funny old business, but I suppose she'd had enough of his antics.'

I pause, tea in hand. 'What antics would those be?'

'Going off to London and living the high life too often is what I heard. Those theatrical types are never going to be reliable, but I suppose Mrs Berrow fell for his winning ways.'

'He was having affairs?'

'So rumour has it.' She puts a hand to her mouth. 'I shouldn't be gossiping.'

'I won't repeat anything. Shall we go over these forms?'

It doesn't take me long to realise that Bet has a problem with reading, which she tries to conceal. Her face flushes with embarrassment. I tell her that it will be quicker if I go through the bumph myself, and she sits back thankfully and drinks her tea. I sort out the information that bureaucracy demands, add a covering letter and pop it all in an envelope.

'That should get it sorted. If they send you anything else you're not sure about, just tell me and I'll call in.'

'You were so quick doing that, yet it beat me. Thanks so much.'

'It sounds like Hector Branch wasn't much good with form filling, so you're in good company. There's a solicitor there, trying to make sense of everything.'

Bet turns one of her buttons and glances at me. She hesitates, then takes the plunge. 'Mr Branch was like me — he had word blindness, struggled with reading.'

'Oh, I see. That must make life tricky. I suppose Mr Branch got people to help him.'

'That's right. His wife did, but then she died and Clarence went away to boarding school when he was seven.' She tugs down a sleeve. 'Nancy used to deal with things for Mr Branch and read them to him sometimes. She was paid as a cleaner, but she was a secretary too, in many ways. They'd work together for an hour or so most days. She didn't have much schooling, but she was bright, on the ball and a good reader. I envied her for it.'

The fire flares just as there's a spark in my brain. Bet moves across to poke it and add more wood.

'It sounds like Nancy and Mr Branch got on well.'

'They did. He missed her when she left, mooched around the place.' She turns back and her face is red, perhaps more than the fire's heat warrants.

I lower my voice. 'Did you ever worry they got on too well?'

Bet sounds alarmed. 'I've no idea what you mean.'

'I expect you do. Mr Branch had been widowed and they spent a lot of time together. I've heard Nancy was a bonny woman back then, and it sounds as if he enjoyed her company.'

Bet blurts, 'She was engaged.'

'Yes, but sometimes things happen.'

'I'll just freshen this tea,' she says, hurrying to the kitchen.

When she returns, I keep my voice quiet, reassuring. 'I'm going to be frank with you, Bet. Mr Branch told Miss Laidlaw something before he died. It worried her. I'd say that's what she wanted to talk to you about, but she didn't get a chance before she was killed. I wonder if it was to do with Nancy and the time she'd spent in Mr Branch's company.'

Bet puts her hands to her face. She's gone from flushed to ashen. 'Oh goodness, Daisy. This is . . . well . . . this has knocked me for six, I can tell you.'

I pour fresh tea for her and hand her the cup. 'I realise that. Is Leslie Hector's son?'

Bet stares into her tea, gulps some and then nods. 'Nancy told me one day, just before she left Granville Grange. She was terribly upset. Mr Branch wanted her to stay on there, but she wouldn't, said she couldn't face the shame and she'd handed in her notice. She was just about to get married, you see. Her husband never had any idea and then he died young.'

'She and Hector didn't consider getting together once she'd been widowed?'

'Nancy wouldn't have wanted it all to come out. It would be hard to live down in a small place like this. Then again, maybe Hector Branch didn't offer — Nancy was lower class, after all. Oh, goodness, I promised never to tell anyone!'

'Does Leslie have any idea?'

'I'm sure he doesn't. Mr Branch would never have said, and as far as I'm aware, I'm the only person Nancy told. I did wonder if Martha suspected something. She's got eyes in the back of her head, that one. Not much passes her by. But we've never spoken about it.'

My conversation with Martha comes back to me. 'I expect that's why Hector Branch wanted Benny Mathis to take the job at Granville Grange. It meant that could Leslie live there too and he could see him now and then.'

'That's right. They moved to the gatehouse when Leslie was in his early teens.'

I'm wondering about Captain Branch. Had Lucinda said something to him about Leslie? Their argument in the street might have been about more than her leaflets. Perhaps the captain had found a reference to this undeclared son in his father's papers. He might have worried that Lucinda would tell Leslie, and he'd stake his claim on the estate.

'Did Clarence Branch know about Leslie?'

'Oh no, I'm sure he didn't.'

I'm not convinced. And if Joan Dean is aware, through conversations with a confiding Hector, there's yet another layer of complexity.

'I shouldn't have said anything. I've got such a headache now.' Bet shakes her head. 'It's one of the reasons I've always stayed in touch with Leslie. I owed it to Nancy after what she'd been through.'

'I'm glad you did tell me. It's important, because Lucinda was very worried about it.'

'Oh Lord. Poor Leslie. If he finds out, it'll be the most awful shock.'

When I say I have to go, she's so glad to see the back of me, she doesn't ask if I'm going to tell the police. I'm not about to add to her store of worry.

CHAPTER NINETEEN

JB is staying in London overnight so it's me, Tybalt, Oberon and cocoa. I'm in my dressing gown, dealing with fan mail and listening to *The Barretts of Wimpole Street* on the wireless. JB is playing Captain Surtees Cook, so he's here in voice. I've been working on a reply to a dyspeptic-sounding letter writer.

Dear Mr Berrow,

I listened to You Can't Take It With You *on the wireless recently, and I have to say that I was very disappointed to hear you in this nonsensical play. I don't understand why we have to have this kind of baloney about a New York family and their strange ways and oddities. You'd be better sticking to the bard and solid British productions. Surely we have plenty of talented writers of our own.*

Yours sincerely,

George Denison.

I check the dictionary and finish my reply.

Dear Mr Denison,

Thank you so much for taking the time to write to me. I'm so sorry to hear that you don't care for New York life. I can assure you that there are plenty of odd and strange people in my neck of the woods.

Maybe you'd be more comfortable only listening to home-grown talent.

With very best wishes,
Jeffrey Berrow
PS. May I point out that 'baloney' is a term first used in New York, which is a spelling variant of the Italian 'bologna' (sausage).

Satisfied with my sprinkle of spite, I stick the letter on the post stack and finish my cocoa. Tybalt has hopped up for a tickle under the chin when the rumble of a motorbike breaks the silence. The engine cuts right outside and there's a knock at the door. Tybalt jumps down and heads for his favourite window seat. I pull my dressing gown tighter as I answer.

'Hello, Leslie. This is unexpected.'

'Sorry to arrive like this, but I wanted to talk to you and it's difficult at the hotel. My fiancée lives in the next village, so you're on my way home. I hope Mr Berrow won't mind.'

'He's not here at the moment. You'd better come in.'

The distinctive scents of autumn blow in with him — smoke, mould and a sourness that hits the back of the throat. Leslie's navy balaclava and leather jacket are covered in droplets of misty rain. I tell him to hang them over a chair near the fire.

'Would you like cocoa or tea?'

'No, thanks. I can see you're ready for bed. I won't linger.'

I'm relieved at the refusal and the indication that he's not going to hang around. I sit opposite him and attempt an encouraging smile.

He runs a hand over his damp, flattened hair. 'I've come to see you because something's been needling me. I wanted to talk to someone about it and you came to mind.'

I'm worried that he might be about to divulge some personal problem, because he'll probably regret telling me later and I'm no expert when it comes to the male mind or dispensing advice. He might need the likes of Helping Hannah the agony aunt. 'What about telling your fiancée?'

'Elaine?' He shakes his head quickly. 'I can't mention it to her, she'd just say I was causing problems. Her family have been up in arms about what's happened with Benny, treating me as if I'm some kind of criminal myself. I was worried she'd break it off with me, but we're just about OK and I don't want to cause any more upset. So you came to mind because you're quick on the uptake.'

'Thank you.'

'I'm not sure at all what to make of it. I was in Oxford a couple of months back and I saw something.' He takes up the poker and traces lines through spills of ash on the tiled hearth. 'My uncle Benny hasn't always been on the right side of the law. He did black market stuff earlier in the war. Trading game he'd poached and such. He stopped when things got hot.'

'At least he did call a halt.'

'True. I used to be on at him about it. Fool's game, if you ask me. And then he got himself arrested for something much worse. Nice poker this, good and solid.'

'What did you see in Oxford?'

'There was a chap from London, Artie Baldwin. Benny used to do some shady business with him a couple of years ago.'

'Black market business?'

'Yeah. Artie did deals all over the place. I met him once at Benny's house. Talk about a smooth operator! Anyways, I was biking past the train station and I saw Artie chatting to Dr Jessop. I remember asking myself, what on earth can those two have to talk about? I mean, they're not likely to have met socially, are they?'

'No, it's unlikely.'

Tybalt leaps down from the window seat and pushes against Leslie's leg. 'Hello, little puddy tat! Aren't you gorgeous?' Leslie gives me his gap-tooth smile. 'What's his name?'

'Tybalt. He's got a brother called Oberon. That's all you saw, Artie and the doctor chatting?'

'Not quite. I'd slowed the bike and I saw Miss Laidlaw coming out of the station. She used to go down to London sometimes, Red Cross and other do-gooder work. She stopped and said something to Dr Jessop. Artie doffed his hat to her. Then she hurried off.'

I'm intrigued by the snapshot of the GP, the spiv and the elderly lady meeting. 'Would Miss Laidlaw have realised who Artie Baldwin was?'

Leslie is still making a fuss of Tybalt, the long, sweeping strokes from head to tail that he loves. He glances up. 'Possibly, it's hard to say.'

But she did visit Granville Grange, and might well have seen Artie around Benny's house. 'Are you telling me because you want this passed on to the police?'

He gives an embarrassed laugh. 'It's something and nothing, probably, and I don't fancy seeing any more of that inspector. I didn't want to say anything to the doctor and get on the wrong side of him, in case I ever need treatment!'

He's making light of it now, but I can tell that he's been worrying at it. 'I expect you're right and it was just a coincidence,' I reassure him, while contemplating that it might have been a chance meeting that led to complications and violence. 'People do cross paths at stations, don't they? I wouldn't lose any sleep over it.'

Leslie nods, dons his jacket and his balaclava. 'Well, I'll let you get off to bed. See you tomorrow, sleep tight!'

I lock the door after him, check that the cats have water and dispose of a chewed field mouse in the gubbins room. It's almost ten, too late to ring Peter Thaxted. I sit by the fire for a while, searching for shapes in the embers — one of my father's favourite late-night amusements. Once, he swore that he could make out an elephant, although neither my mother or I could detect it. Tonight, I reckon I can see a long boot, an unpleasant reminder of Captain Branch.

I stretch and snuggle into my dressing gown. It occurs to me that both Susan and Leslie have fretted about things they've seen, not wanting to upset people they regard as

186

powerful in their community. Another remark comes back to me, something Vera said, and I wonder if it might have anything to do with the unlikely conversation between the doctor and the spiv. My scalp tingles with excitement as a possibility comes to mind. Then I'm suddenly overcome by self-doubt and castigate myself for flights of fancy. What am I doing, meddling in these people's lives? It's all very well wanting to stave off boredom, but hardly right to do it at others' expense. I've only been here five minutes and I could cause unnecessary problems and make myself deeply unpopular. Iris Jessop is expecting. The last thing she needs is suspicion being cast on her husband.

I'll sleep on it.

* * *

After breakfast the next morning, I ring Fernfield police station and speak to a chirpy constable. Inspector Thaxted is unavailable, so I leave a message.

'Your name pops up a lot around here these days,' the constable sniggers. 'You his girlfriend?'

'Just make sure he gets the message.'

I slam the receiver down and busy myself tidying. I'm pumping up my bike tyres when the phone rings. An operator asks if I'll accept a reverse charge call from a Mr Tattersall. When I agree, there are a number of clicks and I hear her say, 'Go ahead, caller.'

'Hello! Hello! Is that Miss Daisy Moore?'

'Yes, thanks for ringing, Mr Tattersall.'

'That's OK, like. I got your letter.'

'Have you heard about Percy Etherington?'

There's a weariness in his voice that I hear in so many people. 'Aye, I have, and about Robert. You've seen him in hospital, you say?'

'Yes. He's had a number of operations and they'll give him a prosthetic leg. He has problems with speaking.'

'I'd like to write to him, if you can give me the details.'

187

I give him the hospital address and press on, aware that I'm running up JB's phone bill. 'As I said in my letter, Robert was upset about a woman he saw in the hospital. He said she was Percy's girlfriend. Can you tell me anything about her?'

'Percy did have a girl for a while, like. It was when we were stationed in Dover. Not sure it was anything serious. I only saw her the once. Robert did catch up with Percy when he was on leave one time and she was there. I remember Percy grumbling that she talked all the time. It didn't last much longer. He found her overwhelming, I'd say.'

'What was her name?'

'He called her Tish. I never knew her surname, like. I didn't take to her, to be honest. She was pushy and full of herself.'

I wasn't much further forward with just the name Tish. 'Can you describe her?'

'Pretty. Medium height, fair hair, good figure.'

'How did they meet? What was she doing?'

'Oh now, I'd have to rack me brain, like. No clue where Percy met her. She was working at a troops' canteen somewhere around Dover. I can't imagine why she'd be in Oxford. Are you sure Robert's not imagining things, like? Being poorly like that, it can do funny things to you.'

'I'm not sure who he saw, but I wanted to enquire because he was convinced that he'd spotted Percy's girlfriend.'

'It's kind of you to take the trouble. There's plenty who wouldn't. That's all I can say, really. There's been a lot of water under the bridge since then. I've lost a lot of me mates in the battalion.'

'I'm sorry. I do appreciate you calling me.'

'Yeah, well, we just have to get on with it now, don't we? If you see Robert, tell him I was in touch and I'll write to him.'

I assure him that I will, ask him to call me if anything else comes back to him and put the phone down. Tish, in a canteen somewhere around Dover. There were plenty of those watering holes for the troops, some of them mobile.

Finding her now, with just her first name, would be difficult, and Robert Etherington's sighting, with his vision restricted to one eye, might be a figment of his imagination or mistaken identity.

It's turned very cold, so I search for a hat to wear before I set off for town. There are several of JB's on hooks in the hall and I try on a couple before settling for a tweed, blue-check flat cap which keeps my ears snug.

* * *

A mile outside of Fernfield, I hear a car approaching and glance around, alarmed that it might be Captain Branch on the warpath again. It's Peter Thaxted, and he's signalling to me to pull in. I rest my bike against a tree, walk to where he's parked and get into the passenger seat.

He turns off the engine and angles himself to examine me. 'Fetching hat. Is it Jeffrey's?'

'Yes, I don't have one. Most of my stuff burned in a house fire.'

'I heard about that.'

'Did you? From who?'

'Rosalind. Your bike isn't quite aligned. The front wheel is out of true.'

'Yes, it has a mind of its own.'

'Like its rider. I got a message that you wanted to speak to me.'

'I've information for you.'

He straightens, curving one arm around the wheel. 'Go ahead.'

He has that bland, disinterested face, but I'm not fooled by it. I'm determined to get something from him first. 'Did you interview Captain Branch?'

'I did. He states that he was out for a walk on the morning Miss Laidlaw died, so no alibi. However, there's no evidence to place him at the scene. He admitted that he and Miss Laidlaw had disagreed over her views on German food relief and he tore up a leaflet she tried to give him. But an argument isn't a strong motive for cracking her skull.'

'What about if he'd expected to inherit from her?'

'He said that he had no such expectation, and although he appeared unaware of its terms, he wasn't named in her previous will.'

'Who was?'

Thaxted hesitates. 'Various charities.'

'Have you found anything significant in Miss Laidlaw's diary?'

'No. It's extremely virtuous and uneventful.' He takes a paper bag from his pocket and offers it to me. 'Pear drop?'

'Thanks.' I take a green one. 'Branch may have a motive you've not turned up yet.' I explain my sighting of him and Nurse Dean in the cemetery. 'I asked her about it and she said that he was thanking her for her care of his dad, which sounds unlikely and would hardly have involved her wagging an angry finger at him.' I then describe my subsequent meeting in the dark with Captain Branch. 'He was rattled when I told him I'd seen him rowing with Joan Dean.'

Thaxted takes a breath. 'You told him that, on a lonely road, at night, when he was already furious with you? You need to be more sensible.'

'I can take care of myself. I learned that driving buses through the dark in London, so don't talk down to me.' He goes to speak, but I hold up my hand. 'There's something else. Leslie Mathis is Hector Branch's son.' I enjoy the shock that washes over his face, although I'm not sure if it's surprise or annoyance.

He says with an alarming softness, 'How did you get hold of this?'

'I talked to a lady called Bet Leyland, who was a good friend of Nancy Mathis. They worked together at Granville Grange. Nancy helped Hector Branch with paperwork because he had word blindness, as has Bet. I got a picture of them being close and I wondered if that was linked to the lie that Hector had divulged to Lucinda. Bet told me that she's the only person who knew — apart from Hector and Nancy, although Martha might have suspected. Leslie has no idea.'

Thaxted polishes the wheel with his thumb. 'I've been interviewing staff that Lucinda mixed with at the hospital and in her charity work. Staff from Granville Grange were going to be my next port of call.' He crunches the last of his pear drop. 'Nurse Dean. Perhaps she also found out about this paternity, when she took care of Hector.'

'That was my idea too, as she spent time with him and he might have confided in her.'

He continues, as if I haven't spoken. 'It sounds as if she's approached Captain Branch about this. Perhaps she's threatening that she'll go public about it and asking for payment to stay silent.'

'I wouldn't put it past her. She'd certainly have the cheek.'

'There's only one way to find out.'

'Would Leslie have a claim on the estate?'

'I'm not sure. He's illegitimate, so possibly not. Even so, it wouldn't be welcome news to the captain. Right, I need to interview both of them again.' He adds sternly, his eyebrows lowering, 'Stay away from Captain Branch. He could be a dangerous man if he has something to lose. I don't care if you disarmed bombs with your teeth during the war. That's an official police warning. JB is fond of you and I don't want him holding me to account if you come to harm.'

The implication being that it wouldn't bother the inspector too much. I open the door, summoning my most sarcastic tone. '*Thank you so much for the vital information, Miss Moore.*'

Thaxted might be saying thanks, but he's started the engine, so I can't hear. It's just as likely that he's cursing me. I watch him drive away. I'm glad now that I haven't told him everything.

CHAPTER TWENTY

Dr Jessop makes me turn my neck from side to side and then up and down. I've come to see him with invented shoulder pain. He presses the muscles and listens to my chest. 'Been doing any heavy lifting?'

'No. I did some maintenance on my bike the other day.'

'Maybe that was it, or you slept in a bad position. I'd say it's muscular pain. Your lungs are fine.'

I button up my shirt. 'They should be, with all the fresh air I get riding my bike. I shouldn't have bothered you with it really, although it's been bugging me.'

'What I'm here for.' He's writing notes.

I'd passed a decorator painting the hall on my way in. He has a tuneful but piercing whistle and he's currently amusing himself with 'The Trolley Song'. I wait until he pauses. 'Are you glad to be back home, doctor?'

'Absolutely. The Dolphin has its charms, but home is best.'

'I could smell the fresh paint as I came in.'

'Yes, Iris is in charge of that, keeping the decorator on his toes. I just wish he'd whistle more softly.'

'You must be busy, with demobbed men arriving home. Nurse Dean told me that her workload has increased.'

He glances up at me. 'Did she? I suppose that's certainly the case.'

I've come fishing, but I'm not at all sure how to cast my bait. Dr Jessop is a carefully spoken man, in control and unlikely to trip himself up. 'I've told Leslie he should come and see you,' I lie. 'He's been under the weather since his uncle Benny was arrested for the attack on Mr Koller. But at least he's relieved that his uncle had stopped doing business on the black market.'

The doctor's hand pauses momentarily, then he continues writing. 'Goodness! Leslie's uncle certainly took risks.'

'Yes. Apparently he did deals with an Artie Baldwin, a spiv from London.'

His voice has a slight roughness. 'He kept pleasant company.'

The decorator is now entertaining us with 'You Always Hurt the One You Love'.

Jessop throws his pen down. 'Oh goodness, this is unbearable! Just a moment, please.' He strides to the door and snaps at the decorator to stop whistling. 'I can't concentrate in my surgery, man!'

'Sorry, doc, didn't realise I was disturbing you.'

'Well, you are, so desist!' He slams the door and retrieves his pen. 'I'm sorry about that.'

'At least he whistles in tune.' I return to my theme. 'I wasn't surprised about Benny Mathis. Lots of people get drawn into the black market on all kinds of levels. I'm not condoning it, but I suppose sometimes it's desperation, not just greed. I met a bus driver in London who was fined for obtaining eggs on the black market. His little boy was unwell and he wanted to build him up. I was sorry for him. He had to pay a hundred pounds.'

'A sad story indeed, and the punishment was surely excessive.' Dr Jessop finishes his notes and screws the cap back on his pen. He leans back in his chair. 'You have a mature head on your shoulders, Miss Moore. Put some heat to your neck, that should relieve the tension. You can take aspirin if you want, but you're young, you should heal quickly.'

I can see that I'm not going to draw him out further. 'I hope Mrs Ward will, too. Is she going to be in the hospital much longer?'

He tidies his notes. 'Hopefully not.'

'That's good news. Nurse Dean can keep an eye on her again when she returns to us.'

Dr Jessop has had enough of me now and becomes brisk. 'Mrs Ward's medical care will be arranged as I see fit. Good morning, Miss Moore.'

I'm satisfied with my visit, even if it has cost me a shilling. The doctor played his cards well, but his little freeze when I mentioned the black market told me what I needed. But what has he been trading and why, and did it lead to Lucinda Laidlaw's death?

Oddly enough, there is tension in my right shoulder now. My mother would have said it was my punishment for telling lies, which according to her, made Our Lady blush. Given all the lies that are told constantly around the world, Our Lady must have a permanently flushed complexion.

* * *

I spend an hour with Felix, who is much brighter and sitting up in bed, reading and making notes. We share the scones I brought from the bakery, scattering crumbs on the sheets.

'We'll have to clear those up, or the nurse will be cross,' Felix says. 'I made a list of more books I'd like from my room, if you could bring them.'

'I'll fetch them next time.'

'What would I do without you? I'm so grateful.'

'You're doing me a favour, giving me the chance to escape the hotel.'

He pushes his glasses up his nose. 'Any news about the murder?'

'I'd say it's all in hand. Don't worry about that, but can I pick your brain now you're better?'

'You can try.'

'Did Lucinda ever mention any concerns about Dr Jessop?'

'The doctor? No. I don't remember her talking about him.'

'Someone saw her at Oxford station one day and he was there.'

Felix plumps up his pillow. 'She did go to London by train a couple of months ago. She was quite agitated about it, said it was ages since she'd been there. When she got back she was very introspective and tired. She sat in the garden on her own.'

'When was that?'

'I'm not sure. August, I'd say.'

'Did she tell you the reason for her journey?'

'No. I assumed it was to do with her refugee work.' He rubs his eyes. 'Lucinda's solicitor came to see me. I inherit the house and almost twenty thousand pounds. Also, five thousand from Hector Branch. I keep thinking I've dreamed it.'

'You're a wealthy man now. I'm *so* glad we're friends.'

He laughs and then says anxiously, 'But, I wondered . . . should I give the five thousand to Captain Branch? He is the son, after all, and I don't want to annoy him or cause offence.'

'That's up to you, but I wouldn't, in your shoes. Captain Branch is a nasty piece of work. Never show weakness.' *And there's another son to factor in now.*

'You're good for me, Daisy, you always say the right thing and you give me a boost.' His eyes shine. 'When I'm a qualified architect, I might buy some land, build my own house. I've started preliminary sketches. Would you like to see them?'

We flick through his sketch book and chat for a while longer, then I dispose of the scone crumbs and leave him to visit Robert Etherington. I check with a nurse that he's been informed of his brother's death.

'He took bad after hearing the news,' she says. 'Stayed in bed for a couple of days and wouldn't talk at all, but he was up this morning.'

Robert's sitting by his bed, dressed but dozing. I pull up a chair and tap his arm. He focuses and manages his scowl/smile.

'Hello, me again. I'm so sorry about your brother, Mr Etherington.'

He winces, shrugs.

'I wanted to tell you that I heard from Frank Tattersall. He phoned me.'

'What say?'

'He confirmed that your brother had a girlfriend called Tish in Dover, but he couldn't tell me her surname. He said that you met Tish once when you were with Percy.'

'Right! Tish.' He slaps a hand down on his healthy leg and nods eagerly.

'It would be hard to find someone just by the name Tish. I asked at reception if they knew of a staff member here called that, but I drew a blank.'

Etherington is sitting upright, alert and saying something that sounds like '*ninam*'.

'Sorry, I don't understand. Have you got your notepad?'

He slips it from under his pillow and takes the pencil from behind his ear. He slowly writes one word and shows it to me. LAETITIA.

'So, Tish was a shortening of Laetitia?'

'Yeah.' He says more slowly, 'N-i-c-k-n-a-m-e.' Then he writes again on the pad. JOKE.

'Percy called her Tish as a sort of fond name. But what about her surname?'

He shakes his head. 'Ask.' He points to LAETITIA. 'Here. Not right.' He's fired up now.

I'm aware that just this little prompt to his memory, the fact that he's been taken seriously, has meant so much. How awful it must be, sitting here day to day, passive, trying to be understood. He has so little in his life, smoking awful cigarettes, staring at the walls or magazines, the only injection of excitement when he's taken for physio or limb fittings. This is important to him.

'Laetitia is an unusual name,' I tell him. 'I'll try asking the hospital staff again. Have you seen her around here since?'

'Nah.'

'When you say, "not right", do you mean there was something odd about her?'

He grimaces, squeezes his hands. Says again, frustrated, 'Not right.'

'Ok, I'll do my best.'

'Ta. Get . . . leg soon.'

'Good.'

'Want home.'

'I can imagine. I'm sure your dad would love to see you. Frank said to tell you he's going to write to you.'

At reception, I wait in a long queue and try again, asking if there is a member of staff called Laetitia.

The woman behind the desk gives me a long-suffering look. 'Tish and now Laetitia! This is like twenty questions. I am busy, dear.'

'I realise that, but this is on behalf of a severely wounded soldier. It would bring him great peace of mind. It's an uncommon name, you'd spot it easily.'

She huffs, but calls to a colleague to deal with the person behind me, goes to a drawer and starts rifling through a card index. She has to break off several times to answer the phone, but finally shakes her head.

'Sorry, dear. No Laetitias in there. A Lucy and a couple of Lindas, that's it.'

It was too much to hope for, although I had been more optimistic armed with a proper name. Where do I go from here? I'm sure that Robert Etherington did see Tish. I want to confirm it for him and solve the riddle of what he means by 'not right'.

* * *

Back at the Dolphin, my head is full of the various people who touched Lucinda Laidlaw's life. It's as if they're all jostling for space and my attention. Is it like this for Peter Thaxted, or is he far more composed, with his suspects clearly in his sights? I imagine that he has a cool brain, whereas mine is fevered. I now have another question in my mind about Lucinda's visit to London and why she was so preoccupied on her return. From Felix's comment, it was an unusual journey for her, and she'd conducted most of her charitable work by letter. I suspect that it's important. What had caused her agitation prior to the trip?

I deal with an order for cleaning materials, then ring Inspector Thaxted. To my surprise, I'm put through to him.

'Good afternoon, Miss Moore, how can I help you?'

'Any luck with your interviews?'

'My enquiries are ongoing. Some of these matters are delicate. Mrs Leyland confirmed her story about Leslie's parentage. I didn't reveal you as my source.'

'I expect she was very upset.'

'She was, but rest assured I put my kid gloves on with her. I can safely say that she believed she'd done the right thing by the time we finished talking.'

'I'm happy to hear that. Inspector, I wondered if I could see Miss Laidlaw's diary?'

'Why?'

'I might be able to bring a fresh eye to it, spot something.' I want to search for any references to a London trip in August.

There's a sound like papers shuffling. 'I'll put it through the letterbox at her house. I suppose you might find it there and read it. Please return it to me when you've finished.'

I put the phone down. There's something else that's been niggling at me and I want to deal with. I check Susan's whereabouts. She's hanging around Leslie in the kitchen, cutting pastry shapes for the top of a pie and giggling at his jokes. I take the master set of room keys, nip upstairs to hers and unlock the door. It's such a small room, it doesn't take me long to search and find what I'm after. I go through it, replacing items carefully. I leave my discovery open on her bed and go back to the kitchen, asking her if she can lend me a hand with something.

She follows me upstairs. When she sees that I'm heading to her door and opening it, she squeals, 'Hey! I locked that!'

I turn to her. 'Yes, and I unlocked it.'

'You've no right!'

'No, I haven't, but I don't expect you're going to make a fuss or report me.'

She follows me into the room and I close the door. I've left the suitcase I found under the bed open on top of it. It's full of goods: bars of chocolate, bags of sweets, items of clothing, cosmetics, soaps, shampoos and magazines.

'This is all stolen, isn't it, Susan?'

She flops onto the bed and nods. I sit at the other end from her. 'Did you steal it all around here?'

'Mainly. And in Oxford. You gonna grass on me?'

'It depends on if I believe you're telling me the truth. Did Miss Laidlaw know about this stuff?'

Susan clutches her chest. 'No! How would she? I always lock my door. I nicked it over a long time and kept it in here. She only found out about that tat in the charity bin.' She scoops her dull hair behind her ears. 'I've never had nothing to call my own. It's just some things. No one missed them. I never took nothing from the hotel, honest.'

She's always grubby, her hair in need of a wash, despite the fact that she has some fragrant stuff in the suitcase. I picture her taking her consolation prizes out and treasuring them each night before securing them under her bed. They're all she has in the world. She's a sad girl and I feel like a bully. I can't see her attacking anyone for the sake of her pilfered bits and pieces.

'OK.' I stand and go to the door.

'Is that it?' She's staring at me. 'Aren't you going to tell on me?'

I shake my head. 'It's up to you what you do now. You can guess what Miss Laidlaw would have said to you about your suitcase.' I open the door, pause. 'I'd quit while you're ahead,

Susan. If you carry on, you'll get caught. You have a decent job and accommodation here. I'd hate to see you lose it.'

* * *

Early evening, I cycle to Lucinda's house through a sleety rain. There's a thick envelope in the hall containing her diary, a slim book with a dark red cover, inscribed with 1945 in gold lettering. I take the electric heater to the sitting room and plug it in.

Inspector Thaxted was right — the diary does make for dry reading, with brief entries about petitions, letters and church activities, observations about the vegetable garden, jam and chutney making and knitting patterns. There is a lovely comment at the end of July. A lump forms in my throat as I read it.

It is marvellous to have Felix here. He is such a brave, kindly young man, with a fine brain, and he expresses sadness but no rancour about the way the world has treated him and his family. He is rescuing me from my old-lady ways, shaking me out of my solitary habits. Thea and Otto would be so proud of him.

I flick forwards, and on the fourteenth of August, I find a succinct entry.

To Streatham, to see Maude C. Terribly tired now, but I'm glad I made the journey. Dear old London is so exhausted and drab, as are we all!

I copy that down, and continue through the diary, but find nothing else of interest. On the day before she died, Lucinda wrote:

Felix and I cut down the green beans and cleaned out the shed. We listened to the wireless in the evening. Still dreadful news about Hiroshima and Nagasaki. Felix went to burn the midnight oil and study. I darned some of his socks.

I replace the diary in the envelope and go to the hall, where I've noticed an address book on the walnut stand.

I leaf through but can find no reference to a Maude C in Streatham. If she visited this woman, Lucinda must have noted an address somewhere. I check the pockets of the coats hanging in the hall, but they're empty, apart from a sixpence and a toffee wrapper.

I head upstairs and find Lucinda's bedroom. When I switch the light on, I see a single bed with a crocheted quilt, a dressing table with a mirror and a large, dark oak wardrobe with a curved top and handles shaped like acorns. Above the bed is an intricate framed embroidery in red, green and silver: *To everything there is a season and a time.*

I open the wardrobe, which smells of herbs and rosewater, and rake through the summer clothes, which are grouped to the left. Lucinda had a modest collection of plain cotton dresses in various pastels, skirts, blouses and cardigans. There's a barley sugar in a skirt pocket and a clean hanky monogrammed with a fancy *L* in a cardigan. At last, I find a folded sheet of paper tucked in a beige linen jacket with an address. *36 Catesby Road, Streatham.* I should tell Inspector Thaxted. But if he and his men searched the house and missed this, that's their bad luck. Anyway, he's busy interviewing suspects, so I'll be doing him a favour by checking on it.

I slip the note into my pocket, pleased with my evening's work. I have no idea if this address has any link to Lucinda's death, but I aim to find out.

On the way home, I put the envelope with the diary enclosed back through the letterbox of Fernfield police station, addressed to the inspector.

* * *

That evening, JB is in fine form. He's been asked to audition for the part of Sir Robert Chiltern in a stage production of *An Ideal Husband.*

'I'm slightly old for the part, but my agent says I appear younger than I am.'

'Really?'

He assumes a sulky pose. 'You don't agree?'

'I suppose in certain lights . . .'

'Treacherous factotum. Will you run through some lines with me?'

We sit by the fire and spend a while on a scene. My mind's only half on it, the other half pondering Streatham.

'*What an appalling philosophy that sounds!*' JB begins, his Sir Chiltern a touch too arch. '*To attempt to classify you, Mrs Cheveley, would be an impertinence. But may I ask, at heart, are you an optimist or a pessimist? Those seem to be the only two fashionable religions left to us nowadays.*'

'*Oh, I'm neither,*' says my Mrs Cheveley. '*Optimism begins in a broad grin, and Pessimism ends with blue spectacles. Besides, they are both of them merely poses.*'

'You're in an optimistic mood tonight, me old china.' JB breaks off to light a cigar.

'I suppose I am. Is it OK with you if I take a day off tomorrow?'

'Certainly.'

'I want to pop to London. I've squared it with Vera. She reacted as if I'd said I was going to Outer Mongolia. She commented that she's never been there, she has no wish to, and it's a nasty, dirty place. She warned me to watch myself. When I pointed out that I'm a Londoner, born and bred, she muttered about chaos and danger.'

'What are you going for?' JB asks.

I've decided not to tell him, in case he has conflicting loyalties and reveals anything to Thaxted. I want to claim that supper at Rules. 'Oh, just for a wander and to catch up with a friend or two.'

'That sounds relaxing. I'm staying around here tomorrow. I said I'd give the *kommandantin* a hand with framing a couple of her paintings, but do you want a lift to the station?'

I need to keep this excursion under my own control. 'No, thanks. I'll cycle there and back.'

We return to our rehearsal, but I catch him glancing at me now and again. I maintain an air of innocence.

CHAPTER TWENTY-ONE

Despite the ruins, craters, rubble and scattered debris, my heart sings at being back in the bustle of London. It's a cold, bright, lovely day, the sun glowing on the capital. I sit on the top deck of the bus to Streatham with the window open, so that I can absorb the dusty air and the energy of the streets. I'm beaming, suffused with a sense of ownership and belonging. The pavements are busy, with long queues outside shops, many of which are decorated with Union Jacks and red, white and blue bunting. Londoners are wallowing in victory, and who can blame them after years of devastation? Some bomb sites are being cleared, and there are clusters of prefab housing. I smile when the bus is held up by a rag-and-bone man whose horse has decided to stop in the centre of the road. A small crowd has gathered for the entertainment, some youths yelling encouragement to the animal. I can hear cries of, 'Gee up, Dobbin!'

I called into a bookshop at Paddington station and located Catesby Road in a street map. I alight from the bus at Streatham Hill and walk past side streets of traditional terraced houses with bay windows and short front paths. The fourth on the left is Catesby Road and the front window of number 36 has a poster of Churchill making the victory sign.

The gate has been removed for munitions or firewood and the strip of front garden is planted with leeks and parsnips. Next door, a woman is outside cleaning the windows and she nods to me. There are two frosted panes of glass on either side of the front door, and when I knock, I see a shape appear in the hall.

'Have you come from the council about the wasp nest? They said they were sending a Mr Rayburn.' A small, nimble woman in her late thirties with prominent front teeth.

'No, nothing to do with wasps. I'm sorry to disturb you. My name's Daisy and I'm a friend of Lucinda Laidlaw. Are you Maude?'

'That's right.'

'Did Lucinda come to see you?'

'Miss Laidlaw came here, yes. In the summer.'

'I'm afraid I have to tell you that Lucinda has died.'

Maude's mouth droops. 'Oh, heavens! What on earth happened?'

The woman next door has paused in her cleaning and edged to the nearest side of her window. *Careless talk costs lives* flashes through my mind, except in this case, the life has already been lost.

'Could I come in and speak to you?'

'Well . . . I suppose you'd better.'

She takes me to a beige and brown sitting room. As I step in, I freeze. It reminds me uncomfortably of our home in Walthamstow. It's not just the similar moquette three-piece suite, the pervasive pall of cigarettes and the acrid scent from the coal in the brass scuttle — there are familiar statues of Our Lady and Jesus on the mantelpiece and an oil painting of the Holy Family over the fireplace. I note the Miraculous Medal that nestles in the hollow of Maude's neck. My mother was buried wearing hers. A shiver runs through me.

'Can I get you a cuppa?' Maude asks.

'No, thanks.' I am thirsty, but I don't want to linger. My mother might appear through the door, accusing me of leaving lights on — '*Anyone would say we lived in Buckingham Palace*'.

I note an opened envelope propped on the mantelpiece, the address facing me. It tells me a vital detail about the woman I've come to see and reassures me that my journey has been worthwhile. We sit on the soft armchairs, where I recognise the nubbly texture of the material.

'I'm sorry about your friend,' Maude says. 'She was so nice, with lovely manners. And a real lady, if you take my meaning. Was it sudden, was she poorly?' The veins stand out on her thin neck as she strains forward.

'I'm sorry to say that she was murdered.'

Maude crosses herself. 'Merciful heavens! Where did it . . . was she murdered at home?'

Now that I've read the *Mrs M Crampton* on the envelope, I'm wary about picking my way through difficult ground here, so I equivocate: 'Nearby.'

'Have they caught whoever did it?'

'Not yet.'

Maude presses her hands together. 'Who would do such a thing? Was it a robbery?'

'Not a robbery, no.' I take a moment, look into Maude's mist-grey eyes. 'I hope you don't find this an intrusion, but I wonder if you could tell me why Lucinda came to see you.' I can see that she's unsure, so I add quickly, 'I'm just trying to make sense of the last months of her life and she noted her visit to you in her diary.'

Maude takes a moment. 'It was an awful shock when she turned up out of the blue, just like you've done today. I nearly sent her packing.'

I'm concerned that Maude might still do that to me. 'I can imagine. I expect Lucinda came with good intentions.'

'I did realise that. But when she'd gone, I wasn't sure that she'd done me any good, to be frank with you.' She twists her mouth up, asks suspiciously, 'Are you from round here?'

'I grew up in Walthamstow.'

'Oh, right. How'd you know Lucinda, then?'

'I moved Oxford way because of the war.'

'I see.'

There's a long silence. A carriage clock in a glass case over the fireplace whirrs, striking the hour, and a ballerina twirls out to the tinkle of the 'Dance of the Sugar Plum Fairy'. She spins before disappearing. The clock makes a noise like a creaking bedspring and ticks on.

'I really don't want to be nosy,' I offer meekly, 'but it means a lot to me to understand Lucinda's final months.'

Maude waves a hand. 'I might as well tell you. I'm not ashamed or upset these days, it doesn't hurt as much to speak of it. Time does heal. The neighbours have stopped gossiping and I don't really feel anything now. Relief, maybe.'

'If you can find the way to . . .'

She places her feet together, straightens her frame. 'My hubby did a runner. Nine years ago now. I came home from doing the shopping and he'd gone. Left a note saying he couldn't stand it anymore and not to search for him. I'd bought his favourite lamb cutlets as well.'

'I'm so sorry.'

'So was I, to start with. I was a nervous wreck for months. The doctor had me on tablets. Not now, though. I wouldn't let him in the door if he came back with his tail between his legs.'

'It must have been awful for you.'

'Yes. I mean, we hadn't been getting on too well. Ray started getting funny ideas about Russia and communism and reading strange books. He was forever going on about the Spanish Civil War and collecting for the Republicans. I told him to get his nasty books out of the house. Those communists are atheists. They go around destroying churches, just like the Russkies. We had some awful arguments, but you don't just run off, do you?'

I let that hang in the air. 'Are you a Catholic? My mum was.'

She touches her medal. 'That's right. Ray wasn't. I told him when we married that it was for keeps in my church and marriage vows are sacred, not to be broken.'

No divorce for Ray Crampton then, which makes him a bigamist. 'Is that what Lucinda came to talk to you about?'

Maude rubs little circles on the arm of her chair. 'She told me that she'd been at a meeting of some kind in Oxford about the war, and there were speakers and other people from London there. One of them saw Ray in the audience and recognised him, told Lucinda that he'd vanished from here a while back, left me on my tod. She found out where I lived and came to see me.'

'Had she told Ray?'

'Oh no! She said she wouldn't have done that until she'd spoken to me. I told her I didn't want him back now. If he turned up, it'd only cause a lot of upheaval again and I wouldn't trust him. I'd always be worrying that I'd come home and find him gone. Then I'd have to go through it all over again.'

'That's courageous. There are plenty of women who'd take their husband back — especially given your religion.'

Maude breathes deeply. 'My parish priest urged me to, when I told him about Miss Laidlaw's visit. He said to hate the sin, not the sinner. I hope I'm a good Catholic, but it's alright for him to say that. He wouldn't have to live with the worry. Nine years with not a word! Ray took a suitcase and his rotten books and vanished. If there'd been children, that would have been a different kettle of fish. I'm used to being on my own now. It's my house, my mum left it to me. I've a nice little job supervising at the infants' school and I do lots in the parish with the Women's League. It's not as if Ray went away for a short while to sort himself out and came back because he wanted to, is it?'

'That's true.'

Maude touches her medal again. 'I'll be married 'til the day I die, or Ray does. I see myself as a grass widow. I pray for him, that he'll stay away from the evil clutches of communism. That's the test God has sent me, so I accept it.'

I have to admire Maude, living this in-between existence, although she appears to have accepted her abandonment in many ways. She still has the status of marriage to cling to. I shan't divulge that her prayers for Ray have gone unanswered to date. 'Did Lucinda tell you anything about Ray's current circumstances?'

'No, just that he lived around the Oxford area.'

Lucinda had kept her counsel about Vera then, as I'd have expected. She wouldn't have wanted to heap extra distress on this grass widow. 'How did you leave things with Lucinda?'

'I told her not to speak to Ray, said I didn't want to hear from him or send him any message. She left me her address in case I decided I did want to contact him. But I haven't — out of sight, out of mind and good riddance, I've decided, whatever the priest says.'

She speaks bravely, but there's a tiny quaver of doubt there. Her situation is so odd — married yet not married. Not unlike Vera — or the Berrows, for that matter. I visualise her searching for Ray on that day she came home, the lamb cutlets beside the note on the table. Did she cook and eat them or throw them away? I'd have binned them. She offers tea again, but I refuse, wanting to escape her sitting room with its uncanny mementoes of my old life.

'I hope I don't sound hard when I talk about Ray,' she says at the door.

'Not at all. What he did to you was very cruel.'

I take my leave of Maude Crampton and walk back to Streatham Hill, turning over what I've learned. Lucinda had been an honest, upright woman, if a meddler. She would have accepted Maude's decision, but that didn't mean that she wouldn't have spoken to Ray Crampton about her discovery. After all, his marriage to Maude rendered his bigamous one to Vera invalid, and they were hoping to start a family. If Lucinda did face Ray with what she'd found out, it would have given him a strong motive to silence her.

At Paddington, I loiter by the departures board, confused by a forlorn yearning. What if I don't return? I don't spend much in Fernfield, I've saved some money. I could book into a cheap B & B, seek a job, any job. I'd be here, in the flow of life, at the centre of things. I visualise that other existence I could pursue. But there's unfinished business calling me back.

Duty calls. I board the train.

* * *

Peter Thaxted is waiting for me at Oxford station. I'd phoned him from Paddington, explaining that I had important information.

'We'll have tea in the café,' he says. 'I've had nothing since breakfast and I'm famished.'

Once we're settled with tea, iced buns and anaemic slices of fruit cake, he asks, 'How was London?'

'Wonderful. My hair smells of soot and brick dust, just as it should.' I chew a mouthful of the cake, which isn't too bad. 'Ray Crampton has a motive for Lucinda's murder. He's a bigamist and his wife lives in London.'

Thaxted pauses with an iced bun halfway to his lips, a gratifying flash of surprise on his face. The poor, jaundice-yellow lighting in the café makes his skin resemble parchment.

'Explain, Miss Moore.'

'Ray is married to a woman called Maude, who lives in Streatham. He did a runner a while ago.' I tell him how I decided to follow up on Lucinda's visit to London in August. 'I saw a diary entry and found the name Maude C. She confirmed that Lucinda went to see her and she spoke quite freely to me. She doesn't want Ray back, I gathered that she's content with her situation now. I'm pretty sure that Lucinda would have tackled Ray about it and remonstrated with him. Maybe he decided he wanted to shut her up before anyone else got to hear about his wealth of marriages. And he's often in and out of the Dolphin, fixing things. He'd have realised that Marlin was empty. He could easily have arranged to meet Lucinda in there that morning.'

Thaxted drinks his tea black. He's demolished his iced bun and starts on the cake. 'How did you find Maude Crampton's address?'

'Fairly easily. It was in a jacket pocket in Lucinda's wardrobe.'

He frowns, rubs his brow. 'I'm working with dolts. Or perhaps I'm one myself. I noted the diary entry about Streatham but it didn't seem important.'

'I did have a useful tip from talking to Felix.'

'Kind of you to paper over my deficit.'

I round up a stray raisin. 'It's just struck me that Ray insisted on cleaning up room one. That must have taken some nerve, if he's the murderer.'

'Trying to wash away his sin perhaps, or a need to revisit the scene. Killers often react in strange ways.'

I get queasy, recalling Ray and his bucket with the blood-tinted water. I attempt to erase the picture. 'What's been happening with Captain Branch and Joan Dean?'

'Branch denies that he and the nurse were arguing, as does she. They claim that she was joking with him about his father's tales of his childhood and she was wagging her finger, saying that he'd been a naughty boy.'

'Liars. I saw them, they were both furious.'

'Undoubtedly. Branch put on a good show of being terribly shocked when I revealed that he had a half-brother. It was hard to judge if he already knew. Miss Dean states that she and Hector Branch talked about lots of things, but he was often muddled and he never told her any family secrets.' He stretches his leg out. 'If neither of them budges, it's hard to prove otherwise. There's no evidence to put pressure on them. In the meantime, Branch is talking to his solicitor about Leslie Mathis. I presume that Leslie might learn about his birth status sometime soon.'

'Cat among pigeons.'

Thaxted nods and pours more tea for us both. 'Leslie Mathis has certainly had some surprises recently.'

'Speaking of shocks, Vera's going to be in a dreadful state when she finds out about Ray.' On the train journey back, I wondered if a guilty conscience has been impeding his sex life. He doesn't strike me as an unkind man. He must remember Maude sometimes, ask himself what's happened to her, how she's coped with abandonment. But I can hardly share Ray's sexual inadequacies with Peter Thaxted.

'Bigamy's a crime, whether or not Ray Crampton killed because his secret had been discovered,' the inspector says. 'I dislike dealing with it because it exposes lives in a particularly horrible way. I'll have to investigate that as a separate issue and charge him.'

'Will he be imprisoned?'

'Possibly, depends on the judge. He might get a fine.'

'Maybe his communist beliefs allow bigamy. I expect he regards marriage as a bourgeois institution.'

Thaxted smiles. 'The Bolsheviks certainly denounced monogamy and they introduced rapid divorce. I expect that Crampton's deceit is based on expediency rather than ideology. It was unwise to marry a Catholic if he wanted an escape.'

'Why do Rosalind and JB remain married? Religion isn't a hurdle for them.'

Thaxted rubs his neck, extends it to the left, then right. 'Marriage is a complex and mysterious entity. Perhaps they have the union they both want and need, given their dispositions. They play their parts in a useful status quo. After all, we're all actors in our own lives.'

I recall the inspector's previous observation that the set-up between the manor and the lodge resembled a farce. I file his comment away for later. 'I'd better get home. I said I'd help JB rehearse tonight.'

'Which play?'

'It's a stage production of *An Ideal Husband*. JB has an audition.'

'Not a role for Ray Crampton, then. How are you getting back?'

'On my bike.'

'It's almost dark. We'll put your bike in the boot and I'll drive you, then head to the bigamous baker and see what he has to say for himself.'

It's a beautiful night with a full, frost moon in a cloudless sky. Thaxted drives slowly and carefully, moving his leg with great deliberation.

'Have you heard of any problems at the cottage hospital?' I ask.

He rolls his shoulders. 'What makes you raise that?'

'Vera told me that she saw Dr Jessop with an official there. The doctor was uneasy.'

'There is an ongoing matter in hand. That's all I can say.' He turns the heater up. 'Did London tempt you back?'

The words leave my mouth before I can check myself. 'I expect you wish it would.'

He turns his head to me sharply. 'Why do you say that?'

'You give the strong impression that you find me irritating.'

He takes his time. 'I did at first. You're an acquired taste.'

'Like wine?'

'Broccoli, maybe, or pickled herring.'

I turn away to hide a grin and relapse into silence.

* * *

JB is playing the piano. I can hear 'Embraceable You' as I park my bike. In the sitting room, both cats are lazing on top of the piano, like bookends.

'Hello, me old china. Did I hear a car?' JB is glad to see me, all smiles, guiding me to a chair.

'Peter Thaxted gave me a lift from Oxford with the bike.'

'Very chivalrous of him. And how was it in the smoke? I was worried that you might not return once you were back in the magnetic draw of the darling old city. Vera will be glad that you didn't get consumed by the fleshpots of Soho.'

Just as well he didn't glimpse my hesitation at Paddington. 'It was a fruitful, interesting visit. Tybalt and Oberon are content.'

'They've been listening to their favourite melodies. I'd swear that Oberon was tapping his paw in time.'

I hold my hands out to the fire. 'How was your picture framing?'

'Most pleasant, despite the fact that I had to gaze on roguish fairies grouped in a country churchyard. The *kommandantin* can be fine company for a couple of hours and her cook provided an excellent lunch.' He joins me by the hearth. 'I can see that you're simmering with news. There's an energy field around you. Do tell.'

I give him a full account of my day and my conversation with Thaxted. 'Sorry I fibbed about my reason for going, but I needed to see the lie of the land for myself.'

'You're forgiven. Declan would give you a light penance.'

'Ray won't get off that easily. The Cramptons will be in quite a state this evening.'

JB makes a soundless whistle. 'Bigamy! I wouldn't have credited Ray with having it in him. He's always struck me as a fairly spineless armchair commie.'

'Hidden depths. It must be hard, if vanishing and leading a double life is the only way to escape an unhappy marriage.'

'Indeed. Poor old Vera. She's a conservative soul. This will be an awful shock.'

'Even more so if Ray killed Lucinda to shut her up. The Fernies will have a field day with the gossip. At least it will take the spotlight off Felix.'

'Oh yes, a spot of bigamy will go down a treat.'

I move my chair back a little from the fire's glow. 'Assuming that you wouldn't commit bigamy, what would happen if you wanted to remarry?'

JB reaches to an ashtray for a half-smoked cigar and relights it. 'That's highly unlikely.'

'Some gorgeous actress might sweep you off your feet.'

JB chuckles. 'Believe me, Daisy, that isn't on the cards. No, I'm content with things as they are.'

'And Rosalind?'

'She wouldn't want to "train up another husband" as she so delicately puts it.' He circles a finger at me. 'I doubt Vera will be fit for work tomorrow. I'll phone her in the morning. Can you take charge at the hotel while she's in a tizzy?'

'It's the least I can do, given that I've exposed the problem. And JB, I have more astonishing news. Leslie might also be distracted and upset, even if it equates to him going up in the world.' I divulge the truth about Hector Branch and Nancy Mathis. 'Captain Branch is aware now.'

'Naughty deeds at the big house!' He claps a hand to his forehead. 'Oh Lord! We'll be faced with no manager and no cook. Daisy, are you setting out to wreck my hotel?'

'Don't worry, I'll get in early and sort it all out.' I'm not as confident as I sound, but I'm sure I can make it up as I go along. Susan owes me a favour and can pull her finger out.

JB pours whisky and hands me a glass. 'Leslie is Hector's son! Now, that's going to create quite a stir among the denizens of Fernfield. The *kommandantin* will be all agog when I tell her. And as for the captain, he'll be spitting coals.'

JB carries on musing in this vein. I relax and focus on the hypnotic dance of the flames. I'm sure I can see a map of Italy in a smouldering log.

CHAPTER TWENTY-TWO

Next day at the Dolphin is chaotic and at times I do worry that I've been a human wrecking ball, causing mayhem around me. I picture those huge demolition cranes crashing their way through bomb sites in London.

Dora informs us that Vera has gone to stay with her mother 'for the foreseeable'. The bakery is closed, a notice on the door stating 'unexpected circumstances'. Leslie is mystified, but he's heard from someone, who heard it from a neighbour, that Ray went off in a police car last night. 'It's a rum do,' he says, and I can only nod in agreement. Dora is tight-lipped and will only comment that Ray and Vera's business is their own.

After breakfast, Leslie receives a phone call asking him to attend an appointment with Captain Branch and Simeon Lancaster at Granville Grange later that morning. He's bewildered all over again, wondering aloud why on earth they want to see him. Anticipating that he too might vanish 'for the foreseeable', I consult Dora. She jumps at the chance of being temporary cook, and Susan agrees to take over the cleaning while I cover reception.

I take Mrs Ward a tray of tea mid-morning. She arrived back from hospital the previous day and is less pasty. Her room smells fresher and she's laughing at a comedy on the wireless.

'It's good to see that you're better, Mrs Ward.'

'Thanks, dear. They pumped me full of all kinds of drugs in hospital that did the trick. I have to say, they were marvellous. Couldn't have been kinder. I saw that policemen there, the one who was asking all the questions after Lucinda died.'

'Inspector Thaxted?'

'That's him. He was talking to Dr Jessop and some other chap. He's so ailing, I reckon he should be a patient, tucked up in one of the beds!' She laughs at her joke, almost spilling her tea.

'I'll be on my way, lots to do.'

She waves. 'Can you take that folder away with you? It's Nurse Dean's notes. She left it behind earlier. I don't want it cluttering the place up.'

I take the cardboard folder, tuck it away in the drawer at reception, deal with enquiries and a new guest who's staying for three nights. I'm on tenterhooks, wondering when we'll hear from Leslie and what kind of state he'll be in. I'm also anxious to find out about Ray Crampton. During the afternoon, there's a lull and I tidy the reception desk. When I open the drawer, I see Nurse Dean's folder and the label along the top.

PATIENT
Mrs A Ward
c/o The Dolphin Hotel
82 High Street
Fernfield

I open the cover and read the label inside with astonishment.

District Nurse in attendance
Laetitia J Dean.

I sink down onto Vera's stool, tracing a finger over the name, trying to absorb this. Joan is Tish. I work through how Robert Etherington might have seen her — she went to the Radcliffe, probably attending some course or introductory meeting about her new role as a district nurse in the locality. She was striding along a corridor and Etherington recognised her as he was going for a fitting for his leg, or to have some other treatment. But why is he so worked up about her, why is she 'not right'? I recall that Joan claims to have come from a sanatorium in Sittingbourne, whereas Frank Tattersall said that the woman he'd called Tish worked at a canteen in Dover. She could have changed jobs during the war, but from serving tea and buns to nursing? There's only one way to find out.

I pick up the phone and ask the operator if there's a sanatorium in Sittingbourne, Kent. She confirms that there is and gives me the number. When I get through, I explain that I'm trying to find a friend who I lost contact with during the war, and I've heard she was a nurse at the sanatorium until recently.

'I'll see what I can do. What's your friend's name?'

I give the full name and wait for so long, I assume I've been cut off. Susan wanders past with a feather duster, tickling the plaster mouldings and running it through the stair spindles as she heads to the first floor. She still has a musical cough.

'Sorry about keeping you. No, there's no one going by that name, and I checked anyone who's left in the last year. Sorry. I hope you find your friend.'

I sit, puzzling over this. Troops' canteens will probably have been disbanded by now, and anyway I've no idea who would have run them in Dover. I'm worrying at it when Leslie arrives. He stands at the desk, glazed and tired.

'Are you OK, Leslie?'

'Eh? Oh, yes, thanks. I've had some news, that's all. Nearly knocked me off my feet.'

'Good or bad?' I'm such a dissembler. Maybe all that enforced secrecy during the war has marked me for life.

'I'm not sure. I'll need to think about that.' He leans his elbows on the desk, as if he needs propping up. 'I'm all at sixes and sevens. Elaine might be pleased.'

'Dora's happy to carry on with dinner, if you need a break.'

He focuses. 'No, I'm better working and I've no idea when the bakery will be open. Have you heard anything about Ray and Vera?'

'Nothing at all.'

'The police can't believe he murdered Miss Laidlaw. Ray goes on about the revolution and reprisals when it comes, but really, he wouldn't say boo to a goose.'

He shrugs off his jacket and heads to the kitchen. I call Fernfield police station and confirm that Inspector Thaxted is there. I say that I need to speak to him urgently and I'll call in soon.

Dora reluctantly agrees to take over reception while I'm out. She's flushed and grouchy. 'I was enjoying making that hotpot, but now Leslie's saying it's too salty. Everything's going to hell in a handcart around here. Nothing's been right since Miss Laidlaw died. It's as if there's a jinx on the place.'

Silently, I agree that Lucinda's death has set off a domino rally of exposed secrets. 'It's just a blip, Dora. We'll get back to normal. The new guest, Mr Donnell, is in Seahorse.'

I'm gathering my things together and taking another glimpse at Mrs Ward's file when I hear the door bang. Nurse Dean arrives, shedding her coat, swinging her bag and declaring that she's parched. She behaves as if she hasn't a care in the world, despite being questioned by the police. Either she's an innocent nurse carrying out her daily rounds, or she's adept at concealment and certain that she's covered her tracks.

'You left this in Mrs Ward's room and she asked me to give it to you.' I hand over the folder.

'Thanks,' she says. 'I hope you haven't been peeking. These are confidential medical notes, not for anyone to read.'

'I understand that.'

'Well, good. I was in a rush this morning, never realised I hadn't put it away.' She narrows her eyes at me and adds with a note of pure poison, 'You don't half get involved with lots of things around here. I can't imagine how they managed without you before you arrived.'

I've speculated that she'll have worked out that I've given Thaxted information, or that the captain will have told her about my comments. Her remark proves me right.

I raise my thumb. 'That's my job, keeping tabs on everything.'

* * *

At the police station, I'm directed to a room off the corridor to the kitchen. I give the door a quick tap and walk in. The light is on but there's no one in the chair behind the desk, which is covered with paperwork. A striped tie is curled around a bottle of tablets.

'Hello,' a disembodied voice says. 'I'm down here.'

I follow the voice to the side of the desk near the window. Thaxted is lying full length on the floor, toes pointing at the ceiling, eyes closed. He has a rolled-up towel wedged vertically beneath his spine. His stick rests against the wall beside him, his hands are folded across his stomach.

'Hello, Inspector. You're like an effigy.'

'I have to stretch my spine and ease my leg.' He peers at me. 'Stop looming and sit.'

I pull a chair over and sit by his feet. 'What's happened with Ray?'

Thaxted rubs his eyes. 'He grew very emotional and came clean about bigamy. He confessed that Miss Laidlaw challenged him after her visit to Streatham and advised him to tell Vera the truth, but he denies having anything to do with her death.'

'Where is he now?'

He points. 'In our custody cell, until we can check if any customers were with him in the bakery the morning of the murder. Vera came to see him about an hour ago, marching in as if she might commit murder herself.'

She'll have sat with him in that little room where I visited Felix, wondering what's hit her. 'If Ray didn't kill Lucinda, he must have been terribly relieved that luck was with him and he was safe again.'

Thaxted sways gently from side to side, hands on hips. 'His luck didn't last long, thanks to you.'

'Did he do it?'

Thaxted eases himself up to a sitting position. It's warm in the room and he's wearing an open-necked white shirt that drains what little colour there is from his face. 'I'd say not. I could be wrong, but the man has no personal anger in him. It's all hot air, directed at the class system.'

'Leslie told me that Ray wouldn't say boo to a goose.'

'I tend to agree from my interviews. What's your news?'

I start to speak, but he says, 'Hold on, I need to get up and it won't be a pretty sight, so move away.'

I take my chair back to the desk and bend down to retie my shoelace. I hear the crack of a knee, a muttered curse and deep, laboured breaths. Once Thaxted is seated opposite me, I straighten up. 'This is quite a long story, but I'll try to keep it brief.'

He lifts his collar, places his tie around his skinny neck and knots it. 'If you could.'

'It started with a man called Robert Etherington who's in the John Radcliffe. I met him when I visited Felix. I had no idea that what he told me would lead me to Nurse Dean.' I talk him through Etherington's concern, the information I found in Lucinda's ring binder, my conversation with Frank Tattersall, the name I'd seen that afternoon in a patient's folder and my phone call to Sittingbourne. 'Nurse Dean — Laetitia/Joan/Tish — has been lying about where she came here from.'

Thaxted shakes two tablets from the bottle and downs them with a glass of water. 'You're a dogged, organised person.'

'Apparently.'

'With an eye for detail.'

'Why do I get nervous when you compliment me?'

'Because, Miss Moore, you've been withholding information from me and, frankly, it really, really annoys me.'

'That's unfair. You're busy, it was vague information from a man who's severely injured and who can't communicate well. I wasn't sure that it was anything to do with Lucinda and I didn't want to bother you until I had hard facts.' I sound so lame.

He smooths his tie. 'There are times when I could happily wring your neck. You pretend to be helpful, but you often have your own agenda.'

'What does that mean?'

'Oh, don't play the innocent with me. You asked me about the cottage hospital and Dr Jessop. When I was speaking to Leslie Mathis earlier today, he told me about his uncle's involvement with the black market. Leslie's a decent chap, engaged to a bank clerk, wants to stay on the right side of the law. He needed to get everything off his chest, so he informed me about seeing the doctor, Artie Baldwin and Miss Laidlaw at Oxford station. He confirmed that he'd told you.'

'Dr Jessop is one of my suspects.'

'Is he now? One of *your* suspects!'

'Yes, because I reckon that Lucinda recognised Artie Baldwin as a black marketeer. She'd probably seen him visiting Benny Mathis at Granville Grange and she'd have wondered why the doctor was with him. Something's been going on at the cottage hospital and Lucinda might have discovered that Dr Jessop had been breaking the law. The doctor hasn't got an alibi.'

Thaxted is sitting back, steepling his fingers. 'Hasn't he?'

'No. I asked him what he was doing that morning and he was on his own at the surgery.' I'm right about that, so why am I losing ground?

Thaxted shakes his head, a man about to give disappointing news. 'But you see, a pharmaceutical firm called the doctor twice that morning. They were long conversations, placing him in the clear.'

'He didn't mention those.'

'Why should he, to you? As I've had to point out to you before, you're not the police. Please feel free to apply to join the force if you wish.'

I utter what I believe is called a hollow laugh. 'So I can be a dogsbody or a typist, make the tea for the chaps? My eye for detail would surely be encouraged. I'd flourish, wouldn't I? I'd make inspector in no time.'

Thaxted rubs his jaw. 'Fair point. Also . . . I can't see you taking orders.'

'That's a fair point too.'

'How did that go for you in Whitehall?'

'It was a curious combination of team work and individual effort. Hard to explain. There weren't many rules or orders, apart from complete secrecy.'

'Interesting and clearly suited to your talents.' He lays his hands palm down on the desk. 'Why is Joan Dean — or whoever she really is — lying? What isn't right about her and bothering Mr Etherington?'

'She's concealing something.'

'Those were rhetorical questions.' Thaxted picks up the phone and asks for two cups of tea and some biscuits. I take that as meaning he's not about to wring my neck any time soon. Then he dials a number, asks for Dover police and draws a notepad towards him.

'Hello, this is Inspector Peter Thaxted, Oxford police. I have a query regarding a troops' canteen in Dover in recent years. I see, thank you. Yes, I'll wait.' He covers the phone. 'Putting me through to someone.'

A constable arrives, bearing a tray of tea and biscuits. 'I'll be on night shift, sir, as we have a person in custody. Hope you like the biscuits, my sister made them.'

Thaxted nods and waves him away, speaking again. 'Hello, yes, a canteen for soldiers.' He listens, making notes. 'And do you have a phone number for me?'

He ends the call, drinks tea and takes a biscuit. 'St John's Ambulance ran several canteens around Dover. Let's see what they have to say.' He dials again, shoulders hunched, resting his forehead against his right hand as he explains why he's calling.

I munch through the jammy biscuits and finish my tea as I listen, reflecting that he's got terrible posture. He might benefit from practising the Alexander Technique. A colleague in Whitehall taught my team some of the exercises after we all developed aching necks and backs from poring over our paperwork. I haven't the confidence to suggest it to Thaxted in case he gives me his sarcastic treatment. I'm treading on thin ice with him as it is.

At last, after a series of questions, he finishes the call, claps his hands and stares at me. 'Laetitia Dean, called Joan, worked at a canteen from 1940 until February this year. She was a volunteer who made tea and handed out sandwiches. The canteen had a little First Aid post attached. She did some bandaging and sorting out cuts and bruises — basic skills. Our nurse has no nursing qualifications.'

I'm brimming with excitement. 'She's a fraud!'

'Exactly. A fraud and presumably a serious danger to patients.'

'That explains her library books! I saw her exiting the library with copies of a medical dictionary and a nursing handbook. It was odd and I wondered why she needed them. She must be staying up at night, learning about illnesses and treatments. And now I understand about Mrs Ward.'

'What about her?'

I describe the doctor's dissatisfaction with the nurse's care. 'Her lack of expertise meant that Mrs Ward developed an infection and had to be taken to hospital. Also, she commented that Nurse Dean was heavy-handed.'

'This all adds up to a very unpleasant picture.'

'It's a strange thing to do, pose as a nurse, and especially one who has to work alone.' I have a sneaky buzz of admiration for Joan's sheer nerve. All those comments she made about illnesses and their remedies, her casual diagnoses.

Thaxted shakes his head. 'Quite canny of her, in fact, to apply for a solitary role that takes her out and about. If she worked with others in a clinic or a ward, she'd probably have been rumbled by now. I expect Dr Jessop has reservations.'

I can't help a smile. 'She observed that you need to take iron tablets.'

'Did she now? I'll give her some unpleasant medicine before this is over.'

I get up and walk around, straightening a wall calendar of scenes by the Thames. 'Lucinda didn't make any more records about Robert Etherington's concerns. I wonder if she found out about Joan Dean?'

'She did, although at present I've no idea how.' Thaxted taps his notes. 'The man I spoke to in Dover informed me that a Miss Laidlaw phoned in September, asking him about Joan Dean.'

I take my seat again. 'Let's recap — we've answered some questions, but there's still a central one. Did Nurse Dean murder Miss Laidlaw because she'd found out about this fraud? What do we do now?'

'*I* need to speak to the cottage hospital, Dr Jessop and various other people and *you* should go home.'

'Can't I stay and find out what they say?'

'No, that won't be necessary.' He stares at the plate. 'What happened to all the biscuits?'

'Oh, I ate them. The raspberry jam was delicious.'

'Ask Warren to bring me some more on your way out. I have a long evening in front of me.'

There's no mistaking the tone of dismissal. As I open the door, Thaxted calls, 'Please remember that, like you, Miss Laidlaw was a persistent woman and her persistence got her killed. Be careful, Miss Moore.'

CHAPTER TWENTY-THREE

I hurry back to the hotel through the raw evening. A strange smell greets me when I open the door and find Dora vigorously spraying 4711 cologne around reception.

'Leslie let the potatoes boil dry,' she explains. 'He's only half here today, not got his mind on his work at all. Maybe he's got love troubles.'

Love child troubles, anyway. 'Dinner will be on time though?'

'Oh yes, all sorted. Mr Berrow rang to say that he's staying in London tonight. Leslie's covering reception this evening and I'll do tomorrow. I'm available overnight as well.' She's full of beans. 'I spoke to Vera and she said she'll be back after that, but I told her that I'll do extra hours as long as is needed.'

'How is she?'

'She didn't say much, just that there's some silly mix-up with the police about Ray's suppliers and it'll all be sorted soon. Storm in a teacup.'

I suspect that she could say more, but she's turned away. 'Is there anything I need to do before I go home?'

'No, everything's fine. Nurse Dean had to pop out to a patient and said to keep some dinner warm for her. You go on. See you tomorrow.'

* * *

At home, I feed the cats and make a sandwich, which I eat sitting by the fire. Tybalt stalks in, grooms himself on the hearth rug, then settles on the window seat. I let my mind roam around the suspects in this case. Ray, Joan and Captain Branch all have motives for wanting Lucinda out of the way, and any of them could have accessed the hotel on the morning of the murder. Ray and Joan had a lot to lose if Lucinda had revealed information about them. At present, my money's on Joan. There's an offbeat edge to her, leading me to believe that she could lash out if challenged.

I'm reading through a few new fan letters that have arrived, placing them in date order, when there's a knock at the door. I'm half expecting to see Rosalind, but I find Dora, dressed in a heavy wool coat, a long silk scarf and a round hat with a velvet bow at the front.

'I hope you don't mind me popping round. I just wanted to discuss the situation at the hotel with you. I'm worried about things.'

I'm taken aback, but I invite her in. She opens her coat and sits by the fire, saying she won't stay long. Her colour is high, she's a tad breathless and she's clutching her bag tightly on her lap.

Her tension makes me assume that something major must be troubling her. 'It might be best to speak to Mr Berrow if it's an important hotel matter, Dora.'

'Oh no, it's you I wanted to talk to.'

'Right. I'll help if I can.'

The red velvet bow of her hat catches the glow of the fire. 'You're always helpful, Daisy, and you're always so interested in people.'

'Kind of you to say so, but it's part of my job at the Dolphin to take an interest.'

'But you do go the extra mile, don't you?'

'I'm not sure what you mean.' There's something peculiar in her tone.

'You're a thorough type of person. Vera says so too.'

'Thanks for the compliment.'

'Mind you, I'm not sure you rate us much. We probably seem like country bumpkins to you after the excitements of London life.'

'That's not my view at all.'

'Sounds it, from some of the things you've come out with.'

'I dislike prejudice. It doesn't help in life.'

'Depends, doesn't it? Depends on what you've got to lose.'

Dora's in an odd mood. 'Has something upset you?'

She rocks her feet back and forth, pulls her coat collar down. 'Actually, can I just pop to your loo?'

'It's to the left off the kitchen.'

'Thanks, won't be long.'

I go back to JB's fan mail, aware of a distant flushing and running water. I'm reading Mrs Jenny Moir's adulatory letter when there's a shift in the air. As I turn my head there's a shadow, a loud crack and the room goes dark.

* * *

When I come to on my chair, my hands are tied behind my back and my ankles secured with a belt. The room swims into focus and I see Dora sitting opposite me, still in her coat and hat, her bag on the floor beside her.

'Wakey-wakey. Have a nice sleep?'

'What's going on?' My head is throbbing, a pain in my right temple radiating outwards.

'Must be strange for you, having to ask that. Usually, you're clued up about everything that's happening.' Dora sniffs righteously and folds her arms.

I'm trying to work out how long I've been unconscious. Judging by the height and brightness of the fire, no time at all. I flex my wrists but there's almost no movement.

'You're tied nice and tight,' Dora assures me.

'Why are you doing this?'

'I'll be more than happy to explain, if you're not sitting comfortably.'

I remember that Dora gave me the message from JB. She realises that I'm on my own tonight. It's not a comforting recollection. 'Yes, you'd better.' Her stony eyes reflect an anger I've never noticed before. In that moment, I realise how far off the mark I've been with my suspects. 'Did you kill Lucinda?'

'Bravo! I did indeed. Like you, she couldn't mind her own bloody business. Interfering bitch, wanting to be everyone's conscience.'

'Is this about Ray and his bigamy?'

Dora makes a noise in the back of her throat. 'You're so like Lucinda, trotting off to Streatham, poking around in things that are none of your affair.'

How does she know about Streatham? Vera must have discovered something and told her. I've no idea how this is going to end, but I assume that Dora isn't planning to leave me in the best of health after her confession. I'm wondering if I can rock my chair violently enough to surprise her and get an advantage. Although what that will be, with my hands and feet tied, is beyond my fuddled brain right now. I try not to move my head when I speak. 'Keep this short, I've got an awful headache.'

As she starts to speak, the phone rings. She waits for it to stop, sitting impassively, like a granite monument. It stops, then rings again, at least a dozen times.

'That's probably Mr Berrow. He'll worry when I don't answer. He'll ask someone to come and check on me.'

Dora shrugs. 'Doubt it. You're not that important, even if you've a high opinion of yourself. Save your breath. You haven't that many left.' She flashes me an unpleasant smile. 'You ferreted out lots of things, but you never realised how close me and Vee are. We were in the same class at school together and she's very dear to me, always has been. I had a sister, but she died years ago and Vera took her place for me. I've always minded her, you see, and vice versa. She was my rock when my fiancé was killed. Ray too. He couldn't do enough for me. He's got such a big heart.'

Yes, big enough for two wives. I'm attempting to ignore the band of pain around my forehead. 'That's very touching. You found out that Lucinda had discovered Ray's bigamy?'

'Oh yes. Overheard her talking to him about it one day when he was repointing bricks at the back of the hotel. Lecturing him, more like. I was cleaning in the room above and I had the window open. On her high horse, she was, all schoolmarmish, warning him he needed to tell Vera or she'd have to herself. Poor old Ray was in a state, begging her to give him time. She told him he had until the beginning of November, and then she'd have to speak to Vee. I wasn't having Vera upset like that. She's trying for a baby and that kind of shock wouldn't help.'

I squint through the pain. 'But surely you'd want her to know that she's not really married, that Ray's a cheat and a liar?'

'Why? It was done; she and Ray have been together a while. He's a decent man and good for Vera, even though he's a daft commie. Vee really loves him. I gathered that the wife in London didn't care about him or where he was. She can't have been much of a wife if she couldn't hang on to him. Why upset the apple cart? Men tend to roam, can't help themselves, and what you're ignorant of can't worry you. I bet there's plenty of bigamists all around us. I didn't want our Vera's name being mud.'

'Worried about the Fernies?'

That makes Dora bristle. 'You may mock, Miss High-and-Mighty Clever Clogs, but you're the one tied up.'

'I give you that. Did you tell Ray what you'd overheard?'

'Course not!' She holds the lapels of her coat firmly. 'I didn't want him upset, or telling Vera. I decided I'd deal with the problem for them. Least I could do, after all they've done for me. That's what it's like, when people are true friends.'

'Murder is a strange interpretation of friendship, Dora.'

'It had to be done. There was no other way. That meddling pest had to be stopped.' She sneers, 'She was like you, reckoned she was better than the rest of us.'

'So, you told Lucinda you needed to talk to her.'

'I did. I stopped her in the street and explained that Ray was upset and had confided in me. I suggested that we discuss it in private, see if we could find a way of making it all less stressful for Vera. We agreed the place and time to meet. I was waiting for her. She never knew what hit her, I suppose, just like you didn't when I knocked you out. Years of cleaning — they give you strong arms.'

'It was handy for you, that Lucinda had asked Felix to come along, that he was late and put himself in the frame.'

'Wasn't it, just? How she reckoned that asking him to be there would help is beyond me. He's like a long streak of piss, that one.'

How is she planning to kill me? Another blow to the head? Suffocation? A knife? My mouth is dry. 'What led you to me?'

'Poor Vera rang me earlier. She'd come back to the flat to pick up some things and there was a phone call from Maude Crampton. Your visit raked it all up again and set her thinking, made her come over nostalgic. She reckoned that maybe it would be good to talk to Ray, see how he was doing. Also, she'd had a letter about an insurance policy maturing for a tidy sum and it needed his signature. Amazing, how money prompts people into action.' She shakes her head contemptuously. 'She checked the address Lucinda had left her and it didn't take her long to trace Ray through the Fernfield operator. Poor Vera found herself talking to that Crampton woman, all because you interfered. Can you imagine how upset that made her? Ray in jail and this Maude bending her ear. Not that you care, as long as you get your glory. She's in such a state. It was bad enough for her, hearing about Ray, but that was a right slap in the face.'

'I'm sorry, it is terrible for her. But it's no secret, the police have told Vera. Why do you want to hurt me when the information is out there?'

Dora's hands go into fists. 'I killed a woman to protect Vera and keep her marriage going. I thought she was safe, and Ray too. They love each other, they've got a good life together and hopefully some day soon, they'll have a family. I'd sorted it all out for them, and then you went and stirred the whole thing up again, spreading muck just to prove how clever you are. It's all your fault! You reckon you're so superior to us all, sneering at the town and the people who live here. You don't fit in here and you never will.' She leans forward, spittle on her lips. 'I hate your bloody guts and I'm not having Vee seeing you around, reminding her of what's happened every day. You never stop with your questions, poking and prodding folk. I had to come and deal with you in case you ever found me out.' She reaches down for her bag, opens it and takes out a large syringe. 'It won't hurt and it'll be quick. More than you deserve.'

My bladder twinges and I tighten my pelvic muscles. I refuse to let this woman see my fear. 'You won't get away with it, Dora. The police will work it out.'

'I'm not so sure. That lanky inspector's too muddled by all those pills he takes.'

'What's in the syringe?'

'Morphine.'

'Where did you get it?'

'Dr Jessop's bag of goodies. Don't worry, I've read up how to do it.'

Am I supposed to be grateful that she's studied how to finish me off? I'm visualising throwing myself forwards when Tybalt springs from the window seat onto Dora's shoulder, making her start. I seize my chance and rock forwards, cannoning into her. She falls sideways into the fireplace, the sleeve of her coat and her trailing scarf catching the flames. I bang my head as I land, the jarring pain winding me. I'm on the floor, stunned, while I watch the fire lick up her scarf and race to her hat. Dora's screaming and twisting, Tybalt has vanished, paws flying. Not again — this is where I started, with a cat and a conflagration.

I work my way to my knees and I'm trying to pull Dora away from the fire with my teeth gripping her other sleeve when there's a banging on the door. I loosen my grip to yell for help, then try again to get hold of her, but she's flailing about and my strength has gone.

I fall backwards, smoke creeping down into my lungs. Dreamily, I muse that it's a peculiar way to go, toasted with Dora. Is my mother taking revenge from beyond the grave? JB will be really annoyed that I've done this to his home.

There's a crash, voices. I see feet and someone's lifting me and then there's lovely cold, clean air.

CHAPTER TWENTY-FOUR

JB drives me home from the cottage hospital the next morning. He insists on placing a blanket over my knees.

'I'm fine, I'm not an invalid,' I protest.

'Humour me, it creates the illusion that I'm doing something useful. This reminds me of the first time I met you, when you smelled of bonfires. Are you a fire sign — Aries, Leo or Sagittarius by any chance?'

'No, Aquarius. When I get home, I'm going to lie in a bath. Are you sure the lodge isn't too badly damaged?'

'The inspector's quick-acting constables put the blaze out sharpish with the hearth rug. Just a smudge of smoke discolouration over the fireplace that can easily be painted.'

I rub my wrists. 'Dora tied a mean knot.'

'Dora! My goodness, what a tale! Really, I'd never have imagined that she'd get so vicious. I always found her friendly and helpful.'

'You didn't see her wielding a syringe of morphine. Have you heard how she is?'

'She's in the John Radcliffe with burns to her arm and neck, but she's not so bad.' A smile twitches his lips. 'People you come in contact with end up in hospital, Daisy. Hope you're not planning to send me there.'

It's an uncomfortable subject and I'm conscious of my mother's censuring presence. I plait the fringe of the blanket. 'If it wasn't for the inspector, I might not have survived last night.'

'He does have his uses.'

'Have you spoken to him?'

'Briefly. He said he'd call by later today.'

It was Inspector Thaxted who'd been ringing me the previous evening. He'd released Ray after a flour delivery driver had confirmed his whereabouts on the morning of Lucinda's death. When Thaxted rang Vera to give her the good news, she'd burst into tears, telling him about Maude Crampton's phone call and how she'd confided in Dora about my involvement. Operating on some sixth sense, Thaxted had worried when he couldn't reach me by phone and he'd dispatched two constables to Brize Lodge to check on me.

At home, I spend ages in a bath, shampooing my hair gently to eliminate the lingering smell of smoke. My head still aches from the blow Dora gave me with the paperweight she'd brought with her. I swallow aspirin with a tot of hot whisky and sleep for a couple of hours, but I don't get much rest as my dreams are filled with the sounds of Dora's screams.

Tybalt makes an entrance when I'm dressed and sitting by the fire with a copy of *Stage and Screen*, reading about the release of *Brief Encounter*. He hops onto my lap and starts paddling. JB is smoking a cigar and reading his fan mail, chuckling as he turns the pages.

'Is there a medal awarded to cats, JB? Tybalt deserves one after last night. If he hadn't jumped on Dora's shoulder, who can say what might have happened?'

'We could call him Sir Tybalt from now on.' JB takes the poker and moves it to the right and left of Tybalt's head, knighting him. The cat takes no notice.

'Listen to this, Daisy! "*Dear Jeffrey, if I may make so bold—*" no, you may not, Miss Crowley — "*you're a marvellous actor and, really, you should be in more films. You'd be a terrific romantic lead.*

If you're ever down Basingstoke way, please call for a cup of tea and a slice of cake, and could you send me a signed copy of your next theatre programme, if it's not too much trouble? Also, a couple of photos for me and my mum April, and she'd love a little note saying hello, as she adores your work." Honestly, why don't I just send her a vial of my blood? I don't suppose it would satisfy her.'

I'm composing a suitable reply in my head when I see a familiar trilby pass the window and Peter Thaxted knocks at the front door.

He takes his coat off and sits while JB goes to make tea. Today, he's wearing a navy suit that fits him better, masking his skeletal thinness. He crosses his legs, tilts his head to one side appraisingly. 'You're pretty chipper, considering. How's the head?'

'Sore, and I have a lump where Dora bashed me.'

'Uh-huh. And how's the head in here?' He taps his temple.

'How do you mean?'

'It's the second time this year you've been in a fire.'

'Oh, I see.' I don't want to discuss that. 'Yes, too much excitement. I must be like Tybalt — nine lives.'

I see him take the hint and back off. 'Has Jeffrey updated you about Dora?'

'Yes, he said she'll be OK.'

'We got a brief statement from her for now. You certainly enraged her.'

'I realised that she and Vera were friends, but I hadn't guessed how close. I was reflecting on how much Dora always hung around the hotel, quick to take on extra duties. I'd got the impression that she didn't like her own company.'

'Yes, a lonely woman, lost her fiancé in the war, lives on her own, and Vera's like family. Dora was often at their flat in the evenings and at weekends.' He takes his trilby from where he's perched it on his knee and twirls it. 'We searched her house. She's been knitting baby garments, ready for when Vera and Ray produce the longed-for child. Dora was lined up as godmother. The way she saw it, she had a lot to lose as well

235

as Vera if Ray's secret was exposed. She has a major emotional investment in the Crampton household. I'd venture more than they've ever realised — an unhealthy fixation, almost.'

That makes me wince, causing Tybalt to extend a protesting paw. Thaxted yawns and shakes himself.

'I didn't suspect her at all,' I admit. 'Did you?'

'Yes, and my suspicion was growing stronger. She was quite intense during interview and she did find the body. She was the only staff member whose movements I couldn't pin down during that morning, and she was upstairs in the hotel. I made enquiries into her background and personal life, established how dependent she was on the hotel and the Cramptons for a social life. It was obvious that she didn't care for Miss Laidlaw's pacifism. In many ways, she was my number-one suspect. I didn't have motive until you unearthed the bigamy. I was about to pull her in again for questioning.'

I'm somewhat crestfallen. 'You were ahead of me all the time.'

'I never considered it a race, Miss Moore.' He rocks his leg gently. 'When Vera told me about Maude Crampton's call, Dora's awareness of that and your visit to Streatham, I tried to get hold of Dora. I couldn't track her down and when you didn't answer the phone, the alarm bells sounded.'

'Thank you for sending your cavalry to my rescue last night.'

'Just doing my job.'

JB brings through a tray of tea. 'Help yourselves. I have to make some phone calls, so I'll leave you to it.'

We drink in silence for a minute or so. JB's voice echoes faintly from the phone. Thaxted reaches for Joe Casey's photo and holds it up to the light.

'Sad about Joe. He was such an artless, warm person.'

'Were you friendly with him?'

'I met him once when I drove my mother over to visit Rosalind. I called in to see Jeffrey and Joe was here.' He's suppressing a smile. 'You remind me of him in some ways — worldly and yet naïve. An interesting combination.'

'What makes you say I'm naïve?'

He clears his throat. 'Ask me again in six months. I might have changed my opinion by then.'

I've had enough of obscure remarks. I place a hand over Tybalt's warm head. 'What's happening about Joan Dean and Dr Jessop?'

Thaxted adds more sugar to his tea. 'We checked out Miss Dean's background and it's clear that she forged references and evidence of qualifications, either on her own or with help. She's been arrested for impersonating a nurse. All her cockiness crumbled quickly. She was stunned at being exposed, dissolved into floods of , and so far she's been too unwell to be interviewed. I'm fairly sure that when he finds out, Captain Branch will acknowledge that she's been blackmailing him about his father's secret. A murky young woman, all told.'

'How did Lucinda manage to get in touch with Dover?'

'Ah yes. She found another friend of Percy Etherington's from his battalion and tracked Miss Dean that way. Joan has stated that Miss Laidlaw hadn't spoken to her. Perhaps she was going to but fate intervened.'

'And the doctor?'

'Jessop's also been arrested, for selling drugs from the cottage hospital on the black market. I've been on his tail for a while. According to him, life had got terribly expensive and he needed the money for home improvements. I wouldn't be surprised if he's struck off. People in Fernfield had better stay healthy for now, given that their medical services have been depleted.'

'It's awful about the doctor. Iris must be devastated.'

Thaxted cups his jaw. 'He broke the law, stole from people who need drugs, exploited his respected status. I wouldn't waste any sympathy on him. His wife — that's a different matter.'

I'm shaky inside, the events of last night flickering all the time at the edges of my mind. 'You can't make an omelette without breaking eggs, but there's a lot of misery around this case.'

'I'm used to it. You take it easy and try not to dwell on it.' He fits his trilby on, snaps the brim. 'Sorry for saying I wanted to wring your neck, by the way.'

'It's OK. Discounting Dora, I'm sure you're not the only person who has that fantasy.'

He gives a dry laugh and rises. 'I have a great deal still to do today. You've been a real help, Miss Moore. I'm so sorry you were injured in the process.' He dons his coat, picks up his stick. 'I'll let myself out. Say goodbye to Jeffrey for me.'

He tips his hat as he passes the window. I wave, but I'm not sure he sees me. I'm so tired suddenly and my limbs are light and achy. The rhythmic rise and fall of Tybalt's breathing lulls me into a doze, broken when JB breezes in.

'I've got a part in a film early next year. Crime drama, set in London. I'm a small-time crook.'

'Congratulations!'

He bows. 'Declan wishes you well and he'll say a prayer for you. We agreed that you solved the case by forcing Dora's hand and making her break cover, so I've won the bet and you're coming for supper at Rules as soon as you're better.'

I watch him collect the tea things and build the fire up. I was so intent on solving this murder, and yet now that I've succeeded the satisfaction I anticipated isn't quite there. Instead, my mood lowers. I'm reminded of days when I spent hours cracking a cipher and finally completed the task. The hot glow of achievement burned briefly but was always followed by a certain lingering melancholy.

I take myself out for a walk in the dying afternoon, kicking conkers along the lane and throwing up rustling leaves.

* * *

I return to the Dolphin with some trepidation two days later, wondering if Vera will ever speak to me again. Leslie has rallied round — with JB's permission, he's got Bet Leyland in to do the cleaning and Vera's back at work that morning.

Susan comes close to me as I'm hanging up my coat, her eyes shiny with excitement. 'I can't believe that Dora bashed in Miss Laidlaw. She was teaching me to knit. Ever so kind and patient she was too, because I'm so ham-fisted, I kept dropping the needles.'

'It is hard to understand. She bashed me too. You never can really predict what someone is capable of.' *Like setting fire to their home and not admitting it, or keeping stolen goods stashed beneath their bed.* 'Can you knit now?'

'Sort of. But I'm not much good. Suppose I need to practice, but it won't be the same without Dora encouraging me. I can hear her now, "Elbows in, wool nice and even."'

'Susan, have you heard anything about Iris Jessop?'

'Ooh, yeah, she's gone to stay with her mum and dad in Oxford. Fancy the doctor being on the fiddle!'

Vera asks us all into the parlour after breakfast has been cleared away. She's pale, but there's a fighting glint in her gaze and she's done her hair and make-up. She's wearing her silver bracelet, so I assume that Ray has been forgiven, or is on the path to redemption.

She stands by the window. 'I just want to say a few words. There's going to be lots of gossip, so I'm knocking it on the head. My Ray's done wrong, committed bigamy and he'll no doubt pay for it, as he should. But I love him and I'm sticking by him.'

There's a silence, then Leslie starts applauding and we all join in. Vera blushes.

'Good for you, Vera,' I tell her.

She's tight-lipped. 'Just to say, Daisy, that there's no hard feelings. Dora did a terrible thing. I can hardly credit it. All those years of being so close and I never saw her as much as raise a finger to anyone. Never even heard her shout or show real anger. I'll never get over it. I can't blame you for searching for the truth. I'm sorry you got hurt and I'm glad you're better.'

'I'm sorry too, Vera. I wish that these things hadn't happened. They've had an awful effect on everyone.'

Susan's twitching and twisting her hair around a finger. 'It's amazing, what's been going on right under our noses. I can't get over it all. And Leslie's a toff!'

Bet Leyland raises an eyebrow at me and I smile guiltily.

Leslie sits up and preens himself. 'Like you, Vera, I might as well head off the rumours. I've found out that Hector Branch was my dad. It's all been an awful shock, but there we are. I'm still trying to get my head round it, to be honest. My solicitor is discussing whether or not I might be able to claim an inheritance.'

'What about Captain Branch?' Susan asks. 'I hope his nose is out of joint. You're his brother now!'

'Well, half-brother.' Leslie sounds uncomfortable. 'He hasn't really spoken to me. He let Mr Lancaster do the talking.'

'He won't be so quick to come in here acting all snooty. Maybe he'll have to let you move into Granville Grange and share it. You'll be ever so important,' Susan breathes.

'Don't be daft, Susan,' Vera tells her. 'None of your flights of fancy, thank you very much. We have quite enough to deal with and we all need to keep our feet firmly on the ground.'

I'm reassured by Vera's familiar, tart tone, but I smile at Susan, who's glowering at being told off.

'It's going to be a difficult time for me,' Vera continues, 'what with Ray and Dora and all the commotion. I expect I'll be wobbly. And there's one other thing.' She pushes her hair back and her voice trembles. 'I've just found out I'm expecting.'

Susan claps again and we all pile in with congratulations.

'Yes, well . . . anyway . . . I'm hoping, Daisy, that you'll be able to take over my duties when I have to take time to deal with all that I have on my plate now.'

'I'll be happy to, Vera.' It's the least I can do, even though the prospect doesn't thrill me. And after all, it's one of the reasons JB employs me.

The day settles down. I find a new plug for the top-floor bathroom, sort a laundry delivery and take a tray of tea to Mrs Ward.

During the afternoon, I catch the bus to the hospital and visit Felix. He's heard about Dora and I bring him up to date on what's happened with Ray, Vera, Joan Dean and Dr Jessop.

'Fernfield has many hidden depths,' he says, 'and you've dived very deep in them. Daisy, you should join the police.'

'That's what Inspector Thaxted suggested.'

'You'd be a wonderful detective. You have a talent for these things.'

'No, I don't like uniforms or being bossed about.'

He laughs. 'Me neither. The rules in here are so constricting, and every five minutes a nurse tells me what to do or forbids me something. But never mind. This morning, I've been told that I can go home at the end of the week. Joy!'

I leave him elated and head to see Robert Etherington. I find him shuffling up and down the corridor on crutches, trying out his new leg. He's sweating and straining, but he makes it with me to the day room, where he sinks into a chair and wipes his brow.

'I found out what wasn't right, Robert.' I explain about Joan Dean and how she's been arrested.

He raises a triumphant fist. 'Not right! Liar! Just lies.'

'Exactly. She's a fraud. She might never have been found out if it wasn't for you, and she could have hurt a lot of patients while she was practising on them.'

'Good, good.'

'The police arrested Lucinda's murderer too.'

He flexes his hands. 'All good. All right now.'

I'm not sure I can agree with that sentiment. I say goodbye and walk to the train station. Tonight it's my promised supper at Rules.

* * *

JB's car is parked at Oxford station, so we drive home later that evening. I laze beside him when he starts the engine, fairly drunk, full of potted shrimp, roast chicken and caramel gateau. We've had too much white wine and Father Hickey insisted on brandy chasers. On the way to the tube, we sang drunkenly, with the priest conducting us.

'Father Hickey was a little flat at times tonight,' I remark. He'd been good company, but his gaze had drifted inwards.

'His friend Abe has gone away for a while. He misses him.'

'Oh, where's he gone?'

'I'm not sure.' JB's tone is evasive. 'He's a stage designer, so I expect he's off in some far-flung regional theatre, enduring an awful bed-and-breakfast.'

'Anyway, it was a lovely evening. Thank you.'

'Factotums should receive praise when it's due. You've far exceeded my expectations, Daisy.' He adjusts his driving gloves. 'I realise that you miss your war work. Fernfield doesn't generally offer you much of interest, and I assume that murder won't come along to stimulate you every week. But you are going to stay as my right hand for now, aren't you?'

I'm not sure what I want. I'd experienced the profound, familiar wrench of homesickness in London. Boarding the train, it was as if I was leaving a lover. I reply as honestly as I can. 'I've no other plans.'

'Thank goodness! I'd really miss you now, if you weren't around. We jog along well, don't we? No spats or misunderstandings.'

I catch his anxiety. 'We get along famously, JB. I couldn't ask for a better employer and housemate.'

'Excellent.'

I scan the houses passing by. Iris Jessop might be behind one of those doors. 'I wonder what Iris will do now.'

'Lie low for a while, have her baby, hope the law will be lenient with her husband.'

'She had so many plans.' Suddenly, I recall what's in my bag. 'JB, are we anywhere near Peter Thaxted's house?'

'Not far, but it's after eleven, late for a social call.'

'I'd like to put something through his letterbox.'

242

'It's not much of a detour, I suppose.'

After ten minutes of driving through residential streets, JB pulls up outside a grand, detached Victorian villa. I tell him I won't be a minute. I walk up the paved path in a not very straight line. There's a gap in the curtains and I glimpse a bowed white head inside the window, illuminated by a reading lamp.

I take the pamphlet about the Alexander Technique from my bag and slip it through the letterbox, easing the brass square back into place so that it doesn't make a noise. Then I hiccup loudly and clamp my mouth shut. He raises his head, listens, lowers it again.

I turn back and slip into the warm car. JB has lit up a cigar, his head shrouded in a smoky haze. It's a clear night now, with a huge buttery moon and needles of frost in the air. On the way home, JB teaches me the words to an old Oxfordshire song, 'Near Woodstock Town'.

Life could be worse. I'll stay for the time being.

THE END

Thank you for reading this book.

If you enjoyed it please leave feedback on Amazon or Goodreads, and if there is anything we missed or you have a question about, then please get in touch. We appreciate you choosing our book.

Founded in 2014 in Shoreditch, London, we at Joffe Books pride ourselves on our history of innovative publishing. We were thrilled to be shortlisted for Independent Publisher of the Year at the British Book Awards.

www.joffebooks.com

We're very grateful to eagle-eyed readers who take the time to contact us. Please send any errors you find to corrections@joffebooks.com. We'll get them fixed ASAP.